AUTHORIZED PERSONNEL ONLY

Barbara D'Amato

A Tom Doherty Associates Book
New York

NOTE: If you purchased this book without a cover you should be aware that this book is stolen property. It was reported as "unsold and destroyed" to the publisher, and neither the author nor the publisher has received any payment for this "stripped book."

This is a work of fiction. All the characters and events portrayed in this book are either products of the author's imagination or are used fictitiously.

AUTHORIZED PERSONNEL ONLY

Copyright © 2000 by Barbara D'Amato

All rights reserved, including the right to reproduce this book, or portions thereof, in any form.

A Forge Book
Published by Tom Doherty Associates, LLC
175 Fifth Avenue
New York, NY 10010

www.tor.com

Forge® is a registered trademark of Tom Doherty Associates, LLC.

ISBN: 0-812-59016-3
Library of Congress Catalog Card Number: 00-057270

First edition: December 2000
First mass market edition: January 2002

Printed in the United States of America

0 9 8 7 6 5 4 3 2 1

ENTHUSIASTIC PRAISE FOR BARBARA D'AMATO

"Written in such terrifying terms readers will find it easy—no, mandatory—to stay up all night to finish the book."
—*Publishers Weekly* (starred review)

"A sure-footed thriller . . . chillingly believable. . . . D'Amato's plotting wins the day. . . . A marvelously paced double mystery."
—*Booklist*

"The meatiest and most straightforward of Suze's three procedurals to date. D'Amato's headline sleuth, Second City journalist Cat Marsala, had better watch her back."
—*Kirkus Reviews*

"This fast-moving novel is sprinkled with interesting insights into police work and computer buffs will enjoy the constantly changing cyber strategies kidnappers and law-enforcement officers use to outsmart and confound one another."
—*School Library Journal*

"Combining elements of a fascinating police procedural and a psychological suspense story, Ms. D'Amato's novel is as edgy as a new pocket knife, as terrifying as a trip through a haunted house. Not just one story but two crime plots are interwoven with skill and intelligence."
—*The Dallas Morning News*

"From the first page, [D'Amato's] crisp dialogue makes the book a one-sitting read."
—*Arkansas Democrat Gazette*

"In the hands of the award winning Barbara D'Amato, both themes seem so fresh readers will believe *Authorized Personnel Only* has introduced new concepts. The story line is a combination police procedural and thriller. . . . What makes it so good is the depth to the characters."
—*The Midwest Book Review*

"Not for the easily creeped-out."
—*The Anniston Star*

OTHER FORGE BOOKS
BY BARBARA D'AMATO

Killer.app

Good Cop, Bad Cop

Help Me Please

To Natalia Aponte

ACKNOWLEDGMENTS

Thanks to Mark Zubro for seagulls, and to Edward O. Uthman, M.D., for his discussion of autopsies

MONDAY

CHAPTER ONE

Monday, 1:30 P.M.

"WE LOST SIGHT of them in traffic, squad," the voice on the radio said.

"Get a plate?"

"Never got close enough." It was 3-32, a car from the Third District talking. The Third was well south of the Loop.

The dispatcher said, *"Where you at?"*

"Eighteen hundred south on Michigan. Breaking off."

"All units in the eighteen hundred south Michigan area, we're looking for a two-door green Ford containing two male whites, approximately twenty, twenty-five years old. Heading northbound. These two gentlemen held up a currency exchange on Jeffrey and are armed. Repeat, they are armed."

"In broad daylight," Suze Figueroa said.

Bennis said, "Yeah. What's the world coming to?"

Officers Norm Bennis and Suze Figueroa were rolling east in their squad car on Roosevelt Road heading toward Lake Michigan, minding their own business, which basically meant minding the business of the law-abiding or not-so law-abiding public out there. They had both front windows down for air. Chicago squad cars don't have air-conditioning. Figueroa was driving. Bennis wanted to drive all the time, but Figueroa loved squad cars, loved the lights and siren, and reminded him of department rules. In a two-man car, the manual said each man should drive four hours. Even if one of them is a female.

"Hang a right on Michigan," Bennis said.

"Aye-aye, Captain."

"Now mosey into the right lane and slow down."

"Jeez, why don't you just drive and be done with it?"

"Told you I would."

"Never mind."

Bennis was thirty-six years old, a black man who was medium height and built like a wedge, wide shoulders, narrow waist and hips, fairly skinny legs but a great runner. Figueroa was twenty-six years old, Irish and Hispanic. Bennis had been on the job ten years longer. That made him the boss. He thought.

"Comin' up in the rearview," Bennis said.

"What?"

"Your basic two-door green Ford with two extremely basic male whites."

"I hate it when you're right."

The Ford passed them, going slower than it had coming up behind. It moved sedately into the right lane ahead of them. Obviously the driver didn't want to be pulled over by a cop car for some minor violation. This was fine with Bennis and Figueroa, though. It put the Ford right where they wanted it. Figueroa hit the lights and siren. Bennis was on the radio.

"One-twenty-eight. We got them on view, squad," he said reading off the Ford's license plate.

And at that moment, the Ford took off like a bat.

"Shit! Move it!" he said.

"Like I couldn't guess." Figueroa floored the accelerator. They flew past Eleventh, Ninth, and Eighth Streets—there was no Tenth—all of which came in from the left and dead-ended at Michigan Avenue. The Ford screamed around three or four cars, then cut into the right lane again, just barely clipping the front bumper of a Toyota Celica. The Celica's driver jammed on his brakes—a poorly considered move that caused him to lose control and swerve onto the sidewalk, where, thank God, there were no nearby pedestrians—and Figueroa swore at him under her breath, fighting the wheel to pass him on the left, then swing back into the right lane.

Ahead the brake lights of the Ford went on, just for a split second, but giving Figueroa some advance warning. It swung sharply right, fishtailing as it turned onto Balbo.

The Ford's driver was heading straight toward the lights at Balbo and Lake Shore Drive. Ahead of him was Lake Michigan. His choices were only left or right, unless he planned to sleep with the fishes.

Bennis said, "Eastbound on Balbo," to the radio.

"Ten-four, twenty-eight."

"Not anymore," Figueroa said.

The Ford shot through the intersection with the light against it, screeching sharply left. A blue pickup got out of its way too fast, sideswiping a Jeep.

"Nobody knows how to drive anymore," Figueroa said.

At one-thirty in the afternoon, Lake Shore was busy but not as full of cars as it would be at three when the rush hour started to build. The Ford sped up, going forty, then fifty, then sixty, cutting back and forth around cars, one lane to another. Buckingham Fountain flew by on their left.

Most of the traffic saw the light bar on their squad car and some even pulled over to the right, giving the Ford a free lane and more space for more speed.

"Don't lose him!" Bennis yelled.

"Good thinking, boss."

"Northbound on LSD," he yelled at the radio.

At seventy miles an hour they passed everything on the road. The Ford was weaving, dodging traffic, sliding around the stopped cars at the Jackson intersection, then the Monroe crossing. Speeding up, with the yacht club on the right, it was running too fast into the curve at the north end of Grant Park.

"Oh, shit! There he goes!" Bennis said.

The Ford slewed sideways into the center guardrail, flattening a section, and then spun out across the southbound lanes, miraculously missing six southbound cars, and up the embankment onto the golf course Mayor Daley was so proud of. A golf course in the middle of the city.

Figueroa piloted the squad car bumpily over the flattened rail more carefully than the Ford, and then she cut across the southbound lanes in a gap in traffic.

Ahead of them, the Ford churned into the soft earth of the golf course, the driver still trying to get away from the cops. Golfers ran for the trees, scattering clubs and bags and hats.

Figueroa drove the squad car across the grass, following the Ford.

"Hey! You're messing up the green," Bennis said.

"It's a rough."

"It's a rough now, that's for sure. At least stay in his tracks. The mayor's gonna kill us."

"They're getting out!"

Figueróa shoved the gearshift into park. Bennis was already out of his side, running. The two men jumped from the Ford and ran. The one from the passenger seat turned. He was holding an automatic weapon.

"Bennis! Look out!"

Bennis was chasing the driver. The first guy took a one-handed Rambo stance, feet spread wide, automatic weapon held in his right hand only, and fired at Bennis. He missed, and Figueroa thought, *Thank God.* Figueroa didn't have time to pull her sidearm and she didn't need to. By the time he fired she was on him, just plain jumped him with all her weight, which wasn't much, but if a hundred and ten pounds hits you dead-flat-on, you notice it. She grabbed the gun. Her momentum carried the guy backward with her on top of him and then she rose up and let herself drop on him hard, one knee right in the middle of his abdomen. The air went out of him with a sound like a popped balloon and so did all the fight.

When she looked up, Bennis and the other guy were disappearing over the hill toward Randolph Street and half a dozen squad cars with their light bars flashing were coming up Lake Shore Drive.

Monday, 3:30 P.M.

"I'M SAYING THAT Gentleman Bandit guy had to have the IQ of a rutabaga," said Corky Corcoran, leaning heavily on the bar from his side.

"But handsome I heard," Sandi said from the customer side of the bar.

Suze Figueroa said, "Well, see, that's the thing. When they're handsome they think they can get away with all kinds of stuff."

"Who?" said Kim Duk O'Hara. There were nine of them, just off second watch, all unwinding in the Furlough Bar.

"This armed robber," Corky said. "Weren't you listening?"

"No," said Kim Duk.

Corky laughed. "See, this happened on my next-to-last day, just before I pulled the pin." A former cop, Corky had left the department two years earlier. "Got in all the papers, too. What a send-off! The robber—they called him the Gentleman Bandit—specialized in convenience stores," Corky said.

Mileski said, "Those places! Just banks by another name. Cash withdrawal by Smith & Wesson, twenty-four-seven. Have some cigarettes and Twinkies while you're at it."

"No, that's 7-Eleven," the Flying None said.

"Twenty-four-seven means twenty-four hours a day seven days a week," Corky said, waving his arms hugely and smiling. Mort groaned deeply. Corky and Mort co-owned and ran the bar, Corky having bought a half interest just two years back. Mort was also a former cop, but unlike Corky, didn't talk much.

He was irritable and crabby, which didn't seem to bother his customers. Figueroa believed that cops took a perverse delight in crabby bartenders. Still, most of the cops who hung out here thought Mort had driven his first partner away with his bitching and moaning. The partner had sold out to Corky. Corky was the perfect foil for Mort; he just laughed when Mort snarled.

He said, "So what I'm sayin' is in he goes. I mean, he's done maybe fifteen, eighteen stores we know of by that time, and he's gotta know we're looking for him, but he goes in anyway."

"Yeah, well, he also got away with it fifteen, eighteen times," Kim Duk said, making a not-bad point.

Corky merely beamed on Kim Duk. "It was the media called him the Gentleman Bandit because he's polite, see? Sheesh. Make him a hero, right? So anyway he goes into this convenience store on Kedzie. He's swaggering; he's cool; he's handsome. And he's got a thirty-eight. Goes behind the counter and tells the sweet young thing to please give him all the money out of the cash register and all the cigarette packages she can stuff in this big brown bag. And she does."

"I would too," said Kim Duk.

"Says stuff like 'if you don't mind,' and 'thank ya kindly, honey.' Then he's ready to go. But he wants an efficient getaway. Now, his other masterful jobs have been in Ravenswood, South Shore, Old Town, Back of the Yards, I mean all over the city, but not right here in the middle of the Loop where there's a hell of a lot of one-way streets, so he asks her, 'Say, honey, what's the best road to the Kennedy Expressway?' Being sweet, see? She says, 'Take Randolph Street.' "

"You're kidding me."

"Never. So he says thanks and good-bye, and I'm here to tell you he actually gives her a quick kiss on the cheek, and he quick-steps out of there. Soon as he's out the door, she dials 911 and informs Dispatch about the robbery and says, 'He's gonna be taking Lake Street to the Kennedy.' Naturally, the 911 operator asks how she's so sure, and she tells him. And we get the word. So my partner Jimmy-Jones Sharpe and I are out there on Madison, scream a couple of blocks over, and pick him up. It's easier than netting minnows in August."

"If they were all brain surgeons," Norm said, "we'd never catch 'em."

"I would," said Mileski.

"Jeez. Mort," Corky said, swabbing the bar surface with a rag, "do you have to leave beer goo all over the counter?"

"Keeps the yuppies away," Mort said.

"No yuppies is one thing," Corky said. "But how about basic sanitation?"

Mort snarled and leaned against the ice maker. They were the odd couple, Corky cleaning and Mort bitching.

"So, Susie," Corky said, changing subjects while he scrubbed the counter, "I hear you're a hero." The bar behind him was the only thing close to trendy in the place. Five tiers of wall-length glass shelves totally filled with bottles spread before a not-too-clean mirror. The mirror was a source of constant wrangling between Mort and Corky. Mort believed that washing it would destroy the ambience, though he would never have used the word "ambience." Even the word "character" wasn't one he admitted to knowing in this context. He said, "You ain't gonna hookerize my bar."

The Furlough was a typical cop hangout, dark, no ferns, small windows that hadn't been washed since Eisenhower was president, and every kind of booze known to humankind. God forbid the district commander should stop in and ask for something they didn't have.

"Don't call me Susie. It's Suze."

Norm said, "Rhymes with booze."

"Or coo—" Mileski began.

"Do *not* go there!" Figueroa said.

"So you're a hero," Corky repeated.

"Please! I'm not."

"Tackled a guy with an automatic weapon. Saved Bennis's ass. What I hear."

"Guy thought he was Rambo," Figueroa said. "Shooting one-handed. Those pieces rise when you fire them, which is why you gotta hold them two-handed, but the idiot didn't know that. He was firing way over Bennis's head."

"Still," Mileski said, "that wasn't bad action."

Figueroa said, "You know what I was thinking when I decided to tackle him?"

"You're going to tell me. I know that much."

"That it would take way less time and agony to tackle him 'by hand' so to speak than to spend the rest of the day and evening sitting in front of a round table inquiry explaining why I 'discharged a firearm.' "

"You got *that* right," Corky said fervently.

"Sad but true," said Mileski.

"And the hell of it is," Bennis said, "that the asshole I was chasing got away. Ran down the slope to Randolph. I mean, I was right on his tail, but when he got where there were pedestrians, he took a bunch of cash out of his pocket, paper money from the currency exchange, and threw it up in the air."

"No shit?"

"Yeah, and people just fell all over it. I couldn't get *through*. My guess is when he got to Michigan Avenue he grabbed a cab."

Figueroa said, "Some of the money from the currency exchange—a whole lot of money—was in the car, but I guess he'd stuffed his pockets with whatever he could grab."

"Say, you know what," Mileski said. "At least that guy wasn't *so* stupid."

"Yeah. I bet he was smart enough to keep some, too," Figueroa said.

"It's a funny old world," said Corky, setting up more glasses.

Speaking of the world, there was nothing on earth, Figueroa reflected, as satisfying as letting your guard down after work, coming in and having a beer to unwind. Especially among others of your kind, who understood your problems. You *need* it. Non-cops just don't understand. Other professions unwind after work too, but she believed cops were different.

She had always secretly kind of liked being the only woman in the Furlough after the tour. It gave her a sense of being one of the guys. But they had a new female officer these days.

Sandi Didrickson, the Flying None, was bellied up to the bar. The gang called her the Flying None for a couple of reasons, partly because she came in after the tour, drank three beers, the first two fast, and then after the third glided out, flying on wings of hops.

Figueroa was a-one-beer-and-I'm-outta-here kind of person. For one thing, she needed to get home to the kids and Sheryl. The nurse was supposed to leave at five o'clock.

"But *why* didn't they let you through?" the Flying None said. Of course this was the other reason for her nickname. Sandi wasn't the sharpest knife in the drawer.

"They wanted to pick up the money."

"But they could see you were a police officer."

Bennis said, "And I'm sure that was a *huge* deterrent, Sandi."

Figueroa stood up. "Bye, guys," she said.

Everybody mumbled something or other. But as she pulled on her jacket, Bennis caught her eye and mouthed, "Thanks."

CHAPTER TWO

Monday, 4:45 P.M.

FIGUEROA'S HOUSE WAS painted a dark plum red with cream trim, which looked better than it sounded, stick-built in 1890 or so of thousands of pieces of yellow pine that had cured in the following hundred years to the hardness of cement.

It was on a street full of other Victorians—at least, Figueroa believed they were Victorians, although one of the cops she worked with said they were really Queen Anne style. At any rate, they were large ornate wooden structures, all about the same age, with occasional squat ranch houses of late 1940s to early 1950s vintage cowering on lots between the grander, older places. Driving down the street, you could easily see that at some point not long after World War II the owners of some of the big old places had had to raise money and sold off their side yards.

Most of the old places had the contrasting color trim style, which had been rediscovered a few years ago and was considered accurate to the period. The one next door to Figueroa's was a deep dusty blue with pale green trim. The one next to that was pumpkin and gray.

But this wasn't a wealthy neighborhood, just middle class, just getting by. People kept saying someday the rehabbers would discover these houses, but so far that hadn't happened. The houses were kept freshly painted, mostly, but gutters sagged here and there. The roofs of some showed patches of unmatching shingles—people saving up money for a few years in anticipation of a full reroofing. The yards had not been professionally landscaped, and although they were maintained with a great deal of pride, the work often had been done with more pride than skill. Now, in the last week of May, some grass already looked scalped and feeble from too-aggressive mowing, and much of the shrubbery was overpruned.

The neighborhood was extremely convenient, being just three miles northwest of the Loop. The street itself had all the usual Chicago problems—clogged drainage, not enough parking, and too many potholes.

Suze Figueroa found a parking spot only two and a half blocks from the house. Her secret personal horoscope held that if the parking space was less than two blocks away, that was a good omen and the rest of the day would be especially fine. If it was more than three blocks, bad luck, watch out for trouble. In between? Well, that was like partly cloudy. Or scattered showers. Not very predictable.

Figueroa put her handcuffs in their case and the case into her back pocket. Then she used her cyber-clicker to lock up the car.

She drooped from the heat and a full day's hard work. It was four forty-five when she reached the house and let herself in the back door. Her son J J would be home soon, on the five o'clock bus from school. At seven years old, he stayed after the regular school day to play soccer. Her sister's two daughters, Maria and Kath Birch, would be home at five-fifteen; Kath, who was twelve, from band practice and Maria, the teenager not quite from hell, from a friend's house, where they would ostensibly have been doing homework. Doing homework at that age meant trying out new colors of eye shadow and talking about tenth-grade boys.

As Figueroa closed the back door behind her, she looked around to make sure the house hadn't been broken into by crazed maniacs. Alma Sturdley, the nurse—actually a certified caregiver, not an R.N.—was in the kitchen making tea.

"Hi, Miss Sturdley," Figueroa said.

She would have liked to call the nurse Alma, but Miss Sturdley was determined not to be so informal, and refused to call her Suze, so she was stuck. They had hired Alma Sturdley from a pool of three possibles, and had picked her because she looked so *clean*. By and large, they were happy with her.

Sturdley said, "Good afternoon, Ms. Figueroa."

Since there seemed to be no crazed maniacs, Figueroa pulled out her sidearm as she went through the hall to the coat closet, where she dumped her raincoat. She stopped there and locked the trigger guard on her .357 Magnum Colt Python revolver. In a house with three children, there was no place for a loose loaded gun. Even after Figueroa had made it safe, she put it back in its holster under her arm. Like most cops, she felt exposed to the whims of malign fate without it.

Crossing the hall, she leaned into Sheryl's room.

"Hi, babe!" she said. "How's it going?"

"Bastard," Sheryl said. For some reason, when Sheryl wanted to say "better" she said "bastard." It was one of the few predictable words she used.

Sheryl had been injured in an accident on the Kennedy Expressway six months earlier when her car flipped end over end off a ramp. For several hideous days, Sheryl's husband Robert, Suze, Kath, Maria, and J J thought she'd die. Once she was stabilized, the broken bones healed quickly. But although the body recovered, the effects of the closed-head injury, as the docs called it, were horrifying. Even now, four months after being released from the hospital, Sheryl couldn't walk without help because her entire left side got mixed messages from her brain. She also had a big problem with formulating words.

"Well, I'll be back down in a few minutes," Figueroa told her.

"Good," Sheryl said, perfectly clearly.

Figueroa went up the narrow rear service stairs, which all these old houses seemed to have. The front stairs were quite grand, rising in a graceful curve from the hallway near the front door. A curving railing with turned spindles framed the stairs and a huge oak newel post stood proudly at the base.

The back stairs were steep, cramped, and unadorned. In her imagination Suze passed the ghosts of a dozen Victorian maids carrying piles of towels and sheets from the basement laundries, damp hair straggling loose from their tightly pinned rolls, sweat running down their necks, in those days before air-conditioning.

J J and Suze lived on the third floor, where there were four bedrooms, two of them unused except for boxes of stuff nobody could bear to throw out, and a couple of racks and piles of winter clothes. Sheryl's husband Robert and their two girls had their bedrooms on the second floor, which had five bedrooms and two baths. When Sheryl recovered, they fully expected to move her to the big bedroom Robert occupied. Right now it was safer to have her on the first floor so they could get her out fast in case of fire.

Figueroa let the nurse go, started to stir up peanut butter cookies, and got out the ingredients for dinner. Pasta tonight. Rigatoni marinara. Extra garlic.

Peanut butter cookies, she reflected, are truly not brain surgery. A cup of peanut butter, a cup of sugar, brown and white mixed, a cup and a half of flour, butter, salt, an egg, and mix it all up while the oven heats. Cookies made a house smell happy, however simple they were. Roll the dough into balls, mash them down with a fork. The cookies baked while Figueroa sliced onions, garlic, zucchini, and fresh tomatoes for the marinara sauce. She set the veggies aside to wait for dinnertime.

Then she spent just a few minutes sitting on the end of

Sheryl's bed, telling her about the day. The funny parts, not the dangerous stuff.

The man in the backyard watched the inner wood door open inward, and then the screen door open outward. A twelve-year-old girl came out, dwarfed by two huge black plastic garbage bags, which she carried with arms thrust around their middles, as if she were waltzing with two fat grandmothers.

"Why do I alllllllways have to take out the garbage?" she said over her shoulder.

Someone inside answered, patiently, "You don't always do it. You do it Monday and Wednesday." A slender, dark-haired woman came to the back door, still talking as she opened the screen. "Maria does it Tuesday and Thursday. J J does it Friday and Saturday. And you know this." The girl grinned at her.

The woman leaned against the door frame, studying the girl. "Oh, wait a minute, here. Kath, you're pulling my chain, right?"

The girl started to giggle. "Got you, Aunt Suze."

"Yeah, yeah, yeah." She laughed, too. "Hop to it."

The man had watched the woman closely, his eyes slightly narrowed in recognition. The screen door closed. The inside door stayed open.

The girl walked down the cement path to the alley, not hurrying.

She had on such a short little gray flippy skirt, the man thought. And just a fuzzy pink sweater over that lithe little-girl chest. He stood unmoving, only half hidden behind two blue spruces that guarded one side of the path. He didn't expect to be seen. People rarely looked anywhere except straight ahead.

The sweet little girl moseyed closer, dancing little-girl dance steps despite the big bags. One of the bags hiked up her skirt on the left side. He could see the white underwear she wore.

Such a dangerous thing to let your nice little girl go out to the alley all by herself wearing almost nothing. Why, look. You could almost see downy hairs standing up on her smooth thighs. Such a short skirt. Such a short, short little skirt. Such soft skin on such smooth, slender legs.

She swished past him, one bag brushing the spruce nearest the path with a sound like a fingernail on a blackboard, the other just catching its bottom for a second on a terra-cotta pot filled with scarlet geraniums.

He could smell her smell, that wonderful, soapy, shampooey smell of little girls.

She turned right at the end of the path and started down the alley toward the place near the short driveway that led into her father's rickety wooden garage. Three big garbage cans stood at the junction of the alley and driveway. He heard her feet scraping gravel in the alley as she went.

He watched her come back, doing a little skipping dance. *Skitch-skitch, tap-tap!* She went in the back door, and the screen door slammed itself behind her, but he could hear no voices. That meant the dark-haired woman most likely had left the kitchen. And the inner door still stood wide open.

Quickly he walked up the path to the house. He held his hand up as if to knock, just in case anyone was inside. Pausing just a second or two to gaze through the screen and make sure no one was near, he let himself in the back door.

CHAPTER THREE

ALMA STURDLEY HAD left at five o'clock. The deal was for her to be in the house from eight A.M. to five P.M., while Robert and Suze were at work and the kids were in school. Since on Figueroa's present shift she left early in the morning, Sheryl's husband Robert Birch waited until Alma arrived. On days when Figueroa had to work late, she called Robert at work and he would get home early. Also Maria was supposed to let Suze know if she planned to go to a friend's house, so Figueroa could get hold of her if they needed the teenager to come home and take over. The whole thing was pretty complicated. Alma fed Sheryl and bathed her, got her to the bathroom, washed her clothes, and so on. Alma also put Sheryl through her prescribed daily exercises, a full series in the morning and a second series in the afternoon. Sheryl could walk a little, but only with support because of the weakness on her left side. Alma was at the house Monday through Friday, which meant the family took care of Sheryl on Saturday and Sunday, and of course nights. A special therapist came in for an hour and a half five mornings a week at nine—the maximum the insurance would pay for—Monday, Tuesday, Wednesday, Thursday and Saturday for specific muscle work that Alma couldn't supervise. This odd schedule meant Sheryl never had to go more than one full day without her muscle-stretching and leg exercises, and the electrical stimulation of a few muscles that wouldn't contract without it. A neurological consultant came every Thursday and administered tests. She arrived at four-thirty and stayed an hour, so that day nobody had to be home until maybe five-thirty, as long as they were sure she was here. Alma could let her in before she left. Figueroa called every Thursday at four forty-five to be absolutely certain.

"Hey!" Kath said as all six of them finally got collected around the dinner table. Sheryl was in her wheelchair, held upright in place with a woven chest belt, just to be on the safe side. It seemed an indignity, and usually she could sit pretty well by herself, but she had fallen out once and hurt her jaw badly. Her right side was extremely strong, overcompensating for the weakness on the left. The problem was that if she started to tip, she could grab something with her right hand, but she wasn't usually able to recover her balance.

Figueroa stood in the doorway, just about to go out to the kitchen.

"Hey what?" she said.

"The band is going to the inauguration! We're gonna march in the parade! Isn't that great, Dad?"

"How much is it going to cost us?" Robert asked.

Kath's enthusiasm faded slightly, but she was ready for this question. "Maybe nothing. We've got more than six months, so we're gonna do lots of bake sales and car washes and sell candy."

Sheryl's head bobbed up and down as it did when she was excited. She said, "Abate money."

For some reason Kath understood her best of all of the family and translated. "She said, 'That's great, honey,' " Kath told them. Proud of her mother.

Even Kath could not understand her all the time, not even as much as half the time. The muscles of Sheryl's mouth just did not do what the brain wanted them to. In addition, Sheryl was frequently confused. Figueroa believed that the months of limited mobility, the huge life change from being a competent, self-reliant human being, a highly paid computer engineer to a terribly ill, dependent, and physically weak person had disoriented her. Maybe it was the efforts the brain made to reconstruct itself, the irregular fits and starts of improvement and backsliding, but something gave her bouts of hallucinations.

Figueroa left Kath to explain all the excellent details of the planned Washington trip to her dad. She didn't want to hang over them, and she had more dishes to get from the kitchen, anyway. Being the odd person out in the household was often difficult. Figueroa was sure Robert appreciated the work she contributed, and he seemed to appreciate the care she gave Sheryl. After all, the nurse was here only nine hours a day, five days a week—forty-five hours that left a hundred and twenty-three hours a week when the rest of them had to cope. Particularly when it came to bathing Sheryl and getting her to the bathroom, Suze was afraid that the basic, unpleasant care might damage Robert's relationship with her. There were men who can step into a caregiver role and feel closer to their wives, but Robert did not seem to be one of them.

The rigatoni marinara in a huge bowl was keeping warm in the turned-off oven. She brought it into the dining room, checked to see that the grated cheese, the salad, lemonade, and milk were already on the table, and finally sat down.

"And we're gonna reenact that really famous picture of the Revolutionary War band. You know the one. Mrs. Spears says it's called 'Yankee Doodle,' or 'The Spirit of '76,' and it was painted by Archibald McNeal Willard. There's two drum players, and a fife player. I get to be the fife."

"Well, that makes sense," Maria said in the voice of the older, condescending sister. "After all, you play the flute."

"Yes, isn't it *excellent*?" Kath asked.

"Is the flute player the one with the bloody bandage around his head?" J J asked.

Kath said, "Yeah! I get to have it all gross and bloody."

J J said, "Way cool! Do you get to meet the President?"

"Sure, I guess. Maybe."

J J said to Suze, "Can I go, Mom?"

"I don't think so, honey. You're not in the band."

He made a disappointed face, so Suze said, "And besides, since it'll be January, you'll probably have a basketball game."

"Oh. Oh, yeah."

Robert said, "How come there's no meat in this?"

"It's got marinara sauce. The doctor said we should all eat less meat and more veggies."

"Well, I like it with sausage."

Figueroa sighed. "Next time I'll make a side of sausage."

She snuck a glance at Sheryl. Even though Sheryl couldn't talk properly, when she was clearheaded, Figueroa thought she was entirely aware of all the nuances of everything that went on in the house. She gave Suze a small lopsided smile of sympathy with the right side of her mouth.

Not for the first time, Suze thought that she and J J had to get a place of their own soon. But she couldn't leave Sheryl right now. She was still too fragile.

The kids giggled and teased each other and told Sheryl and each other extremely dumb jokes. J J said, "Why do seagulls fly out to sea instead of in to the bay?"

"I don't know," Kath said.

"Because then they would be bay-gulls. Bagels, get it?"

Maria groaned.

This was much better for Sheryl than being solemn. When their mother, Suze's and Sheryl's, came over to visit, she spoke in a whisper, as if Sheryl were dying, and shushed the kids. *Jeez!* Figueroa thought. *Talk about a totally wrong approach.*

"My turn to take out the dishes," J J said. He was such a good little guy, doing his part.

"And Maria's turn to load the dishwasher," Kath said, the younger sister just checking to be on the safe side.

"J J, bring in the cookies while you're out there. Okay?" Suze said.

"No prob, Mama-san."

"Where did that come from?" she asked Robert, but he only shrugged.

"School," J J said, returning. "Second grade is China and Japan."

"Oh. Well, what's third grade?"

"Dunno."

"The Fertile Crescent," Kath said. "Mesopotamia and all."

"Oh." Suze stared at the platter of peanut butter cookies. "J J, did you eat some of those?"

"No, but I *will*!"

"Seriously. I thought—" Mmm. She really thought there had been a bigger pile of cookies when she left them to cool. But then, it had been a long day. She was tired. Her brain might be on overload. Who knew?

At two A.M., when the house had been quiet for a couple of hours, the man started toward the stairs. He suspected that the old, shrunken boards that floored the attic might creak, so he had stayed quiet as long as he could. He had been lying on a lumpy pile of discarded winter clothing, and he was now very stiff and sore. Plus, during the day, the attic was unbearably hot, and it had cooled as slowly as grease congealing.

So fortunate, he thought, to have both back stairs and main stairs. But then, that was life. Sometimes you got good luck and sometimes you got bad.

Passing slowly across the splintery wood, he stepped onto the narrow back stairs. Probably the attic had housed servants once upon a time. There was some dumb floral wallpaper still clinging in faded shreds to the wall next to the landing.

When the stairs reached the third floor, the wallpaper got newer. White roses on a blue background. The third floor, he guessed, had either housed the more important servants or maybe a nursery. Or both.

Here he became very, very quiet. He peered into the dark third-floor hall.

It was fascinating, he thought, how you could close your eyes and still know what was what and who was where. The third floor smelled warm and woody and like fabrics, but not dusty, so you knew it wasn't used just as storerooms; people lived here. There was a faint smell of bubble bath. That meant there was either a woman, a girl, or a young child, which confirmed what he already had observed about the family. Also, there was an outdoors smell, like grass or earth, probably earth, the more he thought about it. So maybe the kid played outdoor sports.

He stepped the last two steps down into the third-floor hall.

The nearest door was open. Did he dare risk peering in? Stepping as softly, he thought, as snowflakes falling on feathers, he moved forward carefully until he had covered about a yard or so, and he could see diagonally into the bedroom. No perfume smell, some leathery smell. In the dim spill of light from a streetlamp, he could just make out a form in the bed. Very small. Hockey stick on the wall, baseball mitt on the wall, both as decorations, and a soccer ball on the floor as if it were in constant use. Shouldn't leave things on the floor. People could trip and fall. *Wall, small, ball, hall,* he giggled silently to himself. *And that's not all.*

Yes, the boy child was in this room. That certainly was obvious, wasn't it?

The child snuffled and the man backed slowly out.

On the stairs once more, he stalked very carefully down to the second floor. There was a light at the far end of the second-floor hall, maybe forty feet away. He could see an open door a little distance from him, but the two closest doors, one on the left and one on the right, were shut. He leaned next to the keyhole of one and inhaled. There was an aroma of flowers, roses or lilacs maybe, he didn't know much about flowers, but he decided it was perfume, not live flowers. So—maybe one of the girls was in there. Maybe the soft, smooth little one with the short little skirt.

He sniffed the air, savoring the scent as if it were the bouquet of a fine wine.

He gave up on this for now and went down to the first floor, where the landing presented him the choice of continuing down to the basement or entering the kitchen.

It was the kitchen for him. A yellowish alley light shone through the window over the sink, and although he didn't dare turn on any other lights, it was enough.

He stood for a minute or two, just absorbing the smells and glorying in the thrill of being in other people's intimate space, a ghost in the innermost room of their house. Wasn't the kitchen the heart of a house? And here he was in their heart. And nobody knew.

Then he unzipped and urinated in their sink.

It was a long, long stream and gave him immense satisfaction. There was no bathroom in the attic, and he didn't dare use any of the bathrooms anyway, at least not at night. He suspected that he could flush the third-floor toilet in the morning, after the woman and the boy who lived on that floor had gone down to breakfast. There would be so much moving around and water noise all over the house with the girls getting ready for school—everybody said girls spent hours in the bathroom—and the Suze-person probably cooking breakfast, that nobody would notice.

Now he opened the refrigerator. Light spilled out into the kitchen, blinding after the darkness. Maybe the woman in the downstairs bedroom would see it. Maybe not. It didn't matter. The spaz could hardly talk.

Plus, kids raided refrigerators all the time, didn't they?

What wonderful fun it had been to listen to the dinner conversation. All those sweet little-girl stories. And the spaz woman going *glub-glub-glub*. And him standing on the back stairs, four steps up, eating cookies.

Holding the refrigerator door open with his shoulder, he lifted a bowl from the shelf. Some kind of pasta.

He stood there with the door open. Slowly, he fed himself with his fingers, eating right out of the bowl. Not bad, but the stuff needed some meat. The hoity-toity male voice at dinner had been right about that.

He put the bowl back, confident that no one would notice any food was missing. In a house with three children, how could anybody ever remember exactly how much food they had? He would, of course, if it were his house. But other people were such slobs.

He rinsed his fingers in the sink, swishing the urine spots away, too. When the sink was clean, he went back to the refrigerator. In a drawer he found some sliced salami. It was in a square plastic deli package, about three-quarters full. He took two slices, careful to leave four, which was still most of it, then closed the plastic down methodically. No one would ever notice.

Delicious.

So now, he thought, it was time to explore the basement.

CHAPTER FOUR

Tuesday, 2:30 A.M.

AN OLD MAN stood in the middle of the street, in front of the Chicago Police Department at Eleventh and State, looking down at his toes on the white line, trying to figure out if it was very late at night or very early morning. His face was almost invisible under a growth of beard and long, uneven hair. What little skin showed, mostly nose and forehead, was gray with dirt. He wore the pants from a rusty brown suit and the jacket from a navy-blue striped suit over a tan knit shirt. All three items of clothing had been given to him at a Salvation Army someplace, but he couldn't exactly remember where it was, now. He wore sneakers he had found in a trash can in Lower Wacker Drive. A pair of socks, mottled brown from mud, hung loosely in folds around his ankles. Despite the heat, he wore a threadbare black raincoat he'd had for as long as he could remember—from the old days when he was still somebody—flapping over the whole outfit.

His hands were quite clean. He had just washed them in a rest room at Union Station, before the transit cops moved him along.

He was staring at the police department headquarters when a horn sounded behind him. He'd been thinking about other things. It was night but he hadn't noticed the headlights coming up. Quickly he shuffled out of the street, hobbling onto the curb on sore feet and arthritic knees. He limped over to stand near the police department doors.

Fifty-one years ago he had married his high school sweetheart. Barbara Jean, sweet as cream, the fall prom queen, he thought. Twenty-four years ago he was still married, happily as far as he could tell. No children. That was not so good. Then he retired. Two years later, his wife had left him, tired of his gloom.

Once upon a time the man had been a police officer. He had retired after twenty-five years on the job, with a full pension, sixty percent of his final year's salary. He found he had no friends who weren't cops. Funny he'd never realized it before. That year he and his wife tried spending the winter in Sarasota—it sounded so wonderful, sunny days, no ice, no snow, no shoveling, no stuck cars—but they didn't know anybody down there and the people they met, though perfectly nice, weren't like their Chicago friends. And they couldn't get used to the climate. Boring. They came back to Chicago. The people he knew best hadn't yet retired. Most of them didn't have their time in. He had started young in the job, twenty-two years old. Most of his buddies came on the job later than he had, in their mid or late twenties, and still had a few years to go.

He tried hanging around the district, tried to pass the time of day with his old friends, go to lunch maybe, but the cops had work to do. They'd talk a little bit, making an effort to be nice, but then they'd go back to the job.

An amazing thing, really. One day you were one of the guys, exchanging rude comments about the top cops, complaining about stupid new department policies, dissing civilians, stopping together for a beer and war stories after a tour. And then the next day here's the crew throwing you a retirement party, all good fellows together, friends, fellow soldiers, brothers almost. They loved you. And then the day after that, you were nobody. Like pulling down a window shade. Out. It was over.

He'd heard about it from other retired cops. Who hadn't? But you never quite believed it would happen to you. Like death. Or getting old. You never quite believed it would happen.

In order to get out of the house, for a while he spent his days sitting on a bench near his old station, the Eighteenth District, over on Chicago Avenue, but it hurt him too much seeing the squad cars going in and out, rabbiting out of the lot, Mars lights flashing, doing stuff that looked so important and glamorous from outside, even though he knew it wasn't always important and almost never glamorous. But he wanted so bad, so bad, *so bad* to be back.

There were a couple of old guys he knew, retired cops his age, and he hung around with them some, but they drank too much and complained too much, and after a while so did he.

So his wife left. He didn't blame her. She was only going to have one life, and it might as well not be spent with a gloomy drunk. He assigned her fifty percent of his pension. He didn't begrudge it; she deserved it. She'd stuck with him many years. But after a few years, he lost the house. Finally, what little was left of the pension seemed just barely enough to buy drink and maybe an SRO hotel for two weeks out of every month. And little by little everything just basically fell apart.

He stared up at the CPD building. They were going to move, he'd heard. Move the central offices to a big new building someplace. They were gonna tear this building down. Hard to believe.

For two years, 1971 and 1972, he actually worked in this building. He was secretary to the Commander of Personnel. Everybody had to go through him to get to the commander. Glory years.

While he leaned on the wall, a couple of young cops came out of the department doors.

"Hey, Pops," the tall, skinny one said. "You gotta move along."

"Oh, sure, sure, officer," he mumbled. He felt in his pocket for the bottle he carried. Just to make certain it was there. He always felt for it when people made him nervous.

"Get going," the shorter cop said.

The tall one seemed uneasy about moving him along so abruptly. "Want to go to a shelter, Pop?"

"Oh, no. No, no, no." Shelters were dangerous. Full of crazies. And dirt. And disease. If it had been zero degrees and snowing, maybe. But tonight the weather was plenty warm.

He began to move away, to show he was complying. They lost interest in him as he moved north.

There was an alley running east off State Street. He'd go lie down there. Roll up his raincoat and use it for a pillow. Done it a hundred times. A thousand.

Half a block into the alley, with the glow from the peach-colored streetlights of State Street reaching faintly all the way back here, he stopped. Unobtrusively, he shook the bottle of cheap wine in his pocket and he could tell just from the weak slosh that it was nearly empty. He'd have to beg for some money before lying down. Couldn't get to sleep without a drink. He fished in the pocket of the raincoat and found the McDonald's coffee cup he carried and used for begging.

Then he realized how late it was. He didn't exactly know the time, had to be two or three A.M., and he'd forgotten again that it was so late because State Street was always bright, there were always cars going by, and the night was hot. But where would he find pedestrians to drop some coins in his cup at this hour? Cops coming out of the building? He should have asked the two young guys for money. Although—no—he could never force himself to do that—except—

When a shadow fell on him, he turned, surprised. You had to be careful on the street, but at this hour the worst attackers—the most unpredictable and most vicious attackers, swarms of teenagers—wouldn't be in a place like this. If they were out at this hour, they'd be at the El stops looking for late-shift workers.

"Can you spare some change?" he said immediately, hearing the desperation in his own voice.

"I think I can help you."

TUESDAY

CHAPTER FIVE

From the *Chicago Sun-Times*,
Tuesday, May 31:
[City News, section B, p. 2]

More than 220 homeless men and women will share a $300,000 settlement among them, an amount decided upon when District Judge Morton Eidesman ruled today that seizure of their personal property was a violation of their rights. Two years ago city workers cleaned Lower Wacker Drive, and in the cleanup the homeless lost their belongings.

The class action lawsuit charged sanitation workers' sweep of Lower Wacker violated the homeless rights in destroying their property.

"It was a denial of our humanity," said William Lyall, one of the plaintiffs. "The judge did the right thing, God bless him."

The city has admitted no wrongdoing.

Tuesday morning, 7:30 A.M.

SERGEANT PAT TOUHY was in her General Patton mode at morning roll call. Touhy had two modes. Clint Eastwood once said to a director that he had two facial expressions and he had given him both. Well, Touhy too. There was General Patton, which was unpleasant enough but you knew where you were with it, or Understanding Superior Officer. Which was a bitch.

You never knew with Ms. Understanding whether the understanding smile was real or a suck-in.

She finished the educational five-minute updating on what probable cause for search meant. Then she said, "Let's get to the day and read some crimes."

"They ever find the other currency exchange asshole?" Bennis asked. "I'd know him if they got him."

"No. And the one you guys got won't talk."

"Shit."

"Except to say Figueroa used excessive force capturing him. Says his liver's bruised."

"Jeez, Sarge," Figueroa said. "He hadda weigh two-fifty. I'm maybe a hundred twenty after two Quarter Pounders with cheese."

"Says you dropped on him when he was down."

"I surely did—"

"You shoulda shot him," Mileski said.

"Yeah. I'll know better next time."

Sandi the Flying None said, "Why didn't you shoot him, Suze? I can't remember why you said you didn't."

Several people groaned. "Humanitarian instincts," Figueroa said.

"Wait a minute!" Bennis said. "Figueroa saved my life. The suits'd better not get any idea of jamming her up!"

"Oh, give it a rest, Bennis," Touhy said. "I know that. The brass knows that. They're going through the motions. Cover their ass. And by the way, Figueroa, get yourself up to Branch 71 soon as we're done here. The ASA on the case wants to interview you before the arraignment. Now, moving right along, we got a problem. The Detective Division had a little medical situation, so some of you—Didrickson, Mileski, O'Hara, Figueroa, and Bennis—are going over to Area Four to do some canvassing for them today. You will also follow up on your own existing cases from yesterday. Bennis and Figueroa—

don't pretend to forget you're still on the pickpockets! We've got a whole lot of highly pricey stores seriously upset."

"Wait a minute, Sarge!" Bennis said. "This means we're doubling. We're working *two* jobs."

"And your point is?" Touhy asked.

"What medical situation?" Mileski asked.

"Last night was the dinner honoring Chief of Detectives Ramon Bartlett on his retirement. Most of the off-duty detectives were there. Maybe two-thirds of the dick roster. They all have food poisoning."

"Some detectives *they* are!" Bennis said.

"What did they eat?" Figueroa asked.

"Apparently they had onion soup gratiné, boeuf bourguignonne, baby peas—"

"I guess it was really barf bourguignonne," said Mileski.

"As a matter of fact, no," said Touhy, who had no sense of humor to speak of, and was certainly not going to put up with one in anybody else. "They think it was the crème anglaise sauce on the dessert. Some of the eggs weren't cooked enough. Or maybe the sauce was held at room temperature too long. Hot weather like this, see. Salmonella, they think. Forty percent of the detectives are off."

"Off for how long?"

"Couple, three days at least. Okay. Here's what we're gonna do. Mileski and Didrickson go as a team, O'Hara all by his lonesome, and Figueroa and Bennis soon as Figueroa gets done with the state's attorney."

Kim Duk O'Hara asked, "But what about speeders and double-parkers and like that, Sarge?"

"I guess Chicago will just have to take its chances today."

At which point they were sent out.

The ASA doing the Herzog case, Herzog being the guy Figueroa had flattened on the golf course, naturally wanted to talk with Figueroa before the arraignment. Because he was important and Figueroa wasn't important, she was supposed to go to him. Fortunately, Branch 71, one of a dozen Cook County criminal courts, was in the same building as the CPD HQ and the First District police station. In a matter of months, this agglomeration of offices would all be history. The First District was moving to new quarters at 1700 South State. The CPD main offices were getting a whole new building of their very own. The courts were going God knows where. And the present building was going to be demolished. "All this history gone!" some said.

Most said, "And high time too."

For now, not only was the ASA and the court and the First District in the present building, but as a matter of fact, Herzog also was in the building, in the men's lockup on the twelfth floor, just below the women's lockup, on thirteen, called the "penthouse" by the cops.

If Figueroa had been in some distant district, she would still have had to go to the ASA. As it was, she gave Bennis a Hershey bar—with almonds, who said she wasn't a saint?—told him she hoped she'd be right back, and headed for the elevator.

The ASA, Francis Xavier Malley, was tapping his foot when she tracked him down in the wide piece of hall that constituted the back end of the Branch 71 courtroom. Court was not yet in session. Besides tapping his foot, he had his arms crossed and his briefcase wedged between his left leg and the adjacent wall. Suze thought, *And we call the perps assholes.*

"Officer Figueroa?"

"State's Attorney Malley?"

"I asked you to come up forthwith. Herzog will be brought in any minute now."

"Came as soon as I was told, sir," she said with just a slight edge in her voice. Back in the academy, an instructor she admired had said, "Don't risk your job for the idiots. There's too many of them, and a new batch is born every day," and he was absolutely right. She couldn't resist adding, "Course if you ever talk to anybody in charge of speeding up the elevators—"

"Let's get to work. Why'd you pick on Herzog in the first place?"

"Pick on him? Have you read the case report?"

"Yeah. Humor me. His PD wants to go to trial. Says Herzog doesn't want to plead. I need to know how you'd do on the stand."

"We were patrolling on Roosevelt Road, heading toward Michigan Avenue. We got a call from the dispatcher about the robbery, and they had the description of the car, a two-door green Ford, which was presumed to be heading our way. Two male whites. Saw them less than a minute later. Soon as we got behind them they rabbited. Isn't the fact that the cash was on them proof enough?"

"Cash can belong to anybody."

"Oh, please! Both of them running like hell? What about the currency exchange operator? He ID the guy? Description match?"

"It matches, what there is of it, but he didn't see his face. He wore a stocking mask."

"Oh, great. What about the other guy? The guy driving the car?"

"What about him? The currency exchange manager never saw his face at all. He stayed outside in the car with the motor running. Anyway, he hasn't turned up anyplace. You people are supposed to find him, not me."

"Okay. Well, what about dealing with the one we have, get him to give the other guy up? Can't you plead this one to a lesser charge? If maybe this one really wasn't the planner—"

"Malley!" said a voice.

A man in a dark suit with a fine white stripe appeared next to Figueroa. Though no expert on clothes, she could tell the suit was probably half the price of Malley's. Therefore, this had to be the public defender.

"Ben," Malley said without enthusiasm. He added, "Ben Jenks, this is Officer Figueroa."

Jenks held out his hand, but while they shook, he said, "Mr. Herzog is pleading innocent."

Figueroa said, "So why'd he run?"

"You know, officer, a lot of people are afraid of the police. He didn't know what you wanted him for."

"Didn't know but he was pretty sure it was something bad, huh?"

Malley said to Jenks, "We've got him dead-bang on possession of an unregistered firearm."

"I think you've also got him on attempting to kill a police officer," Figueroa said angrily.

As if none of this mattered, Jenks added, "Plus, you used unnecessary force in subduing him, Officer Figueroa. He has the bruises to prove it."

"Jeez, maybe he ought to try not shooting at the cops if he doesn't want bruises."

"We ought to get into the courtroom pretty soon," Malley said to Jenks, as if Figueroa were an idle bystander.

"And the guy is bigger than I am, besides," Figueroa said.

"Doesn't matter," Jenks said.

There was a call in the court, and people started to take their seats.

Malley said, "That's all, officer."

As she turned to walk out of the room, Figueroa saw Herzog. He was coming into the holding pen next to a jail guard, and Jenks, the public defender, went to meet him. Figueroa detoured a few feet and said, "Hiya, Herzog."

Then she moved to stand right next to the prisoner, turned and bumped shoulders with him and caught Jenks's and Malley's gaze. Herzog stood fifteen inches taller than Figueroa. One of his thighs was as big as her whole body. He had to weigh 250, minimum.

Jenks and Malley exchanged glances, as Figueroa knew they would. They were both visualizing a jury taking a look at this picture.

Without a further word, allowing herself just a tiny nod but no smile, she turned away and strode to the elevators.

"Oh, this is so cool!" Figueroa pounded the dashboard in a brisk *rat-tat-tat* as they took off in the car for Area Four.

Bennis said, "What's your problem?"

"I always wanted to be a detective. This is truly the very finest!"

"Well, your calm reserve and stolid, conservative personality is a great reassurance to me at all times, given the risky nature of our endeavor," Bennis said.

"Phooey!"

"Hey! Aren't you the young lady who told me that getting home for J J every day was such a priority? Remember how happy you were that patrol cops put in a regular eight hours and then can go home?"

"Well, sure, but—"

"Most people think cops put in long hours. We know better. And thank you, union. But detectives sure as hell do."

That was true and it brought Figueroa up short. It was almost impossible to have an unpredictable twelve- or maybe fifteen-hour-a-day job and take good care of a child. Maybe she could get a part-time nanny, she thought. Oh, sure. With whose money? Plus, right now when he was young was when J J needed her. And there was Sheryl, too, to think about—

Damn.

"Listen," Figueroa said, "J J isn't going to be seven forever. And anyway long hours is gonna be good practice for when I get to be District Commander."

"Oh, right. I forgot that was the plan."

"And for when I get to be Superintendent of Police."

"Oh, of course!"

"I'll make you Chief of Patrol."

"I'm holding my breath."

She ignored the sarcasm. Bennis was her buddy and if now and then he wanted to pretend to be an asshole, that was his business. But with maybe a bit of retaliation in mind, she asked, "Hey, Bennis! How's Yolanda?"

"Yolanda! What'chu asking about Yolanda for?" he said, doing his street-talk imitation. "You know I haven't seen Yolanda in months. I'm going with Amanda now."

"Yolanda, Amanda, sounds incestuous somehow."

"You got a dirty mind, girl! Besides, Deirdre was between Yolanda and Amanda."

"Between? I'm not gonna touch that with a ten-foot pole."

"And since Mileski isn't here, we don't got ourselves a ten-foot Pole."

CHAPTER SIX

"WASN'T THE CRÈME anglaise," Detective Mossbacher said, pronouncing it to rhyme with cream and grace. Which is how Figueroa would have pronounced it, but she had a feeling Bennis would soon instruct her otherwise. "And not salmonella. Worse."

"Worse than salmonella?" Figueroa said, because she knew he expected her to.

"They think it's E. coli. The bad kind of E. coli." He flipped a memo and pointed a thick finger at a line. "E. coli 0157:H7. Probably in the salad."

Bennis said, "Salad is supposed to be good for you."

"No kidding. They think one of the kitchen employees was a carrier and, much as I hate to say this, guys, did not use proper bathroom cleanliness procedures."

Figueroa said, "Ukkk!"

Since the sick detectives had come from every police area center in the city and therefore every area was depleted, the brass had decided to call in a few patrol cops from each district within each area. This spread the drain on the districts. On the one hand, you couldn't strip the districts, but on the other hand, when you have a homicide, you had to collect the facts ASAP. Eyewitness memories fade, or get falsely augmented by gossip or by inaccurate newspaper and TV reports. Trace evidence gets stepped on or blown away.

So Bennis and Figueroa had been sent over to Area Four. In Chicago, patrol officers work out of districts, of which there are twenty-five, and detectives work out of areas, of which there are five. The First District was part of Area Four, which was located way the hell west at 3151 W. Harrison. It covered Districts One, Ten, Eleven, Twelve, and Thirteen. This made it sort of an elongated east-west slice of the very center of the city.

Bennis and Figueroa and the rest of the First District crew had waited in the main room for their assignment. The place seemed quieter than usual to Figueroa, although she had never spent much time here. She thought in the last two years she'd been here at most maybe four times, tops, for one reason or another. Maybe the detectives were all out rushing around at double speed, covering for their sick colleagues.

Mileski and Sandi the Flying None got called in first. Mileski and Sandi got the job of canvassing businesses and restaurants around the scene of an armed bank robbery that had happened last evening. Kim Duk O'Hara got to canvass a luxury Loop hotel all alone about the death by choking of a beautiful young lady—a plum assignment, indoors and in air-conditioned premises. But the ingrate grumbled about it. He really loved tooling around in a squad car with Mars lights and sirens. And who could blame him?

Bennis and Figueroa were called last. "See Detective Mossbacher. Left door at the end of the hall."

Mossbacher was the "Grizzled Veteran." Old-style cop. Red face. Shiny shoes. His hair was cut very short on the sides and long on top. Figueroa's mind produced a picture of him at age twenty-two, a new recruit, short sides and long on top, the "in" style at the time. Probably he had been in style once or twice through the years, and again now, and never in his life changed his haircut.

"Have I got a deal for you," he said, grinning.

CHAPTER SEVEN

THE HOUSE WAS dead quiet. Stifling heat soaked the attic, and it wasn't even ten A.M. yet. His watch still ran, another piece of good luck. Maybe one of those batteries that go on forever because the company forgot to put in the obsolescence factor. After the horrible luck on Monday, he deserved a whole lot of these little pieces of good luck.

The bad luck right now was the heat. The attic didn't even have an exhaust fan, and the dark-shingled roof hung hot right over his head. He could actually feel the direction of the radiating heat—it glowed in at him, coming from the east side of the roof, as if it were a space heater. Afternoon would be even worse.

Didn't these people know you should have an exhaust fan in your attic? Didn't they realize how much money you could save on your air-conditioning if you got rid of the heat up here? Fools!

Then he remembered how much money he had not saved in his life. Of course, that hadn't been his fault. He'd had a problem, that was all, and it ate money. Lawyers ate money.

He was dripping sweat. He hated to sweat. It was unsanitary.

Maybe he could go down to the third floor and spend the day there. It would be cooler, and as long as he didn't fall asleep, it would be okay. None of the family would get home before three-thirty at the earliest, would they? And he knew from yesterday that the cop got home about five, and the man had got home yesterday at six.

Maybe he could sleep on the kid's bed. Who'd notice? Little boys were sweaty, dirty monsters anyhow, weren't they?

He moved slowly and softly down the back stairs, stopping to listen. He reached the third-floor landing. It was so quiet he heard the refrigerator door close, two flights down, although that was partly because the kitchen was right next to the foot of these back stairs. He heard the nurse say, "There. Now let's see."

She was talking to the paralyzed woman. He heard her feet clump across the hall and into the spaz's room. God, what a clumsy, stupid person. He moved down another flight, to the second-floor landing.

"Now, Ms. Sheryl," the nurse said, "how about a nice bath?"

Bath! Oh, God, how he'd love a bath. He had to have a shower or a bath. Had to. Had to. *Had to!*

"Now you just wait. We'll make a nice lukewarm one. Too hot today for a hot bath, don't you think? We could get in a short bath before the therapist gets here."

"Margle. Uz."

Margle uz! he thought. What a retard.

"Or I suppose you might want it after you do all that exercising. No, I guess this is the best time. All right?"

Then he heard the bathwater running, and he got the brilliant idea. Rushing back up the stairs as fast as he could without making a sound, he hurried into the third-floor bathroom and turned on the water in the tub. He held his arm in the stream so that it wouldn't splash. A couple of inches of cool water was all he needed. Maybe a little more.

With the pipes running the bath for the spaz, there would be pipe noise. The old pipes in this old house were predictably clanky. Surely the stupid nurse wouldn't notice a little more gurgling and bumping.

What if she did?

He kept his eyes on the open door to the hall. If she did—? Well, now, if she did—if she did hear, if she did appear, if she did see him, well, these old houses had steep, old stairs. Why, they weren't even up to current building codes. She'd probably just have an unfortunate fall.

CHAPTER EIGHT

Tuesday, 10 A.M.

"POOR GUY!" FIGUEROA said. "The poor old guy!"

Bennis said, "Yeah," very subdued. "He looks just like my grandfather."

"Bennis, your grandfather is black."

"So? Also he probably looks just like *your* grandfather, Figueroa."

"Yeah, he surely does."

"He looks just like everybody's grandfather, you know?"

"Yes," she said, sadly, "I know."

"If you guys are gonna get sick, just leave," the pathologist said.

Figueroa said, "I'm *not*," with more force than was absolutely necessary. And she meant it.

Bennis said, "No ID at all?" He gestured at the clothes and "effects" on the rack eight feet back from the autopsy table. The only effects were a bottle with a label of some cheap wine and an inch or so left in it, and a McDonald's coffee cup. And eighty-eight cents—two quarters, three dimes, a nickel, and three pennies.

The diener, who had stripped the body for the autopsy, said, "Nope. Plus most of his pockets had holes in the bottom."

"Poor old guy," Bennis said, echoing her. That's one of the reasons Figueroa liked Norm Bennis, she thought to herself. Eleven years as a cop and he still hadn't lost his center. He was actually able to be tough on the job without being heartless.

"Well, now let's see." The pathologist, a chubby man in his early sixties, clapped his hands once. He had a Santa Claus beard and wore bright green-and-yellow checked pants finished off with oxblood tassel loafers peeking out under his lab coat. Most of the M.D.s here wore scrub suits and booties. Autopsies were a messy business. Dr. Percolin, however, wore the long lab coat and clear plastic covers over his stylish shoes, leaving his trouser bottoms open to possible splashing. He drew on two pair of gloves with that slapping noise people who wear surgical gloves love to make. *Puts the rest of us nonprofessionals in our place,* Figueroa thought. Although to be fair, Dr. Percolin here was accessible and friendly. "So you're the newbies!" he said. "Well, this is gonna be different. Ever seen an autopsy?"

"Of course," Bennis said.

"During training," Figueroa said. "The academy schedules autopsies for us. And twice when we filled in for one of the detectives."

"You're experts then, huh?" Before they could protest, he said, "Don't mind me teasing you. I've been doing this for twenty-two years and I still learn something new pretty much every day. Which is why I love it, mmm? And by the way, if you ever run into a pathologist who says he knows everything"—he fixed them with a very serious face—"run fast. Guys like that are a menace. Guys like that send innocent people to prison. Always check their results, mmm? But enough of this cheery chitchat."

Percolin studied the exterior of the naked body minutely, using a magnifying glass now and then to aid his eye. Then he directed the diener to make extra photos with a Polaroid CU-5 close-up camera of certain parts, including the nose.

He and the assistant turned the body over. After studying the back for hypostasis, which they found, they turned it again. With the body once again supine, he mumbled the usual intro into his foot-activated mike. "The body is that of a poorly nourished white male, seventy-one inches in length, one hundred and thirty-two pounds, hair gray, eyes brown. Rigor just passing off in the jaw and neck. We have what appears to be an appendectomy scar, normal size and location."

Suze couldn't see any fresh wounds on the body except a slight abrasion on the nose, which the doctor had included in his recorded notes. There seemed to be no obvious cause of death. "Hypostasis consistent with lying on back," Percolin said to the mike.

Mike off, Dr. Percolin pointed at the face and said, "Strangulation, I guess. Say, look at this."

"Dirty," Bennis said.

"I shouldn't have said look at this. I should have said smell this."

"We already do."

"Not that."

The body gave off a ripe, sweaty odor, in addition to the usual smells of feces and urine that cling to death. But Dr. Percolin had his nose right down near the corpse's unlovely neck.

Bennis leaned forward. The old man's chin rested above a filthy chest. And at that instant a bug, a real living insect, crawled out from the left armpit.

"Yo!" Bennis said.

The doc said, "Little critter must've just warmed up. They're real quiescent in the cooler."

The bug dropped onto the floor. The doc and the diener ignored it.

"Let's have you do this methodically. Look at the body as a whole," Percolin said.

Suze looked. The hair around the crotch of the old man was stained, and some of the gold granular stuff might be crystallized urine. The ankles were dark brownish gray with grime, darkest just above where the socks might have ended. But Figueroa said to Dr. Percolin, "The hands and face are clean." The face was unshaven, with a three- or four-day beard, but what skin could be seen was pink and washed.

"So he stopped someplace and washed up," Bennis said. "So what?"

Percolin looked at Bennis and waggled his head. "Not good, officer. You're a detective now."

"Okay. Tell me."

"Now. Like I said before, smell this."

"Yeah, yeah, okay."

Bennis leaned over the corpse and smelled where Percolin pointed. First the face, then the hands. After Bennis, Figueroa smelled, too. She said, "Hey! They're different!"

"Exactly." Figueroa received a big Santa Claus smile. "What do you deduce?"

"He washed his hands with some kind of liquid soap. Cheap stuff, like in public bathrooms and court buildings. I've used it a thousand times myself."

"And the face?"

"Different. It could be one of those pre-moistened towelette things. Lemon-scented."

"Exactly."

"But why not use the same stuff for both your hands and face?"

"Who knows? That's the question, isn't it?"

Figueroa realized that Percolin had gone through this sniffing process before making a cut. He didn't want to confuse the external smells with blood odors.

Dr. Percolin placed a block under the man's neck, angling the head back. He revealed a yellow-brown, papery-dry groove around the front and sides of the neck. With the wrinkled and drooping skin covering it, Figueroa had not noticed the groove before, even when the body had been turned facedown and then onto its back again. "How'd you know that he'd been strangled?"

"Genius," Percolin said. "I wish. Actually, it's about as subtle as saying a guy was shot when he has a circular hole in his chest with powder burns around it. See, his face is swollen. Not so obvious as some cases, because he's old, but enough to notice. And look at the eyes. See these little hemorrhages in the whites?" He pulled the lids back to show the eyes to her. "Petechial hemorrhages, they're called. They're in the other membranes around the eye, too, but you can see them better against the whites. And there are more here on the skin of the face. See?"

"I see. So if a victim is hanged or strangled, you see these petechial—"

"No. Not hanged. Strangled. If the victim is truly hanged, the body falls from a height. There's a sharp drop and all the arteries in the neck are closed down instantly. But when you strangle somebody, the interior arteries running up near the vertebrae go on pumping. But at the same time the veins carrying the blood back are compressed, so the blood has nowhere to go."

"And pressure builds up."

"Exactly. Now let's take a look at the groove around the neck. See, it goes only three-quarters of the way around. The back of the neck shows no groove."

"Strangled from behind," Figueroa said.

"Sure. But we'll put that together with the roughish abrasion on the nose—"

"Strangled after being pushed onto his face!" Figueroa said.

"Or simply held facedown. The cord around his neck was pulled up from behind. And maybe then he struggled. You're a studious type, are you? Hmmm?"

Bennis said with some vigor, "She certainly is."

Santa Percolin smiled broadly and asked, "Or an ambitious type?"

Figueroa shrugged. "A cop is what I always wanted to be. I'd like to make detective. I'd like to do everything there is on the job."

"Well, my dear, why not? You only go around once in life."

He opened the body with a Y incision, from each shoulder to the breastbone and then down to the pubis, filling the air with a meaty smell. He cracked the chest, humming as he did. He detached the organs in one large unit. Most of his work was done with just one knife, its blade about a foot long and very sharp. The diener swung the dissecting tray near the torso and then he and Percolin lifted the organ bloc onto the tray. Percolin cut into the pericardial sac around the heart and felt inside the pulmonary artery for clots. "Heart's not bad-looking, considering," he said to Bennis and Figueroa. "He could have gone on a fair number of years, poor old guy."

Percolin was sympathetic enough, Figueroa thought, without being maudlin. Unlike the doc in her first autopsy, who made hideous jokes at the expense of the deceased to tease the recruits, Percolin respected the dead man's dignity, covering his genitals when not actually cutting there. But he hummed like a bee as he worked: "Roamin' in the Gloamin' " and "You Take the High Road."

As he continued, stepping on the foot pedal frequently to trigger the audio recording device, Dr. Percolin lost some of his jolly Santa persona. Figueroa wondered why the change. Maybe he was finding evidence of another, mysterious cause of death in addition to the strangulation, or maybe an unexpected disease. However, his comments to the recorder didn't suggest it.

Having reached the digestive system in his dissection, he ladled out the contents of the stomach. "No food in here," he said. "Just booze. Smells like scotch. What do you think, Officer Bennis?"

"Scotch. Good scotch, in fact," said Bennis, who was a gourmet.

"I think you're right. Good scotch. Which is a little odd, when you've got eighty-eight cents in your pocket, isn't it?"

But Percolin's pensiveness had begun before the scotch, so that was not the cause.

The dead man had a small ulcer. "Which is no wonder. That's pretty much to be expected with a drinker who doesn't eat," Percolin remarked aside.

He found liver disease, moderately advanced, which was no surprise, either. "I still say he could have got a few more years of life out of this body." No appendix, consistent with the appendectomy scar. Nothing much else. Percolin took samples of blood for a tox screen and the vitreous humor of the eye for ethanol. And tissue samples. And stomach and intestinal contents samples.

"You can start reassembling the guy, Jimmy," he said. "You did the prints, right?"

"Always."

"I knew that."

"I'd like a copy of the ten-print too, if it's okay," Bennis said. "I want to run it through AFIS and the FBI records."

Figueroa said, "That's it? We're done?"

Percolin said, "We're done *here*. The tox'll take a week to ten days."

"That's too long," she said, worrying that they would be sent back to being patrol officers before then.

Percolin said, "Don't worry about it, Officer Figueroa. I'd be astonished if anything special showed up. I think you've got what you've got."

"All right, Doc. Then what's bothering you?"

His pink cheeks bunched up in a smile. "I like you, Figueroa," he said. "You've got all your marbles."

"Thanks. But what is it?"

"Tell you what I'm gonna do. Jimmy, get me some vials and sterile water."

The assistant brought sealed packages. Percolin changed gloves, then opened a plastic stoppered tube. He set it next to the dead man's shoulder. Then he ripped open a package of sterile gauze. The assistant poured water on the gauze in Percolin's hand, and Percolin wiped one side of the clean part of the victim's face with the wet gauze. Immediately, he put the piece of fabric in the tube and stoppered it. He repeated the whole process with the other side of the face. Then the clean forehead.

"I'll see if we can get an analysis of what was used to wash his face. There are several ways to detect very small traces of chemicals. Assuming most of them haven't evaporated. Who knows? The point is to get a profile of the wiping fluid."

Figueroa said, "Don't you mean what *he* used to wash his face?"

"I doubt it. I think we're going to find out what *somebody* used to wash his face."

"The *killer* washed his victim's face?"

"I hardly think it was an idle passerby, do you?"

Bennis said, "No, of course not. But why? Why would you even think so? It's not like he couldn't have washed his hands, say, at the bus depot and then got hold of a Wet Wipes wherever he bought his scotch."

Percolin was grim. "I'll tell you why. I had a peculiar case a week or ten days ago. A drifter—a homeless man, I suppose. Smothered with some extra clothing he carried around in his bag. Not strangled. His hands were quite dirty. But his face had been washed, and the skin smelled just like this."

Out in the squad car, Bennis said, "Does the doc think we've got a serial killer?"

"With just two possibles? I don't know."

"It's far-fetched."

"And a killer who washes faces?" Figueroa said. "It's nuts."

"So? Killers are sometimes nuts. Maybe usually."

"But somebody washed the faces of those two men."

"They washed their own faces."

"Wait a minute," Figueroa said. "There *is* a way we can tell whether it was the killer who washed the dead man's face. We can look at the site search."

"For what?"

"For the used lemon-scented Wet Wipes or Handi Wipes or Wet Ones or whatever. The evidence techs should have picked everything up. If the wipe was lying near the body, the dead man might have used it himself or the killer might have used it and dropped it. But if it's gone, then the killer took it away, which means the killer washed the guy's face."

"Hey, that's brilliant." Then Bennis's expression changed. "No, wait. It's not brilliant. Sorry—brilliant but not conclusive. The victim could have washed his face someplace else and left the Wet Wipes there."

"Oh! Damn! You're right."

They drove in gloom for several minutes. Then Figueroa said, "No, there *is* a way to tell."

"What?"

"Stop the car! I've got to call Dr. Percolin."

"Use my cell phone."

"The victim's nose was abraded while he was lying on the ground being strangled by the killer. Okay. If he washed his own face earlier, the nose abrasion should be dirty. If the abrasion is as clean as the rest of the face, *the killer washed him after he was dead!*"

CHAPTER NINE

"HERE ARE THE files on the earlier case," Detective Mossbacher said. He shoved a large manila folder across his desk at Bennis and Figueroa. "Some homeless guy named James Manualo. Body found in the alley under the El the morning of May twenty-first, and he was probably killed just a few hours earlier. But I doubt you'll get anywhere with it."

"We want to go back over the interviews on the Manualo thing in light of this new killing."

"Yeah, well, two senior detectives worked it for a week."

"Full-time? For a week?"

"Of course not full-time."

"Anyway, we have more information now than they had," Figueroa said. "At least we have another case—" Before the end of her sentence, though, they heard a scream from the hallway outside.

All three of them bolted to their feet and went running out, Bennis and Mossbacher jamming together shoulder to shoulder in the door. Figueroa pushed Bennis hard from the back and he popped out the other side.

Even though the three of them had their hands on their sidearms, as soon as they got into the main lobby it was clear they didn't need weapons. A secretary—what the cops called "a mere lowly civilian"—was standing rigid in the central hall screaming. She was looking at a man who was obviously a detective. He wore civilian clothes, but he wore a sidearm and you could always tell a cop, anyway, Figueroa thought. Blue suit, white shirt, shiny black shoes. The man had fallen to his knees and was vomiting on the floor.

A second man was rushing to help him.

"Back!" Mossbacher barked. "Stop right there, Godfrey!"

"But he needs help."

The sick man staggered to his feet.

"Godfrey! Get away! Paul! Sit down! Don't even try to get up." Mossbacher yelled at the desk. "Anne, call the EMTs!" Godfrey turned and headed for the desk sergeant's telephone, but Anne, the desk sergeant, was already punching in the number.

"I don't need any help," the sick man said. "I'm okay."

Godfrey turned back again to help him.

"Freeze right there, Godfrey," Mossbacher said. "For all I know you and everybody else here can get contaminated with E. coli, and *you* sure as hell don't know it's impossible."

"I don't need the paramedics," the sick man said.

And just as Mossbacher said, "I say you do," the man's eyes rolled up in his head and he fell forward, limp as a dead squid, right in the mess.

Mossbacher said, "Bennis. Figueroa. What are you standing here for?"

"See if we can help," Bennis said.

"You can help by taking the fucking file and getting out of here. Shit, your whole case is just a couple of homeless bums anyhow!"

Figueroa had a message on her pager to call Dr. Percolin. Bennis still held the file of the Manualo case.

"Let's go read that in the Furlough," Figueroa said. "And call the doc."

"Are you nuts? You can't go in a bar while you're working."

"Why not? We really *are* working."

"Oh, stifle that. Everything's image," Bennis said. So they

went back to the First District and sat at a table in the break room with the coffee, candy, and chips machines.

"You know that cop who collapsed at Area Four? Can E. coli take that long to develop?" Figueroa asked.

"Indeed, Suze, my man. It usually comes on in twenty-four hours, but it can take longer. There could still be quite a few more cases."

"When it takes longer, does that mean it's more serious or less serious?"

"E. coli 0517:H7 is always serious, and it's often fatal. The detectives have a real problem." Bennis sounded gloomy.

"How come you always know everything?" Figueroa asked, to lighten him up.

"You should be grateful."

Figueroa used the phone. She came back grinning.

"Your guess was right," Bennis said.

"Yup. The old man's nose abrasion was clean."

"Shit. The killer got him drunk. Flipped him on his stomach. Strangled him while he was lying on his face. Then turned him over and washed his face! This is one cold bastard, Suze."

Her smile vanished. "Yeah. He's gotta be a real madman."

Sergeant Touhy marched in, heading toward the candy machine. "What are you two doing here?"

"Working." Figueroa pointed at the files spread out on the table.

"Oh, good," Touhy said, looking at the papers. *What is this?* Figueroa wondered. *Sergeant Touhy—not crabbing at us, not snarling, not folding her arms and waiting for a better answer? No buffy snorts?*

"What's wrong, Sarge?" Figueroa asked.

"One of the detectives died. The E. coli got to his kidneys."

"Young guy, black hair, skinny, first name Paul?" Figueroa asked, thinking of the man who had collapsed in front of them.

"No. He was fifty-eight."

"Oh."

"He was my partner for a year, back when we were both uniforms."

This was getting worse and worse, Figueroa thought. Touhy with a heart? What next? Quiche and a chilled Chablis in the break room at lunch?

CHAPTER TEN

"HEY, MORT" MILESKI said, leaning both elbows on the bar. "Why did *you* pull the pin?"

"Ah, you don't wanna know." Unlike his partner Corky, Mort had always been a man of few words, and most of them grumpy. The gang was hanging around the Furlough Bar, about ten people just off the second watch.

Mileski said, "Yeah, I do."

"Nothin' much. You don't wanna know."

"Yeah, we all do," Mileski said, sending his gaze around the room very slowly. Everybody did a radio-show chorus of "mm-mmm" and "oh, doubtless" and "yo!" and "we do, we do."

"Ah, hell, I just got tired of getting pissed on."

"By your sergeant? The ungrateful public?"

Mort said nothing. Just shrugged. Figueroa said, "You know you gotta tell us now. You really can't just stop the story there."

He frowned horribly at her, but finally said, "Nah. I got tired of getting pissed on. My last case. I wasn't a detective, see. I'm on patrol, minding my own business, Nineteenth District, I get this radio call, check the well-being."

Mileski said, "Sure."

Silence. Three people simultaneously said, "Go on!" and Mileski added, "Dammit!"

"Oh, all right. All right. Dispatcher says check out a woman at this apartment building. So I go. Well, check the well-being indeed!" Having once started, he seemed ready to keep talking. "Female maybe twenty years old, back bedroom, dead at least three days, hot weather too, mother snuffling and wringing her hands and pacing back and forth. Body's bloated, but you can see the blood on the shirt and bed, and I call it in."

"Yeah. So then what?"

"I figure they knew she was dead for a coupla days at least. I mean, this is all one apartment, and only three bedrooms for what looks like seven people—mother, father, girl, four brothers. So they called when the girl got so ripe they didn't know what else to do. And the brothers are all 'and shits.' "

Kim Duk said, "Huh? What's that?"

Mort stopped, Kim Duk having broken the grudging flow, but Mileski flapped his hands to the side like a conductor and nodded fiercely.

Mort said, "They're like they never heard of 'and so forth' or 'etcetera' or 'and so on.' Or even 'and like that.' "

"I don't get it," Kim Duk said.

"They say like 'I'm going to the store for bread and shit.' Or 'we met him in the alley and bashed him and kicked him and shit.' "

"Oh."

"What ethnicity?" Bennis asked.

"Middle European. The parents speak with an accent. But 'and shit' is the universal language."

Figueroa said, "Yeah. Surely is."

Mileski said, "Go on."

"So I call it in and I close the bedroom door, 'cause it reeks, and I go wait in the hall to tell the guys where the body is. And I'm goin' down the hall past the four brothers and they open their flies and piss on me."

Dead silence. Finally, Figueroa said, "What did you do? Arrest them?"

"By myself? By the time the two detectives come in the door, like twenty minutes later, the brothers are gone. Plus, what am I gonna arrest them for?"

Kim Duk said, "Assaulting an officer?"

"Oh, no doubt, Kim Duk. I'm gonna want to be known as the man who was assaulted by four penises. Make me feel like a big man, wouldn't it?"

"Well, they shouldn't be allowed—"

"Forget about it. I had twenty years in then. I basically quit."

The Flying None said, "Why didn't they like you? Had they killed their sister?"

Mort shrugged. Then he decided to utter a few more words. "Naw. The boyfriend killed her. Stabbed her."

"So then why?"

"Number one, they didn't like cops. Number two, if we picked up the boyfriend they couldn't get to him."

"Get to him?"

"They didn't think the criminal justice system was firm enough. As soon as they found him, they were going to take care of him their way."

Figueroa left the bar in plenty of time to pick up some groceries on her way home to start dinner.

Today's closest parking space was three and a half blocks away in front of a blue, white, and muted salmon house. By her reckoning three-plus blocks was a medium-bad omen. She'd have to watch her back for the rest of the day.

Really, I'm not that superstitious, she told herself as she walked, carrying the bags of groceries. Mainly it gave her something to do while she was walking home.

Robert, of course, got use of the garage, but it was so rickety that someday either a stiff wind or a thick, wet snow would collapse the old structure. *Better on his car than mine.*

It was nearly five o'clock, and this time of year it wouldn't be dark for a couple more hours, but the sun was hot orange in the western sky when Suze walked in the door. She dumped the groceries and then went through her usual firearm-safety routine.

She poked her head into Sheryl's room. Sheryl said, "Umph!" Suze didn't know what this meant, but didn't need to when Sheryl turned away from her. There were tears in Sheryl's eyes, and Suze knew she didn't want anybody to see them.

Suze backed out quickly, saying, "I'm hot and I better wash up. Back in five." And she hiked fast up the back stairs to her floor.

Shucking her jacket, she walked into the bathroom. The first thing she always did, even in cold weather, was to splash water on her face and give it a good rub. She knew that symbolically she was erasing the effects of eight hours in the squad car and cop-shop, and the residue of nasty people, pitiful people, drugged people, bruised people, and angry people.

Next she always washed her hands. She washed her hands as often as she could on the job, very conscious of the fact that a lot of the people she came in contact with could have drug-resistant TB. Partly she was protecting herself, of course, partly protecting Sheryl, who in her condition was terribly vulnerable to lung infections, even ordinary flu and colds. And partly she was protecting Maria, Kath, and J J.

She picked up the soap.

It was damp.

Damp on top, wet on the bottom.

How very odd, she thought. *Alma never comes up here*. Suze took care of the third floor herself, vacuuming and cleaning both her room and J J's. Anyway Alma didn't clean the house or sort clothes or anything like that. Her job was Sheryl. J J and both girls had left home at quarter to seven this morning. Suze had dropped them at school herself on her way to work. The school had an early social hour, which the school called "breakfast club," for children whose parents had to get to work. Robert hadn't left by then, having to wait with Sheryl until

Alma got there, but he had his own bathroom on the second floor. Besides that, he was always out of the house by eight-fifteen at the latest. It was now four-thirty in the afternoon.

Suze went downstairs intending to ask Alma why she'd been up on the third floor, trying to figure out a way of phrasing the question so that it didn't imply any sort of criticism. But when she got downstairs she remembered Sheryl's sadness and then, looking into the room, Suze realized from the twitching of Sheryl's right leg that she wanted to be sat up and leaned forward to ease her aching back. Suze forgot about the soap.

11:35 P.M.

THE WOMAN WITH the shopping cart hesitated at the corner of Eleventh and Wabash. From there she could see into the dark area under the El. The El ran behind police headquarters, down Holden Court. Underneath Holden Court was an alley that cops used as a shortcut to the CPD parking lot. Although it had once been paved, the tar had broken up in the freeze-and-thaw cycle of many winters since then, and nobody had fixed it. Huge potholes pitted the five-block stretch, making even low speeds treacherous. Most of it was now such a mess that to avoid potholes as well as trash, cars took a curving path through it. The sides were wino country. Some larger piles of muck near the uprights of the El were used by the homeless for beds.

The old woman knew the alley was where you could get the best bottles and cans. It wasn't just the winos that threw them around; it was the cops, too. Or cops mostly, to be honest about it. She'd seen more than a few cops toss cans out of their cars before turning into the lot. Didn't want to be caught with open alcohol, she figured.

She peered into the alley. The trouble was the El cut off most of the light from streetlamps and the whole alley was a tunnel into a dark jungle.

Still, with another few cans she could get enough deposit money at the All-Day-All-Nite to buy a bottle of cheap wine. She stirred the cans and bottles in her basket, counting them, but lost count at thirty-one when the ones she'd pushed to one side fell back into the uncounted pile on the other side. Never mind. She'd been doing this a long time and she knew from experience that she needed several more.

She steered the cart into the alley. There were potholes every few feet and she protected the cart from the bounces by easing the front wheels up as she let the back wheels down into hole after hole. Faintly, this stirred memories of pushing Danny in his stroller, leaning the stroller back to go down over a curb. Danny would be—what?—twenty-eight now? No, maybe thirty? She wondered where he was living. Was he married? Did she have grandchildren? Maybe a little girl? She sure would like to see a granddaughter if she existed.

Sometimes it puzzled her that so much of her life had vanished from her memory. She remembered being a child, remembered that clearly. There were bright fragments that rose into her mind unbidden. New snow. And staying home from school when there was a blizzard and her mother making lamb stew. But of the last fifteen or twenty years or so—?

Then the El clattered by overhead and the loud gnashing of metal wheels on metal tracks blew everything else out of her head. Soot sifted down.

It was like being inside a metal dinosaur here, under the tracks, inside its huge splayed metal ribs.

And near one of the uprights was a little drift of five or six Bud Light cans. Wonderful. She laughed happily.

She scooped them up in her arms and dropped them in her cart, saying "Whee!" In a pothole a few feet farther along, a band of light glinted on two amber bottles. She hoped they wouldn't turn out to be broken. Stores were supposed to take them back, even if they were, but just try to tell the clerks that.

They didn't have any respect. And people threw empty bottles anywhere they wanted, just as if they were cans. Nobody had any manners anymore.

The bottles were both broken. She put her hands to her face and cried for a little while, then wiped at the tears, smearing dirt across her cheekbones and nose.

When she took her hand away from her eyes, she saw a figure standing near her, backlit against the distant street glow.

"A lady shouldn't cry," a voice said.

"I'm not crying."

"Yes, you were. But I can make you feel better. Look what I have."

Even against the light, she could see the bottle in his hand. Light shone warmly through the amber liquid. The bottle had that expensive, tailored look. He tilted it, making the liquor lap back and forth enticingly.

"We can have a party," he said. "You'll feel much better afterward."

WEDNESDAY

CHAPTER ELEVEN

From: "Boul Mich Beat"
by Mike Rocco
Chicago Today, Wednesday, June 1

The City Council, in its wisdom, has decided to take up the problem of homelessness. But Councilman Ed Voladivic announced at the start of debate: "Why are we worrying about this? It's summer. The homeless bums out there aren't cold."

And his colleague in insensitivity, Cordell Wasserstrom, said, "I pay thousands for my kid to go on Outward Bound trips and sleep in the woods. What's the problem?"

Well, I'll tell ya, Ed and Cordy. Maybe we don't all want to sleep in the woods. And maybe sleeping on Lower Wacker is more like sleeping in a jungle.

I mean, who really enjoys a cement pillow? And if the great Chicago outdoors is so wonderful, why don't the Embassy Suites and the Holiday Inn and the Omni and the Palmer House go out of business?

Hell, why don't we rent six-foot stretches of Michigan Avenue sidewalk to tourists at big bucks? And six-foot stretches of LaSalle at cut rates. Send your kid to Grant Park for the night. Discounts for the under-twelve set.

Here's a fine new way for the city to make money. No?

BENNIS RECEIVED THE call at 3:21 A.M., and was not pleased. He got moving immediately, though. After he arrived on the scene, he agreed to call Figueroa himself. "Under the El, near Eighth," he said to her. "Can't miss it. You'll see the lights."

"All right."

Suze dressed fast in her uniform, belt, and all the accoutrements, and went down the stairs to the second floor. Since she had her own phone line, the call had not awakened Robert. She knocked on Robert's open door.

"What the hell is it?"

"I'm on call. I have to go out."

"Why do you have to wake me up?"

"You probably'll have to get the kids ready for school."

"Oh, shit!"

"Robert, just give them cereal. It doesn't have to be a hot breakfast."

"Yeah, yeah."

"And don't bother to pack lunches. Give them lunch money. If I'm not home by seven A.M., you'll have to drive them to school."

"Mmmph."

"You'll have to call school, too, and tell them the kids will be late, because Miss Sturdley won't be here until eight. You know they take roll at pre-class, too, so the school needs to be told."

"Damn it!"

"Sorry."

He knows all this himself. He just wants to complain. Why should I apologize?

Suze went on down the stairs. Robert probably would not bother to reset his alarm and so he wouldn't get up before his usual hour. He never got the kids up if he could avoid it. But J J would wake him or would get Kath to wake him. The kids knew Suze could be called out sometimes. They all had alarm clocks.

She tiptoed down the last flight of stairs, even though the kids generally slept as if on an IV anesthetic. Except of course when you wanted them to sleep, which was when they woke up, which was why she was so careful now.

As she hit the first-floor hall, she heard a scurrying sound. Sheryl? Sheryl was often restless. She kicked and writhed as she lay there in bed. She was sleepless a lot, in fact, which wasn't surprising since she was basically bedridden.

Still Suze thought the sound had come from the other direction, maybe the kitchen. She passed through the kitchen on her way to the back door, but saw nothing.

She hoped it had been a mouse and not a rat. One of their neighbors had rats and claimed all these old houses harbored them. Suze didn't think so. The idea of rats made her shiver. Rats in the walls. Creeping along on the other side of the plaster, just inches from your head, for all you knew. Ick! Rats with their dirty yellow fangs and naked ugly tails, living with you without you knowing it, slinking slyly through the house while she slept. Horrible.

By the time she hit the street, her annoyance with Robert and her thoughts of rats had faded, overtaken by curiosity about the murder Bennis had sketchily described, and by the time she parked in the CPD lot on State Street, eagerness made the blood sing in her ears.

She didn't want anybody to be dead. Really, she didn't. But if somebody was dead, she wanted to be the cop to solve the crime.

Harry Pressfield was one of the first-watch uniforms, who worked eleven to seven. He ordinarily left the district just as Bennis and Figueroa came on at seven, and they knew him slightly from chatting in the locker room. Pressfield had found the crumpled body near an El support at three A.M., on his way from coffee break back to the CPD building.

It was easy enough for Figueroa to locate the crime scene. The usual group of cops and equipment had assembled around it. When Figueroa strode up, it was nearly four A.M. Bennis was peering down at the small, rigid corpse.

Mossbacher was here, too. He looked rumply and out of sorts, his eyes red and his nose pink. Was he a drinker, Figueroa wondered, or did he just stay up too late? Unable to sleep after his tour, like a lot of cops? Too jazzed? Too stressed?

The dead person was a woman. This was not immediately obvious, as the hair was bunched under the head and the clothes, wrapped around her like a cocoon, could have been worn by a lot of male homeless. The clothes looked more suitable for a woman, but the homeless wore what they could get. Figueroa was surprised, although she shouldn't have been, that it was a woman. Occasionally hookers were killed in this area. Hadn't been any for a couple of months, though.

And this was an old woman. She wore a dozen layers of clothing, despite the warm weather—a cloth coat that might have been real cashmere, probably discarded when the elbows wore through. Its hem was badly stained. Under it were a flower-patterned blouse with blue morning glories and green vines, chartreuse stirrup stretch pants, and peeking out at the waist some sort of purple tunic or leotard, shreds of purple hanging out. When Figueroa was in high school she had done a report on the Middle Ages and she had explained that the poor people in those days just put a new garment atop other older garments, letting the older clothes underneath wear out, rot, and shred, and eventually fall off like dead leaves. The other students had been horrified, of course, accustomed as they were to washing machines, clean clothes, and new clothes whenever anything wore out. But here was a present-day example.

The woman's hair was gray and thin and caked with dirt. Her arms were like sticks. Her hands were dusty. The eyes were sunken and half-closed. The ankles were grimy.

And the face was clean.

Mossbacher said "Figueroa," as if it were a greeting, and then walked over to the second uniform, a first-watch female officer who looked familiar to Figueroa, although no name came to her mind. Mossbacher gestured to the woman, showing her where he wanted her to put the yellow barrier tape. The woman tied one end of it to a telephone pole, walked the spool across the alley, and ran the tape twice around the leg of an El support. Then she moved fifteen feet farther along a sagging stretch of chain-link fencing. With the holes in the fence too small to push the tape spool through, she puzzled for a few seconds, then pulled out a three-foot length from the spool and broke off the end, pushed the end through a hole in the fence, and pulled it out another hole. Then she tied the spool end to the torn end and continued back across the alley. When she reached the place where she had started, she tied the whole thing off and took out two AUTHORIZED PERSONNEL ONLY signs. These she duct-taped carefully, one north of the body on the telephone pole and one south onto the brick side of a building. Pleased, she stood with her hands behind her back and waited for further orders.

Mossbacher took out his cell phone and dialed.

Meanwhile, Figueroa and Bennis studied the body. The woman lay on her back, legs slightly bent, one arm over her chest, the other out to the side. A shopping cart filled with bottles and cans was a few feet away.

An evidence tech circled the dead woman, taking photographs. He was a man of about forty, with hair cut to within a half inch of his scalp. He wore Levi's and a khaki windbreaker. When he figured he had enough pictures, he put the camera in a blue cloth bag and opened a black case.

"Could you photograph the shopping cart closer up?" Bennis asked.

"Who are you?" the tech asked, annoyed.

"Officer Bennis."

"I don't do what uniforms tell me."

"Officer Figueroa and I are acting detectives. You know about the detectives being—"

"I heard about it. Well, you'd better take direction from me, then. I've been doing this a long time. You don't need pictures of the cart."

"I want pictures of the cart—" Bennis said.

"And I want the cans in the cart printed," Figueroa said.

"Why?"

"Suppose the killer got close to her by handing her a few cans?"

"There's probably fifty cans there!"

"Plus I want the area around the body Dustbusted." Figueroa meant that the tech should vacuum the ground around and under the body, but she was also implying that the trace evidence picked up that way should be studied. "And watch for a Handi Wipes or Wet Ones."

The tech said, "That's crazy. There's wall-to-wall trash and dirt there."

"What the hell's the matter with you?" Bennis shouted. "Your *job* is collecting evidence."

"Shit, it's just a bag lady. She's a wino, man."

"I don't believe this," Figueroa said. "We've got a murder here. Just do as we tell you."

"You're not detectives!"

"What's going on?" Mossbacher yelled. He flipped his cell

phone closed and strode over, hard shoes hitting the ground like hammers.

"These uniforms are trying to order me around."

"Berkley, they're Actings! During the current crisis, you do as they say, understand?" Berkley made a gruff sound, but he pulled out his camera.

"And I want a plat drawn," Figueroa said.

The tech didn't answer, but Figueroa was confident that at this point he'd do as he was told.

Bennis, apparently agreeing with her, said to Mossbacher, "We also need to search through all this crud"—he kicked at a discarded rag on the ground—"to see if there's a Handi Wipes or a Wet Ones. Some kind of pre-moistened towelette." The tech looked daggers at him. He added, "And Figueroa and I are gonna help with that."

Mossbacher jerked his head sideways to Bennis and Figueroa, pulling them over to the squad car. "Got a hint for you."

"Yes, boss," Bennis said.

"For the present, call yourselves 'Acting Detective Bennis and Acting Detective Figueroa' and like that when you meet a tech. Or anybody. They won't know whether you're a fill-in from patrol or a fill-in who's been a dick and is now, say, vice or whatever."

"Yes, boss."

"And what in the world made you wear a uniform?"

"Well, boss, nobody said—"

"*Don't* wear a uniform."

"Yes, boss."

"And another tip. Go easy on the enthusiasm, my little friends. I know you're new and eager. But be cool. We can't fingerprint the whole world. Follow the manual."

"Manual says we canvass next," Bennis said.

"Right."

Bennis gestured at the surroundings. You canvassed for witnesses, hoping to find a shut-in or a gossip who knew the dead person, hoping somebody sick and sitting up all night had been looking out of his window. But what window? Bennis cocked a thumb at the El overhead, the parking lot, the chain-link fence, and the blank brick wall beyond.

"See what you mean," Mossbacher said.

The brick wall was the back side of an apartment building, a five-up, the limit beyond which the owners had to install elevators. Most of the wall that faced the El was windowless, presumably because nobody would want to look at the El anyhow, or hear the noise. One small window on the south corner of the west wall had been allowed in each apartment.

"Not so good."

Bennis said, "Passengers on the El wouldn't see anything going on under the tracks."

Mossbacher said, "Nope."

"How about we look for other homeless people?" Figueroa said hopefully.

Mossbacher smiled pityingly. "You can try," he said.

Figueroa said, "We're gonna have to get a memo to all the roll calls and ask if anybody parking or unparking a car saw the woman. Or whoever attacked her."

"Yup."

"And we also have to circularize everybody in the CPD building, like secretaries and janitors and so on. Ask them the same thing."

"Circularize is not a word," Bennis said.

"Yes it is."

"Plus, secretaries wouldn't be here in the middle of the night. However, janitors might be. And you're absolutely right. We do that right away." He stepped back from the body and all the way over to the side of the alley. From here, the El didn't block the view. On the other hand, it wasn't the site of the murder. "We also go to those two apartments."

"You aren't supposed to go to homes in the middle of the night unless it's urgent." But she was looking where he pointed. From here, the whole west wall of the apartment building was visible. On the third floor of the brick building, the corner window showed lights. On the fifth floor another corner apartment was brightly lighted. "Can if they're clearly awake," Bennis said. "Plus, you can canvass at any hour when you've got a violent crime, and we got a murder. We'll do the lighted places first, though."

Two adults stood in the doorway, a heavily varnished brown door half open and held in place defensively by a man of about thirty-five. A bright red angry baby screamed in the woman's arms. The man was unshaven and his light brown hair stood on end. It was obvious why they were awake at this hour.

"May we ask you a couple of questions?" Figueroa said.

Neither answered.

"You're not in any trouble," she said. The response she got sounded like "vt" and "verstandig" with many other glottal syllables in between, and "politieagent," which sounded odd, but Figueroa understood the basic meaning. Figueroa and Bennis wore uniforms. These people were frightened.

Figueroa paused. With no translator, and in fact no idea of what language this was, she was stumped.

"See out window?" she said, pointing. The small living room was just beyond, and she could see the two windows at right angles to each other. One faced south and one faced west toward the El and the area around the crime scene.

The two adults turned to look at the window. The infant turned deep purple, sucked in a breath, and emitted a blood-curdling shriek. It was furious. Its world was horrible. All was in ruins.

"Colic?" Figueroa asked, almost as a reflex.

"Ooo, colic, ja, ellendig!" the woman said. "Kinderarts!"

Figueroa nodded her head, thinking of the universal language of parents.

Suddenly the father shouted, "Marika!"

Whatever did that mean? Figueroa thought. After a few seconds, he shouted, "Marika!" again.

The baby shrieked. The mother leaned from left to right, left to right, with a little bounce included. The baby screamed louder.

Then there appeared in the room beyond a tiny girl, maybe six or seven years old, rubbing her eyes and trailing a long pink nightgown with a pattern of improbably blue roses.

"Mmmmf," she said.

Her father pointed at Figueroa and Bennis and said, "See?"

The little girl regarded Figueroa and Bennis with no fear, indeed something like quiet, thoughtful study. Figueroa was very aware of the nightgown on the child, new but bought longer than she needed so that she could wear it for several years and save money. She'd had many items of clothing exactly like that herself as a child.

The little girl quickly decided they were okay, and spoke up like a miniature adult. "What seems to be the problem?"

Figueroa explained, over occasional screams of outrage from the baby. Crime in the alley. After eleven P.M. Before three A.M. Searching for witnesses. See from here. Help the police. She was extremely careful to treat the child like a human being and not talk down to her.

When she finished, the little girl said, "You may look," and led them to the window. She was obviously more than a translator; she was an adult before her time. While Figueroa and Bennis looked, the child explained the situation to her parents in their language.

The view of the murder scene, Figueroa saw, was as bad as

she had feared. You looked right out at the El, which passed next to the west wall directly outside. It occupied about half of the entire vista. Beyond it, you could see State Street, but not a whole lot of the CPD parking lot and none of the alley. To the north, you got a diagonal view of the CPD building itself, for whatever that was worth. If you stood right up against the glass and looked down, you could see some of the access strip along the alley under the El.

The little girl spoke up.

"My mother saw nothing. She is very worried about Adrian. Adrian is perfectly all right. Babies *do* cry, you know."

"I know," Figueroa said.

"All the same I think it is very responsible of Mama to be so worried, don't you?"

"Yes, indeed. You have to take babies seriously. Did your father see anything?"

"He says he was walking Adrian at one-thirty. He says there was a man crossing the parking lot. But we see people crossing the parking lot all the time."

"At one-thirty in the morning?"

"Yes. It is a police station."

"True. What did the man look like? Tall? Short? Fat? Thin? Old? Young? Oh, and wait. Which way was he going?"

There was consultation, during which the baby screamed again, turned bright red, went stiff, then subsided into gulps. The mother decided to walk him into the back hall and let them talk.

"He looked like anybody, Papa says." Figueroa sighed. "But he was not old. Not fat. And he was carrying a brown bag. And he walked slowly toward the alley."

"Slowly?" Figueroa had never seen a cop actually stroll the alley or into it. The littered, unwholesome alley was considered something you got over with as fast as reasonably possible.

More consultation.

"Yes, slowly. And then he disappeared under the El."

"When did he last see him?"

After more talk the child said, "He's not sure. He did not see him long. One-thirty is the best he thinks. He was leaning on the window, carrying Adrian, you know. Very weary. That's what he says. Very weary."

"I wonder," Figueroa said, "if you would tell me what language you're speaking?"

"Dutch. We have come from the Netherlands."

Figueroa reached out and shook the little girl's hand. "Thank you, Marika. I really appreciate your helping us."

"Oh, I believe that most people would probably do the same."

Ordinarily a proper canvass is supposed to consist of two teams of two detectives each, supervised by a sergeant, who were to canvass all possible witnesses immediately and go back later if some were not home. In this case there were just two officers doing all the canvassing. Which in fact was not that unusual. In fact, a detective had once told Bennis that he had never in eight years been on a "perfect" canvass.

The only other apartment with a light had been on the fifth floor. Bennis and Figueroa were glad to see light still visible under the door when they got to the fifth-floor hallway.

Their knock brought someone to the door, but whoever it was didn't open it. He said, "Go away."

"Sir, since you're up," Bennis said, "we'd like to talk with you. Chicago Police Department." They had long since developed a certain kind of teamwork in which Bennis used his male-authority voice when that was appropriate, while Figueroa used an unthreatening female voice with families, women, and children.

"Go away. I don't know you."

Bennis said, "Sir, if I hold my ID up to the peephole, you will see I'm a Chicago police officer."

"Can't get up to the peephole."

Figueroa whispered to Bennis, "Disabled, maybe?"

"Look, sir, I—" Bennis weighed the problem of losing his ID and then said, "Suppose I pass my police identification under the door. Would that be okay?"

"Oh, never mind." Bolts screeched. A chain rattled. Finally the door creaked open a few inches. "I guess if you're willing to do that, you're okay."

A gust of stale air emerged, flavored with frozen-dinner smells. Macaroni and cheese. Ravioli. Chicken and broccoli and potatoes. The man sat in a wheelchair, one of the heavy kind with battery power. A gray plain blanket lay over his legs.

"May we talk with you, sir? We noticed your light was on."

"Talk? Why? It's the middle of the night." He backed up and Bennis and Figueroa entered.

Bennis explained. A murder. In the alley. After eleven P.M. and before three A.M. View from here.

"Nope," said the man.

"You didn't see anything? That window overlooks the area." Bennis walked through piles of boxes and magazines to the west corner window. It looked down on the alley from a higher angle than the Dutch family with the baby. It had a better angle on the CPD parking lot and State Street, but it seemed to Bennis as if the height made the murder scene area on this side of the El harder to see.

"Nope," the man said.

"You didn't go to the window?"

"Nope. Writing letters."

The apartment did not have a dining room, but there was a corner of the kitchen most people would have used as a dinette area. It was filled with magazines and books, an old typewriter and stacks of blank paper. It faced south, not west.

"Writing letters?" Bennis repeated. In training they taught you that one nonthreatening way to urge a witness to go on was simply to repeat his last phrase.

The man gestured at the very old Smith-Corona manual typewriter. Besides the newspapers and magazines, several law texts lay there, with markers stuck in their pages or turned over open to a saved place. "Yes! Writing letters. To the *Trib* for one."

"To the *Tribune*?"

"Yes, young man. For God's sake, pay attention. Letters to the *Tribune*. The *Sun-Times*. About the City Council. It's not constitutional, you know. We are entitled to a town meeting form of government. All citizens should be welcome. It's a constitutionally mandated foundation of our governmental system. They still have them in New England. Participatory democracy. It's unconstitutional that they close us out here. One man, one vote. The Chicago town meeting would solve all our problems. Let everybody vent. Get it all out. Clear the air. Say your piece. Then make strides forward into the future, with everybody fully informed."

"Uh, Bennis?" Figueroa said as they left. She looked back to make sure the door was firmly closed.

"You wish a word?"

"Yes, dammit. How can a handicapped person live on a fifth floor with no elevator? Does the city allow that? How does he get in or out?"

"Probably he doesn't go out. I saw a much larger jacket on a clothes hook in the kitchen. Larger than he'd ever wear. Somebody lives with him. Probably he never goes out."

"But what if he's there alone when the other person goes to work? What if there's a fire? What if—"

"Figueroa. Put in a word with Human Services. I agree with you. But I'm betting he won't be grateful."

They knocked on all the other apartment doors. People were home, which, Figueroa thought, was hardly surprising. All said they had been sleeping. All said they had seen nothing because they had been sleeping. Most of them were extremely angry that they'd been awakened, and willing to express their anger loudly.

Figueroa hoped somebody might have been sitting in the dark, looking down at the El, however spooky the image was. But even if somebody had been, residents around here would be so used to police cars and police officers coming and going that they might not have paid any attention to people roaming around. Figueroa had hoped, nevertheless. She got nothing.

It took Bennis and Figueroa nearly three hours to finish the canvass, put the paperwork to bed on the dead woman, and see her off to the morgue. They spent nearly an hour searching the crime scene for a pre-moistened towelette that wasn't there. All of which gave Figueroa and Bennis just time for eggs and biscuits, red-eye gravy, and a lot of coffee at the Snuggery before roll call at seven-thirty. In the forty minutes available to them, there was no point in Figueroa trying to get home and back, but she called in. Sheryl, Kath said, had had a restless night. Robert was irritated, J J was giggly, Maria was languid, and Kath herself sounded sweet.

It was nice to have something predictable, something regular to count on, Figueroa thought.

When they got to the district for roll call, there was a message. Yesterday's elderly dead man had been readily identified by AFIS. He was a Michael Kilkenny O'Dowd, and he had once been a Chicago cop.

CHAPTER TWELVE

SUZE WAS GRUMBLING. "I don't see why we have to spend time on *pickpockets.*"

"We're too important, huh?" Bennis said mildly.

She hated it when he sounded wise and calm.

"It's not that *we're* too important, it's that the murders are too important," she muttered as he parked on Chestnut Street, making a neat one and a half pass parallel parking job in a minuscule space between two cars. "Dammit, Bennis! Three people have been murdered."

"Yes, and if this were *NYPD Blue* or *Homicide: Life on the Streets*, we'd have just one case to work on, wouldn't we?" Bennis said with perfect serenity. "Matter of fact, we're quite lucky Touhy didn't give us the vandalism on the backhoe at the lakefront. Or that one about the Porta Potti missing from the construction site."

"Yeah, fine. Why don't we get a list of overdue library books, too, while we're at it?"

"Figueroa, my man, have you ever lost your wallet?"

"Twice," she said grimly.

"You have much money in it?"

"Once, years ago. I had the rent money. And both times I was devastated. My credit cards, driver's license, Firearm Owner's ID, library card, picture of J J as a two-month-old. Look, I know what you're trying to tell me. Pickpockets can make people miserable. But *they don't make them dead.*"

North Michigan Avenue was retailing's *crème de la crème*. In three blocks you had Bergdorf Goodman, Godiva, Lord & Taylor, Marshall Field, Armani, Brooks Brothers, Cadbury and Mason, Neiman Marcus, Saks Fifth Avenue, Tiffany, and a whole lot more. And those weren't even the most exclusive. There were couturiers so special they never advertised, and you had to know somebody just to be allowed in the door. However, the small exclusive shops were not where Bennis and Figueroa were headed. Pickpockets didn't go into small places with closed doors.

"So," Figueroa said, "these schmucks target the biggest stores?"

"Large stores when a demonstration is going on. Makeup demos especially. Seems you ladies can't take your eyes off a good makeover."

"Give it a rest, Bennis."

They sauntered into Cadbury and Mason, where a woman in a white coat was mixing many colors of Versace powder to match exactly the complexion of an extremely attractive model. The model wore a white smock. The demo person wore a lilac smock. She was working from several pots of powder—beige, sand, mauve, petal pink, rose, and pale amber. Twenty or thirty shoppers, all women, stood raptly watching.

"How are you gonna blend in here, Bennis?"

"Simple. I'll go talk with the chief of security. You blend in."

Following Mossbacher's orders, they had worn plainclothes, so Figueroa blended in pretty well. The crowd ranged from seventy-year-old women in beautiful wool suits and much jewelry, their lavender hair perfectly permed, to young women in business power suits, and harried women in Levi's with children in strollers or backpacks. In addition to the thirty or so people in the crowd, others milled around on the fringe, wandering in and wandering away.

It was an ideal setup for a pickpocket, Suze thought, as she edged closer into the group of spectators, her elbow right up against the purse of a tall blond woman. On her other side was a younger woman in a black spandex jogging suit, her wallet presumably in the belly bag at her waist. That would be harder to get into, Suze thought, but maybe not impossible for an expert. In front of her was a woman with a child in a stroller. The woman wore feather earrings, Figueroa noted, and Levi's, and her wallet was in her back pocket. Figueroa stared at it.

It would take a lot of guts to be a pickpocket, Suze realized. She tried to imagine herself lifting that wallet from that tight back pocket, and simply couldn't imagine how. Wouldn't the woman feel the first touch? Suze shifted position to nudge the wallet pocket slightly. The woman didn't appear to notice. But the wallet was still wedged into the pocket.

All right, she thought. *Assuming I'm good at extracting the wallet from the pocket, the setting is ripe for it. But then what? How soon would the victim discover it was missing? Would I take the wallet and move back out of the crowd and walk to the door, right away? Of course. My first thought would be to get away.*

I wouldn't run. Too noticeable. Walk fast? Hide? Have a confederate who would distract the crowd? Maybe. Pass the wallet to the confederate and stand innocently right where I was?

If you left, even quietly, somebody in the crowd would remember what you looked like, wouldn't they?

The targeted stores were invariably the busiest stores. No surprise there. Bennis and Figueroa hit them all. By noon the two had seen demonstrations of perfumes, lipstick, eye shadow, and nail polish, and just missed one on how to tie a scarf attractively.

They met four chiefs of security and two assistant chiefs. In one case the big cheese was out sick and in the other case he was in Detroit. Their talk with Brandon Ely, the last of the six, was pretty much typical. Of the six security honchos, five were men, one a woman; three were former cops, two Army, and one a graduate of a professional security and alarm program. All were between thirty-five and fifty-five, the assistants being on the young end.

They sat in Ely's office while a lesser mortal brought in Starbucks coffee (at one store it was Seattle's Best, at one it was Water Tower mezzanine's, and the three others their own house blend). Ely's office was cheaply paneled, which seemed to be de rigueur for these guys. He had tan low-pile carpeting, also pretty common. Ely was maybe fifty years old, portly and graying, and was one of the former cops.

He said roughly the same thing as the other security chiefs. "We don't get many pickpockets. What we get is shoplifting."

"And employee theft?"

Grudgingly, Ely said, "Well, yeah. Some."

"Okay," Bennis said. "This most recent theft. What exactly happened?"

"Sans Souci was demonstrating a new perfume. They had a little 'educational' spiel all worked out. A lecture on the different sorts of scents. Basic categories of scents. Spicy, fruity, floral, something like that. They passed around little pieces of cloth with their logo on them and each was scented with a different type of fragrance. Then a short lecture and then they gave out free samples. Free samples draw the crowds. Most of these women could buy a gallon of Chanel Number Five and not blink, but they love free samples. So I'm standing near the Michigan Avenue doors. We had some shoplifting last week, so I'm not sitting here in my office, I'm on the floor keeping an eye out. But very unobtrusively. I'm not standing in *front* of the doors or anything like that. I'm off to one side looking at leather gloves. Trying some on. I didn't look like a store employee."

"This was shoplifting? I thought we were talking pickpockets."

"We are. I'm coming to that. So the crowd starts breaking

up and one woman suddenly screams, 'My wallet's gone!' Her handbag is hanging open and her wallet's missing."

"You were watching the crowd when she said it?"

"You bet. And before. Now, the way things are in a store, with a lot happening all the time, other shoppers wandering around, several aisles, browsers blocking the traffic pattern, you lose sight of people real fast. In fact, you know stores are intentionally laid out so that you can't walk in a straight line right through. They want to slow you down, have you go past a variety of displays of merchandise. Anyway—there are only two doors out of the ground floor. They're big double revolving doors, with side doors next to them for strollers and the disabled and so on, but there's only two sets of them, one on Michigan and one on Pearson. I'm at one and our notions buyer was at the other, studying a display of costume jewelry. You wouldn't make her for a store employee, either, she says, any more than you would have me. She says none of the people who left the perfume demonstration went out the Pearson door. And I'm watching two or three people from the demonstration leave by the Michigan door, and I can tell you they weren't standing anywhere near the woman who got her purse rifled."

"You get a good look at the people near her?"

"So-so. In a crowd like that, maybe four or five people were behind and beside her. The people in front of her, I don't see how they coulda done it."

"Me either. Can you give us descriptions of the people behind her?"

"Yeah, I guess so. Fair to middling, maybe. But frankly they looked like a cross-section of all our customers. And that's not what bothers me. What bothers me is, say you're gonna lift a wallet. Wouldn't it be the first thing you do is get out of the building?"

Figueroa said, "Sure."

"But I'm here to tell you, whoever she was, she didn't rush out the doors."

Bennis said, "Maybe she hadn't picked enough pockets."

"I guess."

Bennis and Figueroa got up. "You'll write out those descriptions?" Bennis asked. Ely nodded. "Fax me at this number. And what I'll do, I'm going to recommend that some of the patrol officers pass through the store from time to time. You understand we don't have enough people to just stand here and watch all day, though."

"I'm not sure we'd even want that. Cops looming over the customers."

"Right," Figueroa said. "It takes some of the fun out of having your nails painted chinchilla if a cop is looking."

Ely raised his eyebrows. Bennis said, "She's joking, sir, but there's some truth to that. We usually try to keep a low profile in stores. What you could do to help, Mr. Ely, is let us know ahead of time when the store is planning these demonstrations."

"Okay. I'll do that. I'll make up our schedule and fax you that, too." Ely was loosening up. In fact, he seemed to find Figueroa amusing. "After all, we can't blow a whistle at the end of a demonstration and yell, 'Everybody check your purse.' "

"I guess not," Bennis said.

"And much as you'd like to, you certainly can't frisk 'em all for contraband."

"Okay, we've wasted two hours. Can we go now?" Figueroa demanded in the elevator.

"Yeah. Over to the CPD. See about the other currency exchange robber."

"Wait. I have to call. We've got O'Dowd's next of kin's name and phone."

Death notification was one of the responsibilities of the

investigating officer, usually the detective. She and Bennis rarely had to do it and she was glad of that.

Barbara Jean O'Dowd sounded much younger than her dead husband, the retired cop, had looked. Figueroa fought down a surge of anger at a woman who could let her husband wander the streets in an old overcoat with just a bottle of wine, eighty-eight cents, and a foam cup in his pocket. Mrs. O'Dowd's address was in Elgin, far northwest of Chicago. Did she ever get into town to see her husband? Did she care? Of course, you never knew what went on inside a marriage, but still—

Procedure said the first people to talk with after eyewitnesses were the family. And Figueroa was going to talk with the family, even if she had to bite her tongue about her feelings. She was aware she was being unfair, prejudging the situation, but couldn't even one family member watch over this man?

"I'm afraid I have bad news, Mrs. O'Dowd."

There was a silence, which Figueroa broke into right away. Even though there was no record of O'Dowd having children, records weren't always right, and she didn't want this woman to think a child of hers was dead.

"We have a Michael Kilkenny O'Dowd who is, uh, he's dead, ma'am."

"Oh, poor Dowdy," the voice said. And that nickname and the sorrow in the tone took away all of Figueroa's anger. "What happened to him? I always thought the end of it would be—"

"Would be what, Mrs. O'Dowd?"

"Drink related. He'd walk into the street in front of a car. Or he'd drink and pass out and freeze to death. But it's warm now, of course. And why am I going on like this? Tell me what happened."

Figueroa told her as much as they knew.

When she had finished speaking, Mrs. O'Dowd said, "What do you need to know from me?"

"Have you seen him recently?"

"I haven't seen him in several years. Eight or ten years at least. And he didn't call. He thought it was better for me if he left me alone."

"Was it better?"

"I don't know."

"Do you—did he—did you have children?"

"No."

"Did he have friends in town here?"

"Not that I know of. I'm sorry. That sounds so sad. He kind of lost them all in the last years. Dowdy just wasn't going to be happy. And he had the grace not to share his unhappiness with anybody. Even though we might have wished he would. He was a man with a lot of grace. I'm sure there were friends he could have called on. But that wasn't him."

Figueroa said, "I'm sorry."

"I'll claim the body when you let me know," Mrs. O'Dowd said.

"All right."

"Officer Figueroa. There were very few women officers in Dowdy's early years. But he never held the view that they were out of place in the department."

"That's very good."

"Do you have family? No, don't tell me. I know that cops don't like to talk about who they have at home. Hostages to fortune. What I wanted to say is, have family. Have friends and things you do and hobbies outside the department. Have friends who are not cops. Because one day, it's all over. Dowdy was just fine as long as he was a working cop, but after that he fell apart. Have friends and keep them and make time for them. Right now. When you think it doesn't matter. Because later on it will matter a lot."

In only thirty-six hours, the man in the attic had become quite an expert on the family's habits. He amused himself by sitting on the step that was just above the halfway-down turn in the narrow attic stairs. He wished he could sweep the stairs. Nobody around here seemed to care that they were dusty. But someone would surely notice if he cleaned.

This position put him out of sight to the boy and the woman cop who lived on the third floor. He listened to their chatter as they got ready for bed at night and as they got up in the morning. It was better than TV. The stairs acted like a kind of speaking tube, bringing up sounds from the floors below, even as far away as the kitchen.

This morning the cop must have left early. She was no doubt the person who came hurrying through the kitchen in the middle of the night, nearly catching him with the ice cream carton. The crabbiness of Mr. Daddy this morning was the result of being left in charge. Sheesh! What a creep! Didn't he know that the father set the tone for the whole household, for good or for bad? It was his responsibility to be firm and commanding.

When the family left for school and work in the morning and only the spaz and the nurse were left, the man crept down the back stairs to the spot just above the turn in the flight between the first and second floors and listened from there. However, it wasn't very interesting. The spaz couldn't talk, and in his opinion the nurse couldn't think.

He went back up to his attic to change shirts. In the night, he had taken a T-shirt and a sleeveless undershirt from the dryer in the basement. They were a little large on him, but he smiled and whispered, "Beggars can't be choosers." And he hated to be dirty. His own undershirt was so similar that he thought he could probably leave it in the big plastic basket of dirty clothes and somebody would wash it. But that would be just too risky.

He had also found a big roll of silver duct tape and a screwdriver and scissors. He carried that nice package up to the attic as well.

Every day the nurse, Alma Sturdley, took her allotted lunch hour off. She didn't leave the house; that was part of the agreement. Someone had to be there at all times in case of fire. But she was able to sit down with a cup of coffee or tea and a sandwich and read a book, knit, or watch television as long as she kept the sound low enough so she could hear Sheryl's bell. Being a responsible woman, she did exactly as she had promised. The fire alarm she could have heard with the TV at full blast. They had tested it twice, and it was loud enough to wake the dead.

She had got into the habit of relaxing at lunch in the sun parlor. This was a room off the living room on the south side of the house. Kath was growing a variety of houseplants there. Robert had installed three chaise longues in the room and J J had insisted that Suze also put in a small television. That way, if Kath and Maria were watching a program he didn't like on the larger TV in the living room, he could go to the sun parlor and see his own shows.

Alma Sturdley liked to watch the Channel 9 noon news or *Hollywood Squares*.

By his second day in the house, the man realized this was a regular pattern and occurred always on the stroke of twelve.

At eleven Wednesday morning he came slowly but firmly down the back stairs from his attic to the third floor. He was very familiar now with which treads creaked so that you had to step near the wall.

He had explored the third floor briefly yesterday, but not boldly. Now that he knew no one came home during the day, he could pretty much do as he pleased.

The little boy's room wasn't interesting to him. But the cop's was.

The blue carpet absorbed any sounds his feet made. The room had blue and white plaid curtains and a blue and white bedspread. There were three paintings of western scenes on the walls, and each had some blue sky or blue water in it. A color-coordinated cop. What next?

A western-look pine dresser stood between the two gable windows. The man made a note of the position of this room and where it lay under the attic he called home. He must be careful not to walk around on the attic floor that lay directly over the ceiling of this room. The goddamned cop seemed alert. He wasn't going to take any chances.

He pulled open the top dresser drawer. Sweaters and sweatshirts. He felt around under them, but there was nothing special hidden there. Shutting that drawer carefully, he pulled open the second. Underwear. Bras, some black, some flesh color. Panties, most of serviceable cotton, but some black silk as well, and some white lace. He picked up a handful, crushing them into a bouquet, and held them to his face. There was only the smell of a light perfume, no woman smell. He was disappointed but not surprised. She seemed like a clean one, always washing the kitchen countertops, making sure all the dishes went into the dishwasher at night, even if she had to help the kids do them. He heard her chattering with them as they rinsed and loaded. That was admirable, as far as it goes, he thought.

He put the underwear back in the drawer and resisted the urge to fold them more neatly than she had. Her arrangement hadn't been bad. He'd give her a B− for it.

Drawer three held socks, scarves, and some jewelry. He held a scarf up to his nose and smelled the woman's shampoo scent on it. So she didn't wash these after every wearing. He felt underneath them, but except for some outdated ID and odds and ends, stationery and pens and pencils, nothing. The bottom drawer held more miscellany. Annoyed, he pushed it in sharply, and then froze. He'd carelessly made a noise. He shouldn't have done that. Better get control of himself.

The closet, then.

In the closet were dresses, shirts, and pants on hangers. A lot of cop stuff. Blue uniform shirts. White dress shirts. Some blue ties. A cop kind of black raincoat with yellow stripes. All of it in order, cop stuff on the far right. Shoes were lined up on the floor, the cop shoes under the cop clothes.

He felt around the shelf above the clothes.

Aha! He knew it! Her extra. It had to be someplace. No cop ever had just one gun, did they?

He lifted down a stainless-steel Colt revolver. Excellent! It had been hell for him, going around without a gun, but if the cops caught you and you had one on you, you'd never get loose.

And then, he realized that the Colt had a trigger lock in place, an ugly thing like a pair of rubber earmuffs locked together. Making it safe for the little darling children. Instantly, he was furiously angry. He could feel his face get red and hot.

Stop. Get control.

Yes. He unclenched his hands. That was better. Maybe he could find the key?

Back to the dresser. He tried the two drawers that had the jumbled stuff in the bottom. And there were several keys, but even a glance told him they were not the size of the small keyhole in the trigger lock.

Where, then?

She might keep it on her key chain and carry it with her. That would be too bad. Wait. She would carry the key to her daily gun with her, of course, but the extra one? Probably not. Why risk losing it?

Okay. If it was here it was not likely to be in the closet. Too close to the gun. She was too careful for that. And he hadn't found it in the dresser. Still, it had to be near at hand to be any use to her at all.

The pictures.

The back of Yosemite Falls was just plain brown paper. So was the back of a creosote bush against the western sky. But behind Mono Lake at sunrise—a key.

The key.

He stared at it for half a minute, very pleased with himself. He held the gun near it so as to be absolutely certain it was the right one, but he did not touch it, and he certainly did not try to pull off the tape that held it in place.

Then he replaced the paintings and checked them carefully to see that they were straight. He made sure all the drawers were properly arranged. He put the gun back on the shelf.

He had never had any intention of taking it. He just wanted to know how to get to it when he needed to.

In Sheryl's room, Alma Sturdley checked her watch. Eleven-fifteen. They had done the morning set of exercises, and she could see Sheryl was tired. Her face paled because she tried so hard. Sometimes Alma had to call it quits, even though Sheryl wanted to go on. Sheryl would hold on to the chair arms and do it again and again, and once in a while Alma actually had to get firm with her, saying, "The doctor could have me fired if I let you do this, dear. Now don't make me worry."

Today they had been working on getting up from a chair without leaning sideways. Up and down, up and down. "You really are getting better, dear," Alma said. She was still not balanced, even though the movement was better. Sheryl's right arm was very strong but her left was still weak and visibly thinner.

Forty-five minutes were left before Alma's lunch break. She decided to go to the kitchen and make tea so that it could cool off, and she could have iced tea with lunch.

She rose from the rocker near Sheryl's bed and said, "I'm going to make tea, dear. Would you like some while it's still hot?"

"Am-bin," Sheryl said.

Alma Sturdley had never been able to understand much of what Sheryl said, even though she'd been here three months now. But she often got an idea of whether Sheryl was enthusiastic about a thing or not. She didn't seem to be enthusiastic about tea, so Alma said, "Well, all right, dear. Maybe later when it's iced."

In the kitchen, she filled the kettle, then emptied some of the water back out. It was silly to boil a whole kettle if you were just making a cup or two and besides a smaller amount of water would boil faster.

Alma Sturdley stood watching the pot, reflecting that it was a watched pot that never boils. Finally, she got tired of watching and turned to look out the kitchen window at the backyard. She heard a bump behind her. Whirling, she stared down the hall, but no one was there. Then the kettle on the burner made a ticking noise. The kettle danced a little hop. The water on the underside of the kettle was vaporizing on the burner, making the kettle jump a little. That must have been the sound she heard.

Alma put her wrapped sandwich on a plate to eat with the tea. She had brought Diet 7UP in her lunch bag today. It was chilling in the refrigerator, but somehow, tea had sounded nicer. She would not begin lunch until noon. She was extremely responsible.

On the second floor, the man waited a full minute next to Kath's room, without shifting so much as a single inch. He cursed the door that had swung itself into the wall.

Either the nurse down in the kitchen would come and see

what had made the noise or she wouldn't. If he heard her coming up the back stairs, he would head for the front stairs, go to the third floor, and boogie up to the attic from there.

A couple of minutes passed, but she didn't leave the kitchen and finally the kettle began to screech.

He turned back to the little girl's room. This time he was careful to hold the doorknob until the door was fully open, making sure it didn't swing into the wall.

Old houses were like that. Nothing was exactly level, and doors swung open on their own.

Had to remember that.

There were stuffed animals on the girl's bed. The bed itself had been hastily made—just pulled together, really. Didn't parents teach their children the proper care of their possessions these days? But then he reflected that the little girl's mother was unavailable right now, busy being a spaz. So why didn't the cop give these children clear orders? Or their father? Somebody really ought to teach them a lesson.

The animals were more carefully placed than the bedclothes. There was a little white stuffed dog, a yellow Pokémon doll, a very old Raggedy Ann, a small brown bear with much of its fur worn off, a large brown bear wearing a Notre Dame shirt, and a green dinosaur with a red tongue and yellow claws. They were lined up in a neat row against the headboard on top of the pillow.

The man lay down on the bed, nuzzling his face into the pillow, between the two bears. He forced his face farther down, squeezing air out of the pillow.

He could smell the little girl.

He took deep breaths, savoring the scent.

After she came out of the coma, the world was so confused that most of the time Sheryl couldn't make any sense of what the doctors and nurses were trying to tell her. Sometimes she tried to hide inside her confusion, refusing to deal with the real world.

The broken bones made it painful for her to move. But as soon as the staff could get her moving, they became relentless. Her memories of the parallel bars would stay with her for the rest of her life. Hold on, walk, walk straight, hold on, hold on, keep going! And the therapist was always on her left, the weak side, forcing her forward.

"There are five somewhat different approaches to rehabilitation after a head injury," the therapist told her, when she was first able to concentrate a little. Or maybe he had told her the same thing many times before and she just didn't remember. The days blurred a lot. Events overlapped.

"The approaches are Root, Bobath, Brunnstrom, proprioceptive neuromuscular facilitation, and Carr and Shepard. They're all helpful. However, most of us believe that Bobath is the most successful for hemiplegia caused by brain injury."

He spoke quite slowly and distinctly, but without talking down to her, which she remembered appreciating and wishing she could speak well enough to tell him that she was grateful.

"Bobath goes on the assumption that the sensation of movement is what's learned, not movement itself. Sort of like what you feel is what you get."

He smiled. She thought maybe she smiled. She certainly tried to.

"A cerebral injury causes abnormal patterns of movement. What we're going to do is elicit normal patterns of posture and movement and so on. Think of this as motion providing normal feedback to the brain. Moving normally will produce normal stimuli to the injured parts of your brain. And of course it will inhibit abnormal patterns."

In one of those completely unpredictable events, like the sun coming out from a tiny gap in the clouds on a rainy day, she said, "Easy."

He was delighted. "Wonderful! Wonderful! Except of course it won't be easy. It will be very difficult. Sometimes it will be painful. I will be merciless. The right side of your brain was injured, and therefore the physical deficit is on your left. I won't let you get away with leaning over to the left. When you do, I'll make you do every motion again and again."

Which they did.

Before Sheryl was allowed to go home, the therapist schedule was put in place. In addition, Alma Sturdley took two days of training in Sheryl's specific daily exercises. The therapist told Alma that even though Sheryl had to do these exercises and do them correctly, she wasn't supposed to do them to the point of exhaustion. If anything, Sheryl was too desperately eager.

"Tire her," he had said, "but just a little bit."

On the stroke of twelve noon, Alma Sturdley picked up her cooled tea, poured it over ice cubes, and walked down the hall to Sheryl's door.

"I'm taking my lunch now, dear," she said. "If there's a problem, you just ring that bell."

The bell was actually a button that sounded a loud buzzer mounted on the wall. Sheryl didn't ring it much, partly because it was a strain for her to reach unless she was lying on her back with her right hand next to it. And also, Alma believed, because poor Sheryl hated to be trouble to anybody.

Alma sighed. Alma thought Sheryl felt she was a terrible burden. And indeed why shouldn't she? She *was* a burden, or at least a responsibility, and for sure her accident made everybody else in the house do the work that a mother would normally do.

But it wasn't her fault. Alma just hoped that Sheryl realized that. You couldn't quite come out and say something like that, though, even with the intent of being kind. Alma also hoped Sheryl believed she was getting better. Alma had seen for herself in the months she had been here that Sheryl's walking had improved. Why, she could stand up all by herself now for a half minute or so, and when Alma had first arrived she could hardly stand at all, even with two people holding on to her to steady her. Her speech had not improved so much. It must be terribly frustrating, all those thoughts locked inside. Alma, who loved to talk, sighed deeply in sympathy.

Sheryl had a small television set in her room. Alma wished Sheryl would watch some of the comedy shows. Surely they would cheer her up. One or two were just so hilarious. But she never seemed to watch, even if Alma turned them on. She rolled on her other side and didn't look. How strange.

Alma sighed again as she settled in front of the television in the sun room. Poor thing. It must be hard.

Alma reminded herself not to show any pity. She had found over the years of caregiving that usually they hated that most of all.

Sheryl lay quiet. Frequently, she tried to lie just as still as she possibly could, and listen to her body. This wasn't always possible. Sometimes her left arm trembled for no reason. Sometimes her left foot would point and straighten, point and straighten, until she thought it would make her crazy. And nothing she could do, no mental exercise, no relaxation technique, no force of will, not even making some kind of counter move to "distract" it, ever stopped it until it just decided to stop on its own.

And sometimes she was just too achy with all the lying in bed to hold still. She would change position as if compelled to do so when the ache in her back or shoulders or neck became unbearable. She'd wiggle, and arch her back, cringe in on herself like a shrimp, then stretch out as long as she could make herself, then do it all over again.

But now she seemed able to lie still for a few minutes.

Grateful, she felt the sheets under her body, and studied carefully the coolness, touched the fabric with her fingertips, sensing, being aware of the temperature, the texture, the light weight of the cloth. Then she drew in a breath and felt the air with her nose and mouth and down into her throat. It was cool, too, and moved smoothly. The air on her skin was her next focus. There was very little motion in the room, very little passage of air. Instead, it seemed to hang rather heavily over her. Air was called a fluid, and she felt very much as if she were under a pool of fluid. The sensation wasn't unpleasant, but the thought was disturbing. Humans were frighteningly dependent on this body of air, but unaware of it. Probably it was a good thing they were unaware of it. Had there been sunlight in the room, she thought she would feel the weight of that, too, not just the warmth.

Stretching, then settling back to motionlessness, she assessed the muscles and joints that she had become so very painfully aware of in the last four months. Nowadays it amazed her that she had casually spent the first thirty-five years of her life hardly thinking about the parts of her body. Just using them as if they were always going to be there, always going to do what she wanted them to do, as if she were the puppet master, pulling the strings to her arms and legs. Maybe infants, she thought, went through a process of discovering the parts of their bodies and trying to get them to do what their minds wanted.

She could almost feel the electricity buzzing in her nerves. Down the spinal cord, her senses running out to the fingers and the soles of her feet, the toes—

But generating the messages was the problem. During the weeks she had spent in the hospital, when she had been so angry at the feet that didn't do what she asked them to, the eye that looked someplace else, the mouth that wouldn't talk, one of the neurologists had told her that her anger was a good thing.

"Brain injuries are bizarre," he had said. "And especially

brains coming out of comas. People who can't move their legs at all will tell you they're just the same as they ever were before the accident. People who can hardly speak will say there is absolutely nothing wrong. It's very, very strange, and I'm here to tell you that nobody really understands why. It's one of the mysteries of coma. We think it's more common in right-side injuries, like yours. There's a theory that the right side of the brain looks for trouble and the left side of the brain looks for okay-ness. So when the trouble monitor is turned off, so is awareness of it."

She had replied in nonsense syllables but he understood her intent.

"No, it's not because they're trying to look on the bright side of things. They honestly seem to believe that they're doing all the things they always used to do. The people who don't react that way get better sooner."

"Ah, ah, ah!" she had said. Or something like that.

"I know you're frustrated. And impatient and angry. But you need to understand that feeling that way is a good sign."

When she was first coming out of coma, Sheryl had heard sounds, and that was all. She couldn't see or speak, and she didn't really feel herself move, but she heard rushing water. Later the doctors told her that the first of the lost senses to return after coma is hearing.

She was at Niagara Falls. She knew it for certain. And someplace around was Maria, who was only two years old. They were playing near the falls.

A week or so later, farther into her recovery, she realized that it must have been the sound of the respirator she thought was the falls, but she had been so sure. And after Niagara Falls she slipped into utter terror. The sound was not falling water, but flames. She had died and gone to hell and she would be here forever.

And devils were stabbing her with their pitchforks. Over

and over, for days, they stabbed her. They were breaking her back. Some of them poked at her eyes. Or shot flame into her eyes.

Now Sheryl put the past out of her mind. Its only use today, she told herself, was so that she could reflect on how far she'd come. She could stand up. She could see quite well now, even though the world sometimes looked to her as if the left eye focused a little higher than her right eye, making her feel spacey and out of sync.

She would walk again. She knew this, without question. The primary problem now was mental. There were times when she wasn't really sure where she was. She would be eating dinner with the family and suddenly be convinced that she was at work. Or much worse, back at the hospital, waiting for some painful test while machines made noises. Because she was aware of her confusion, it was both less and more scary. She could rationalize it. But the idea that her brain could run away with her was deeply upsetting.

Most frustrating on a moment-to-moment basis was language. It was frustrating because she was so sure she ought to be able to master it. She would think the word "cat," picture a cat clearly, and get her mouth all ready for "cat" and out would come the word "evil." Or "fork." She tried very hard not to burst into tears when she couldn't talk, because she knew it bothered the children when she cried.

What she'd been doing lately in reaction to this was cowardly and she knew it, but she couldn't help it. She'd been talking less and less so she wouldn't get upset. Dr. Gregorich would have something to say about *that*.

She could practice now, of course, when there was nobody to hear her. She would say "It's a warm day."

"Bast," she said. "Corner-gah." She started to cry.

With the nurse in some distant room eating her lunch and playing the television, the man was free to come down the last flight of stairs. At the door to the kitchen he paused and studied the downstairs hall.

He had come this far at night. Several times in fact. But it was important to him to see the rooms by daylight, so as to know exactly what was where.

First, on his left as he started down the hall, was a broom closet. Then, on the right, a bathroom. Now he silently examined the bathroom for three or four minutes to fix it in his mind, noticing where the window was, just in case, and how it opened, a sash window with a simple turn latch.

Time to go look in the spaz woman's room. It was just beyond the bathroom, also on the right. The archway to the living room was beyond it on the left. A glance into the living room told him the nurse wasn't there. Sound came from the sunroom television. He crept softly to the bedroom door. The woman might see him the instant his head appeared around the doorjamb, of course, but more likely not. She couldn't possibly spend the whole day staring at the doorway. And even if she did, she couldn't tell anybody what she had seen.

If she saw him, he would be back up the stairs before the nurse could get here.

No time like the present, he said to himself.

He leaned boldly around the doorjamb.

The woman was much smaller than he had anticipated. She lay on her right side, her legs drawn up a bit, facing away from him. There was a red and blue floral quilt over her, pulled up to her waist.

He noted her window, which was just like the bathroom sash window but larger. It was open a couple of inches at the bottom.

He noted the bottles of medications, an insulated carafe, a plate of cookies, a jar of dried fruit, cards made by the children, all on the nightstand. He noted the hospital bed with rails, the rails raised so that she wouldn't fall out. He noted a kind of swinging bar over the bed, which she probably used to exercise.

There were two chairs, one straight and one soft stuffed one. A rack held several dresses and robes on hangers. All of the clothes that he could see buttoned or zipped in front.

And especially he noted the call button on a wire looped over the bed rail, in easy reach near the spaz's right hand if she was lying on her back.

That call button was important.

As he padded carefully back up the stairs to the attic, he ran over in his mind everything he had seen, but the location of the call button was the big detail, first and foremost.

CHAPTER THIRTEEN

AT TWENTY-SIXTH AND California, the Cook County Criminal Courts Building, Figueroa and Bennis caught up with ASA Malley. Malley said, "He's flipped on his buddy."

"No honor among thieves," Bennis said. "And come to think of it, how sweet that is."

"What changed his mind?" Suze asked. "Did you convince him, Mr. Malley?"

"In a manner of speaking. I asked him how it happened he got to go into the currency exchange and take all the risk and his pal got to stay in the car where he couldn't be ID'd. Pointed out that the way it went down, anything goes wrong, Herzog gets caught and the other guy gets away."

"And?"

Malley frowned. He preferred people to listen to his stories and not prompt him. But he liked the sound of his voice more than he liked silence, so he went on. "Says he's gonna do a deal. Gives us the name of his pal. He seems to be one Stanley Sisdel. Lives on West Addison. Herzog picked him up there once."

"That's in the Nineteenth. They get him?"

"Nope. They went there. Turns out to be a rented single room in a real dump. I mean, this guy must have figured on the currency exchange cash to upgrade his lifestyle. You messed him up a whole lot, guys."

"Good for us," Bennis said.

"So where do we look now?" Figueroa asked.

"Who knows? I'm no cop, thank God. Know what else?"

"What else?"

"The asshole in the car? Sisdel? Herzog says he wasn't even carrying."

"No gun? Why not?"

"Case they were caught. I mean, even Herzog realizes that now. Herzog is not real bright. In fact, he's got the brains of a block of tofu. Your guy, Sisdel, is real bright. But Herzog, he's finally worked it out—maybe with a little help from yours truly—he's finally worked it out that if they were busted on the spot, Sisdel was gonna claim he had no idea what Herzog went into the currency exchange *for*. Cute, huh?"

"Very cute," Figueroa said.

"Not a nice guy," said Manny Jiminez, more cheerfully than he should have, given the info he was getting off his machine. Manny looked exactly like the kid reporter, Jimmy Olson, from the old Superman comics. All he needed was a bow tie, Bennis thought. Maybe one of those straw hats with the red band. Manny had a ham and Swiss cheese sandwich on an onion roll on his desk. Figueroa and Bennis hadn't had time for lunch. It was now past two, and the sandwich smelled like heaven. They averted their minds. As much as possible anyhow.

Manny was the Area Four computer whiz. He had just searched NCIC, Cook County, and Illinois for wants and warrants on the missing currency exchange bandit. "Aha," he said, "I have our known but flown."

The name Herzog had given up was Stan Sisdel, but it turned out Stan Sisdel was an aka and Stan was really Harold Valentine, an improbable name for an extremely unappetizing man.

Manny said, "Seems our Harold likes little girls."

"Likes little girls *and* robs currency exchanges!" Bennis said. "A double threat man."

"Triple threat. Felony stuff relating to scams, too, and other stuff."

Figueroa said, "All right, all right. Give us something we can use. Known associates?"

"No known associates. Maybe he's not a buddy-buddy type. I can only give you what I got. DOB 10-04-65. Social—here—place of birth—mm, yes—I'll print all this out for you. Haydn High School, graduated in 1982. Two years of junior college. Became—well, lookee there. A commodities trader. Lasted four months. He seems to have tried some sort of Ponzi scheme. Mostly by mail looks like. Maybe he's not a real slick talker in person. Just a guess. Arrested the first time right after the CBOE booted him. Lemme get that from another source."

"Be my guest."

"And now—ta-da! National Sex Offenders Registry. Nice that we have it. The registry I mean. No reason whatsoever we couldn't have had one twenty years ago. But don't get me started. Course now we got the Registered Sex Offenders Act, too, so they have to register where they live. Who says life doesn't get better? Yes. Here you go. Our Harold was picked up hanging around a junior high school playground. But since he didn't have any record back then, he basically got away with saying there's no law against sitting on a park bench *outside* a playground. Which there isn't. Of course, it wasn't much later that—oh, my, my Harold!"

Figueroa said, "Tell me."

"Harold's a sucker."

"Any crook is a sucker," Bennis said.

"No. A sucker is a sadistic form of a biter."

"A biter is already sadistic."

"A sucker is more sadistic. A sucker is a very, very angry person. True, they bite the victim. In Harold's case he mostly bites little girls around ten, twelve years old. The sucker takes a bite and holds on and sucks. Makes a quite distinctive mark.

A central area of ecchymoses with a starburst pattern around it. One of the vice guys could show you pictures. Very distinctive. Know it in a second, once you've seen one."

"Oh, swell. So if he's so busy biting, what's he doing knocking over currency exchanges?"

"My guess is he needed the money."

"Valentine got nabbed for abducting the kid, not the biting," Calvin Waters said. Any of several special units could be involved in sex offense cases—Violent Crimes, the Youth Division, the SIU. Calvin was from Vice, and was definitely not cheerful. He had deep grooves from his nose to the sides of his mouth and down to his chin. He looked like a sad puppet.

He went on. "There were three or four other cases he was tied to, but they couldn't tag him for sure."

"I thought tooth marks were distinctive," Figueroa said.

"They are in a lot of instances. Especially on stuff like, say, cheese or fudge. But flesh is quite movable. It's what we call plastic. If you get a nice clear mark on firm skin, you can probably match it. But you get the best marks on cadavers. These particular cases—well, you know how live kids wiggle."

"Especially if they're being bitten," Bennis muttered. "I'd wiggle too." He didn't like this whole discussion, Figueroa saw. Bennis had told her he had never wanted to deal with crimes against children, and he'd never agreed to work Youth. He knew he'd be too angry at the parents.

"How come he's out so soon?" she asked.

"Doesn't say. He served thirty-nine months. Supposed to stay a hundred yards away from any playground or school."

"So what do we do, look for him a hundred and one yards from schools?"

"I surely wish you would," Waters said.

"Why so urgent?"

"This sucker type isn't your ordinary fondler. Suckers have a lot of anger. Generally speaking they escalate."

"To murder?"

"Child rape. Sometimes murder. Yeah."

CHAPTER FOURTEEN

Figueroa and Bennis had specifically asked if Dr. Percolin could do the dead woman's post. Apparently he was free and willing, and he was waiting for them when they arrived.

"Got O'Dowd's blood alcohol level," he said. "It was point three five."

"That's high," Bennis said. "Arrested a driver once who blew point three. He thought he was flying a plane into Newark."

"High enough to be comatose. We call point two to point three grossly impaired. For drivers point one is considered impaired."

The dead woman's old clothes lay on a table, and her wallet and driver's license were with them. The license had expired eight years earlier, but told them her name was Abigail Ward.

Old, naked, gray, and small. Figueroa saw the woman as a crumpled throwaway. Percolin, in his dignified manner, had draped a paper sheet over the body, but the old woman was fundamentally naked nevertheless. Even her reddened eyelids and pallid face looked emphatically naked. When Percolin and the diener turned her over, her bones squeaked on the stainless steel of the table. The left elbow made a sound on the metal like a crying cat. Her buttocks were flat and colorless. The knobs of her spine stood out.

Percolin went through the usual introductory remarks about the external condition of the body, but Figueroa hardly heard. She was very much afraid she was going to cry, and by the time she realized it would embarrass her a lot to cry, she felt tears that had already run all the way down her cheeks.

"Suze, my man—" Bennis said, startled.

"I'm not crying!" she said.

Percolin said, "Officer Bennis, Officer Figueroa is not crying, is that clear?"

"Yes, boss," Bennis said. "I hear you."

Percolin stepped on the voice activator pedal. Today he was wearing penny loafers and his socks were yellow. "There are no serious abrasions or contusions on the dorsal or ventral surfaces. A few small red marks on the ventral skin of the abdomen may represent an attack of insects or members of the tick family. The face has been recently washed."

Figueroa stared at the deflated breasts, like balloons that had lost air, their nipples hard brown knots like dried figs. She got hold of her sadness, not eliminating it, but putting it in some back compartment so that her analytical brain could function.

Percolin took up his scalpel and made the Y incision. He peeled the soft tissues back from the chest. He reflected the flaps he had made.

Then Percolin reached for the bone saw. This was much like a circular saw for wood paneling or drywall, but with smaller teeth and a smaller diameter blade.

Figueroa watched the saw cut through the ribs. Percolin wore a Plexiglas mask, similar to welder's gear. There was a smell of hot, burned bone fragments and a fine mist in the air of blood, bone, and tissue.

He removed the chest plate.

"Heart's not at all bad," Percolin said encouragingly, as if he were telling Figueroa that her child might make All-State. "She does have a few little lung problems."

"Such as what?" Bennis asked.

"Must've had TB a while back. Don't get worried. Old case.

It looks like it's all encased in calcium. I'd bet this was before the new drug resistant strains."

"Make my day," Bennis said.

"Also recent pneumonia. Still a little juicy right here in the left lower lobe." He poked the lung with his index finger, producing a *squish-squish* sound like pressing a wet sponge. "Sleeping out. No medical care. Hardly surprising."

Time went by while Percolin worked and Figueroa worried. How did you find a killer who swooped in on people like this who were rootless? People who had nobody? People nobody was waiting at home for? Nobody missed them. She was startled by Percolin saying, "Figueroa?"

"Yes, Doctor."

"You said 'poor old lady' at one point. Well, how old do you think she is, mmm?"

"Seventy?"

"My guess is she's not more than fifty-five. And if we were doing an office pool and closest guess wins, I would say forty-nine."

"Really?"

"Give the driver's license a look. And she's had a baby. Maybe two but I don't think more than that. Probably thirty years ago."

Figueroa went to the effects table. Percolin was close. Abigail Ward was fifty-one.

Once again, Percolin took a good look at the stomach lining. It showed, he said, the changes typical of prolonged alcoholism. He asked Figueroa to smell the contents. She said, "Booze. But I'm no good at telling what. I'm a beer person."

"Officer Bennis?"

He sniffed. "Bourbon. Good bourbon, in fact."

"My opinion exactly," Percolin said.

Figueroa said, "Is there any way to tell exactly what brand,

Dr. Percolin? If it's not generally available, we might be able to narrow down where she got it."

"Yeah," Bennis said. "Suppose the killer took her to a fancy bar."

"In that outfit she was wearing?" Percolin asked. "I doubt it."

"Or brought it along and fed it to her," Bennis said. "We might be able to find out where it's sold."

Figueroa said, "O'Dowd had good scotch in his stomach, remember."

"Problem with identifying it," Percolin said, "is that so much of the alcohol is absorbed so fast. Fifteen minutes, in most cases. And the stomach acids also would be mixed with it. No, wait a minute. What am I saying? It's right here. We can smell it. This last amount was administered after several earlier drinks; the killer must've fed her a whole lot of alcohol. She absorbed the first five, six, seven shots. They weren't mixed with water as far as I can tell, or at least what's left wasn't. It just basically went into her bloodstream and then he fed her more and more until the stomach was nearly paralyzed. So the stuff that's left here might be pretty pure."

"You *could* identify it?"

"You can identify almost anything if you're willing to pay enough for the analysis. Here's one parameter. If this contains urethane, it's probably bourbon."

"We already know it's bourbon from the smell," Bennis said.

"If this gets to court, you want to be going in and testifying that your nose knows?"

"No. I guess not."

"Urethane is a by-product of the production of bourbon and an unfortunate one because it's carcinogenic. But two or three of the top-priced bourbons are quite low in urethane. That might narrow it down without doing some expensive chemical profile. Suppose this bourbon is low in urethane. So let's say it's a high-priced bourbon. How does that help you?"

"Well, there's maybe a hundred bars in the Loop area I know she didn't go to, if so," Bennis said. "And a hell of a lot of liquor stores I know our murderer didn't buy it from."

"Whatever. If that helps you, so much the better. I'll send this off and we'll see."

Percolin used a ladle, identical to a soup ladle but smaller, to scoop a portion of liquid from the stomach. Figueroa sighed sadly.

It was an hour later that Percolin wrapped up. He snapped off his gloves, slapped them into a bin marked DANGER MEDICAL WASTE, and, crooking a finger at them, led them to a small library off the hallway, densely packed with books and journals. "Canadian limit on urethane is a hundred and fifty parts per billion."

"A hundred and fifty parts per billion doesn't sound like much."

"It is when it's urethane. See here, there are some plum brandies that have two thousand parts per billion. But that's not our problem. Look."

His thick index finger ran down a column of figures next to an alphabetized list of the name of various bourbons. "See, most of them run between seventy and a hundred and fifty parts per billion. Some as high as three hundred. These pricey ones, though, are in the fifty parts per billion range. And one of the Makers Mark lines is zero."

"I see that."

"The other thing is, how fast is urethane absorbed? I'm not a chemist, but I'd guess pretty damn fast. We'd hope at the same rate as alcohol so the ratio remains the same. Anyhow, we can give this a try. There may be other ways a chemist can tell bourbons apart. Each one probably has a characteristic chemical profile. For all I know, the FBI may have a library of chemical profiles of all sorts of booze. I'll save some of the stomach contents here, just in case we need to order more tests later."

Most posts took under an hour, as Bennis and Figueroa well knew, and the fact that Percolin had taken closer to two hours all told, plus Percolin's seriousness, plus the fact that he had left cause of death open, impressed them.

Bennis said, "Tell us what's going on. What exactly did she die from?"

"I wish I knew. My best guess is she was suffocated."

"Like the old man yesterday, then?"

"No. Not strangled like the old man yesterday was. I'm going to need some of these tissue samples looked at by an expert." He'd taken a lot of samples, some that he'd stuck on glass slides and blown fixative at, some that he'd dropped into small phials with tops color-coded to identify the kind of preservative inside. The diener had attached case number labels to all of them. But Percolin gestured at three he'd taken from the lungs.

Figueroa said, "What do you expect to find?"

"My wild guess is they'll show she was sprayed with a fire extinguisher—now, hold it and let me explain. There are a number of fire extinguishers made especially for fires in and around computer equipment where you don't want to use water or foam or anything that leaves a residue."

"I'm aware of that."

"They're also used in restaurant kitchens because you can put out a fire without getting any crap in the food. Halon was one of the early ones, but there are maybe a dozen different types now. They all have the same action. They use a gas that keeps oxygen away from the fire. Argon or some such. I think the killer got her drunk, which wouldn't be difficult. When she was lying passed out on the ground, he kept spraying her with the fire extinguisher until she died."

"Outdoors? I can imagine doing that in a closed room, but

outdoors seems like 'using with adequate ventilation.' "

"She was already in run-down health. She was immobile from the bourbon. She wouldn't fight being smothered. And I think the gas they use in the extinguishers is heavier than air. Anyway, at least you should check to see whether there was any wind last night. If there was, maybe I'm wrong, mmm? That's your job, Officer Figueroa. And in a couple of days we'll see what the lung sections tell us."

"Manualo was smothered, O'Dowd strangled, this woman Ward maybe snuffed with a fire extinguisher. Three dead people and three different methods of murder. That isn't very typical of a serial killer is it? Don't they get into rigid habits?"

"Ask a profiler. You have at least one in the department. But if you're asking me as an amateur in the profiling business, I'd say it told you something about the killer's psyche. These murders all cut off the oxygen supply. Within that overarching requirement, I'd say the variations mean the killer is teasing us. And having a lot of fun doing it."

They left Dr. Percolin looking for similars over the past eighteen months. "Love this computer stuff," he said. "Suddenly I can do searches without breathing paper mites and library glue and paper dust."

Back at the district, Figueroa did some net searching while Bennis made phone calls. She reported back to him. "I got last night's weather report. Virtually no wind. Temperature never got below sixty-eight."

"I thought so. It was a sultry night."

"Was that Yolanda or Miranda?"

"Sultry? Neither. You're obsessed with my lady friends. And it's Amanda not Miranda."

"I don't want to hear about it."

"Yah. Haf a Mr. Valentine," the building super said. "Not a bad guy. May be trying to run out on his rent, though. Paid through the end of May. Haven't seen him. Hasn't brought in a check."

The building had deteriorated and had never been beautiful. Yes, Figueroa thought, Valentine needed the cash from the currency exchange robbery.

"You have him make out a form when he rented the room?" Bennis asked.

"Yah. Sure, we always do that."

"I'd like to see it, sir."

After a brief rummaging in a drawer, the form was produced. It had a "previous address" box, which Bennis would bet was false but nevertheless copied in his notebook, a line agreeing to the rent, with Valentine's signature appended, and not a great deal else.

"You get next of kin or anything like that?"

"No. Don't need it. Last month's rent and damage deposit. That's what we need."

"You said he was not a bad guy. Not a bad guy in what way?" Bennis asked.

"I dunno."

"You hang with him at all? Go out for a beer?"

"Nah."

"Well, help me out here. In what way was he not a bad guy."

"Quiet."

"You ever talk with him? Discuss anything? The Bears? Bulls? The Cubbies? Prothonotary warblers?"

"Nah. Talk in the hall."

"About what?"

"Like 'heat's off' or 'hi.' Like that."

"So he was a good tenant. Why?"

" 'Cause you didn't hardly ever see or hear him."

"Valentine? Who's Valentine?" the man with three stiff hairs in a wart on his nose said to Bennis.

"Your neighbor. Lived in the apartment right under yours."

"Under mine? You expect me to know who lives downstairs?" The man slammed the door in Bennis's and Figueroa's faces.

"Lovely," Bennis said.

"Look on the bright side. You didn't want to spend time with that guy anyway."

"Valentine. Right next door?" Bennis said. "Right there?" He pointed to the right, at Valentine's door. There was no name on it, but it was marked 4D in cheap black plastic numerals. The hall smelled of onions.

"Huh? That's 4D," the woman said.

"I know. The man who lived there was named Valentine. Or maybe Sisdel?"

"No kidding? Funny damn name, either of 'em," she said in a slow, dull tone. "Sistel, huh? My ma had a sistel rug on the porch when we were growing up."

"I think that's sisal," Figueroa said.

"Right. What I said."

"Ever see him? Mr. Valentine?"

"Maybe. Come in with groceries maybe."

"Say anything?"

"Nope. Turned his head away, what I remember."

"Valentine. Right next door," Figueroa said to the woman, pointing to the left, toward the door. By now they'd decided to let Figueroa talk with the women, although the stratagem didn't seem to work miracles.

"Uh, yes."

"Did you know him at all?"

"No!" the woman said.

"But you saw him go in and out?"

"Sometimes. No. Not really."

"Ma'am, could we come in and talk with you?"

No response. Suze Figueroa looked past her into a room containing a turquoise sofa entombed in a thick plastic cover.

"Ma'am? Could we come in and talk?"

From somewhere out of sight came a voice. "Mommy? Can I have some potato chips?"

The woman said, "Um—"

A girl appeared at her side. She was about ten and wore a red skirt, white tights, and a white sweater.

"Ma'am," Figueroa said, "if you could just tell me about Mr. Valentine—?"

"Mommy!" said the girl.

"We don't know anything," the woman said.

"Mommy, is that the bad man?"

"No," said the woman.

"I don't mean the lady!"

Figueroa said, "Ma'am, does your daughter mean that Mr. Valentine is a bad man?"

"We don't know anything!" the woman said. She slammed the door.

"Well, hell," Bennis said. "We sure are striking out."

"Or look at it the other way. We know that Valentine lived here. We're pretty sure he hasn't been here in a while. And we're bloody damn sure he was a loner."

"Oh, that's a big help."

"Give me a card." He gave her his callback card.

Figueroa tapped on the door. There was no response, but she called loudly, "Ma'am, if Mr. Valentine comes back, please call this number. Don't approach him. Don't ask him anything. Just call. Please?"

There was still no answer. Figueroa slipped the card under

the door, with just a tiny white corner left sticking out like the sail of a ship. She waited thirty seconds. It disappeared.

The building super had simply given them the key to Valentine's apartment. Sometimes it took you days to get a warrant and they still acted like you were there to steal the spoons. Sometimes they practically urged you in.

"Probably he doesn't like Valentine," Bennis said.

Figueroa turned the key in the lock and the door swung open. "You know we could be accused of trespassing."

"Only if somebody finds out."

"You know if we find any evidence against Valentine, it can't be used in court if we don't have a warrant."

"Then we go away and ask the district to send somebody and discover it all over again."

"Then the super will tell them we've already been here."

"Probably only if they ask him."

"Oh, all right."

They stood still and gaped at the apartment. The furniture was cheap and worn. The curtains looked like original equipment, as if they were JC Penney circa 1930. The walls were a hideous aqua. But the place was spotlessly clean.

There was a plastic or melamine coffee table. On it were three magazines, squared up perfectly with the edge. Two pens and one pencil were lined up parallel to the edge of the magazine and precisely parallel with each other. Bennis and Figueroa headed to the bedroom.

The bed was made, corners army-square. They opened the closet. "Good Lord," Figueroa said. "Who spaces hangers exactly two inches apart?"

"Valentine, obviously."

In the bathroom, the bath towel, hand towel, and washcloth had been folded precisely in half and hung in size order, precisely spaced. Figueroa pulled open the medicine cabinet.

"I figure the guy for an order nut. But what kind of order is this?" The medicines were carefully lined up, all half an inch from the front of the shelf, but were not categorized, the stick-on bandages next to the aspirin, which was next to the Bromo-Seltzer, but the big square Telfa bandages were on a shelf below.

"Believe it or not, alphabetized by brand name," Bennis said. "Look. Band-Aids, Bayer, Bromo-Seltzer."

"After this, when my kid says a little mess is healthy, I'm gonna agree."

The kitchen was even stranger, because there were more canned goods than there had been medications. Campbell's soups were alphabetized in the "C"s, while the Heinz soup came right next to Hershey's syrup. And there was only enough food to line up with the front of the cupboard shelves, no cans in back, no piles.

The sink was dry; the sink sponge was lined up with the edge of the counter and was bone dry.

"Well, he certainly hasn't been here in a while," Bennis said. "This is not a well man."

They took the key back to the super. The super said, "Sure. I'll call. If he ever turns up."

"Great. We know where he isn't," Figueroa said as they got into the car.

"Exactly. The big question is where is Valentine now?"

CHAPTER FIFTEEN

WACKER DRIVE SNAKES through the center of the city of Chicago by edging along the south branch of the Chicago River, then hanging an eastward right-angle bend and following the Chicago River to Lake Michigan. Thus, there is South Wacker Drive, North Wacker Drive, West Wacker Drive, and East Wacker Drive, to the despair of out-of-towners.

For Chicagoans in the know, however, there is also Lower Wacker. This underground semisecret road is a specialty of taxi drivers, because they can avoid the traffic that clogs the street up above where the daylight shines—and there are no pedestrians to slow you down. Lower Wacker gives access to basement delivery ports of major hotels and civic buildings. Part of Lower Wacker is lighted by green bulbs, a strange but atmospheric notion thought up by some Department of Transportation honcho.

Lower Wacker is also home to the homeless. Warmer than ground level in the glacial Chicago winters, and cooler than the sunny streets in the stifling summers, many homeless live in Lower Wacker the year round.

Tunnels branch off from Lower Wacker in all directions, running for miles under the city. Some are unlighted. Some lead to underground iron-groined chambers and low-ceilinged tunnels that have not been traveled or even mapped since the late 1800s when they were used to deliver coal to Loop office buildings.

Last year one of the hotels was replacing cracked cement

steps next to their Lower Wacker delivery ramp. A day or so later, delivery people heard desperate knocking noises coming from the steps. A homeless man, sleeping in a narrow tunnel behind the steps, had been cemented in. They chopped up the steps, dug him out, and later poured another set of steps.

Bennis and Figueroa parked their squad car next to an iron support.

"First we're in Neiman Marcus and Bloomie's, now Lower Wacker," Figueroa said.

"Yeah, these are the enchanting discontinuities endemic to the life of an urban police officer," Bennis said.

"Actually, I can't stand working this way," Figueroa said. "What I want is to spend all my time on one case, the murder, solve it, put it to bed, and start the next case."

"Then you're in the wrong line of work, aren't you?" Bennis muttered.

"There's a man over there. Unless it's a pile of rags."

They approached the sleeping man. He had found himself a large shipping carton and several pieces of fabric. He had filled the carton with a layer of foam packing "peanuts" and laid a blanket over them, creating for himself an insulated mattress that protected him from the dampness of the sub-sidewalk.

"You got the bag?" Figueroa said.

Bennis said, "Whattaya think this is?"

"I guess I only said that hoping it would wake him up." The man didn't stir. Figueroa, well aware that some cops rousted the homeless brutally, said, "Good afternoon, sir."

The man sat up sharply and looked scared. He was unshaven and very thin.

"I wonder if we could speak with you, sir," Bennis said.

"What do you want?"

"We'd like to show you a couple of pictures of some people you might know. We thought that while you looked at them you might enjoy a snack."

The man said nothing but studied both of them, staring them up and down from his sitting position. Finally, he said, "Cops?"

"Yes, sir."

"Don't like cops."

"Can't entirely blame you," Bennis said. "Coffee? Cream? Sugar?"

"We also have these Quarter Pounders with cheese," Figueroa said. "And pie."

Figueroa, who had missed lunch, had to admit that the cheeseburgers smelled irresistible, and fortunately they were to the man as well. "You can call me Nate," he said.

"I'm Norm."

"And I'm Suze."

Bennis showed him photos of the dead woman and two dead men found near the CPD. "I'm sorry the way these look, Nate," he said. "I'm sure you realize—"

"Look dead. I can recognize dead, mister. I'm not an idiot."

"Have you seen any one of them?"

"Don't think so." He took his time and studied the pictures seriously.

"Nope."

Bennis and Figueroa sipped their own coffee, while Nate sipped his. "Anybody else around here we could ask?" Bennis said.

"Hmm."

"We're harmless," Figueroa said, hoping that they were. "And there's more lunch in the car."

While Nate's home was close to the roadway, it was nevertheless out of sight of the traffic, behind a cement barrier-type divider, and the whole area was dim. Figueroa, whose eyes had become used to the dimness, looked up and down the hidden walkway and saw no more people, homeless or otherwise. Cars and trucks kept up a steady hum ten feet away.

"Suppose I got the food from the car," she said. "Would you take us to somebody else around here?"

"Ain't around here. Ain't nobody else much likes the front porch."

"Someplace else, then?"

"Could be."

Figueroa went and picked up two more large bags of burgers, apple pies, and hot coffee. She winced inwardly, realizing a cheeseburger or two was not anywhere close to what this man needed. He needed a home, running water, and regular meals. But she couldn't think what else to do right now, and she had her own goal to keep in mind. By the time she got back, Nate was standing up and Bennis and he were chatting, of all things, about the 1954 Buick Century.

But from there it was into the rabbit hole.

While on the main roadway most of the lightbulbs were working, and some were even enclosed in wire cages, Nate led them into a side tunnel that was oddly broad but with a very low ceiling, and absolutely without lights. There was a yellow glow at the end of it, though, where it vanished into a T-junction. They had their flashlights, of course, but the light, though dim, was adequate for moving along. Both Figueroa and Bennis, without consulting about it, believed that taking out their large Kelites would make them look like cops or, equally bad, sanitation inspectors.

Passages led right and left from the dead end of the first tunnel. The yellow light came from a dim but working bulb that Figueroa took to be just fifteen watts. Nate led them into the left-hand tunnel. This one, as well as its mate that went right, was tiled, oddly enough, in pure white glazed ceramic.

She whispered to Bennis, "You think this used to be a subway station?"

"You don't have to whisper," Nate said. "Yeah, this was gonna be a subway stop. Subway here never got built."

The floor was cement, and the farther in they went the cleaner it got.

"Nate, is this clean because people clean it, or because—"

"It's clean because it's so far from the cars and the riffraff."

"Oh."

"Although somebody drops stuff, we pick it up. Can't just let the place go to rack and ruin."

Figueroa raised her eyebrows at Bennis, who shrugged.

Nate's cronies were four men, no women. Two of the men were black, two were white, and all were grayish. They lived in an alcove far from the roadway. They had two working fifty-watt bulbs, the sudden glare making Figueroa blink. She estimated they were three hundred yards or more from the car, and they had made five turns getting here. She was afraid that if Nate didn't take them back they would never find their way. And she didn't think their radios would work down here.

One of the black guys muttered all the time. One of the white guys had heavy scar tissue like a mushroom where his left eye should be.

Nate passed around the burgers and pies himself. He allowed Bennis to pass the coffee. Then Nate told the group, "I don't say these cops are okay, you know. But they treated me polite, and I think we could look at their pictures. This here's Norm and that's Suze."

The four said nothing. Figueroa, after a few seconds of disappointment, realized that this meant a conditional yes. Nate took the photos and passed them around.

The four made a circle around the pictures, ducking their heads, not letting Bennis and Figueroa watch them react. There was some whispering. Then the muttering man said,

"Back of the yard

"Bool and a card

"Baby it's hard.

"Mami is low

"Mami does know,

"Abby the gal."

It wasn't rap and it wasn't word salad. Schizophrenic word salad, she thought, would have more internal rhymes, like abby-cabby-yellow-cabby-tabby. Figueroa decided it was just this man Mami's personal response to a difficult life. Bennis and Figueroa looked at Nate for help deciphering it. "Mami here says the woman's name is Abby."

Suze said, "Actually, we knew that. Was she a friend of his? Does—did she have friends? Somebody we could talk to?" It was the first rule: find friends and relatives of the victim.

Mami shook his head. Nate said, "No. No friends."

"Does she—did she hang around with anybody we could talk to? It's important."

Mami shook his head.

"Relatives?"

Nate conferred with the man and said, "Never mentioned any."

"Were there any people you saw around her? Asking about her? Or anybody following her?"

"Hey, you. You trying to pin her death on one of us? On a homeless guy?" He was angry.

"No, we're not."

"I mean, that's real easy. Always pin everything on the bums, you know."

Figueroa said, "Listen, you know as well as I do that not every homeless person is a saint. Be real, here. I wouldn't try to tell you that every cop in Chicago is a saint."

This elicited a huge gust of laughter, even from the silent ones. The little guy laughed so hard he lost his breath and had to sit down on the ground. Suze winced. Well, not every cop was a saint, okay?

"If there's somebody going around killing you," she said, "don't you want to know it? Don't you want him stopped, whoever it is? Suppose the killer is somebody dressed up to look like he's homeless? Help us out here."

"You got a point." Nate looked intently at the other four, especially Mami. They shook their heads. "But I don't guess they saw anybody like that."

"Did Abby usually hang around South State Street? Eleventh and State? Like under the El over there?"

More conferring. Finally Nate said, "Yeah. More fool her."

"Why's that?"

"We never go there. That place is dangerous."

Figueroa hesitated. "You mean—recently? You've stopped going there recently?"

"What's recently?"

"Well, the last month or so, I guess."

"Nah. More like the last year or so."

"God, those cheeseburgers smelled so great! I really should have saved one in the car," Figueroa said as they drove back toward the CPD parking lot.

"Well we didn't know we'd have to feed five people."

"And I guess it was sort of worth it."

"Time is it?"

"Five. We missed the wind-down at the Furlough."

"And we oughta take a look at the murder scene at night."

"I can't. I have to go home and make dinner."

"Suppose I drive you home and pick you up about seven?"

Figueroa called home on her cell phone, got J J, promised to provide dinner, then called ahead to the ultra-fast, ultra-thick toppings take-out pizza place the kids liked best and put in an order.

Holding three pizza boxes balanced in a leaning tower, Suze struggled out of Bennis's car.

"Sure you don't want to come in and eat some of these?"

"No, I want to catch up with a guy who can tell me how to find a pickpocket. I'll be back to get you around seven."

"Yeah, that and you don't like Robert much, either, right?"

"If you can read my mind, why do we talk?"

When she got inside, she found Maria had set the table. Kath pushed Sheryl's wheelchair to the open space on the side. There was no time for niceties. Suze dealt out the three pizzas right down the middle of the table and went to get lemonade and milk. She was so tired her body buzzed.

"I have to go back out for a while," she said as they sat.

Robert said, "Speaking of going out, I have to take my managers to dinner Friday night. The new manager for Ravenswood needs to meet the managers of the five existing stores."

"Sure. When do we expect you back?"

"Well, the stores don't close until nine. So, say we start eating at nine-thirty, finish by eleven-thirty. I should be home by midnight."

"No problem."

"What's this?" Robert asked, opening one of the boxes.

Suze said, "Pineapple and Canadian bacon." Before Robert could say he didn't like it, she added, "J J likes his pizza that way. He'll probably outgrow it. The pepperoni and green olives is there, in that one, and the other one is your favorite. Onions and ground beef."

"Mom, how come you have to go out?" J J said.

"Norm and I have some special cases because we're temporary detectives."

"Why are you temporary detectives?"

"Because a whole lot of the real detectives got sick."

"Why did they get sick?"

"They all went to a dinner and ate some food that was bad."

"Why did they eat it?"

"Because—"

"J J!" Robert shouted. "Stop it!"

"Well, all right," J J said, "but just tell me what the special cases are."

"There have been a couple of homeless people killed," Suze said cautiously. She didn't like bringing her work home, and she really didn't like talking about assignments involving death.

"Why are people homeless?" J J asked.

Robert said, "Because they don't want to work."

"Well, that's not really always true," Suze said. "Some of them can't work. Like, they've had an injury."

"Almost anybody can work if they have motivation."

"Or they've been let go because the factory downsized."

"In which case they should look for a job someplace else," Robert said. "After all, a hundred years ago lots of men worked as blacksmiths. Then people stopped using horses for transportation. The industrious men went into automobile repair. You can't wait for the world to find something for you to do."

"Some people have disabilities and they don't have health insurance. And a few years ago most of the mental hospitals closed, so mentally ill people are out on the streets."

"There's always a job somewhere, if you look," Robert said.

"If you lose a job, like the plant you worked in suddenly closes, you can discover you don't have enough money for rent. So you get behind and finally you are put out on the street."

"People shouldn't get bigger houses than they can afford. If you plan ahead and save your money, you won't get caught short. You'll have something to fall back on."

"If you're homeless, then it's harder to get a job because you can't get your clothes cleaned and pressed and you don't look carefully shaven."

"A lot of them are just drunks and druggies," Robert said.

"Well, those are addictions. Good people can have problems. Well-meaning people can have addiction problems. Or sometimes like I said, they have a mental problem but nowhere to go for help," Suze said.

Kath said, "Somebody should make good housing for them. I read that most shelters aren't safe."

"And here we are," Suze said, "in a nice house, with good food and a roof over our heads. We should be grateful. And sympathetic."

Robert said, "They're nuts or they're drunk or they're on drugs or they're lazy. Why make homes for people like that? Susanna, I don't think it's good to give children the idea they don't have to work. I work all day, and nobody ought to pay me if I didn't."

Suze said, "Oy," under her breath. Then she realized there hadn't been a sound from Sheryl since dinner started. She looked at her sister. Sheryl was trembling, her head bobbing on her thin neck and her right arm twitching, the left held like a claw up against her chest. Suze jumped up.

"Honey? What's wrong?"

Kath and Maria got up too.

Suze checked her eyes and her pulse. "I think she's just having an anxiety attack," Suze said. "Robert, can you help me get her to bed?"

"Sure."

"Kids, you eat," Suze said. "I want to get you started on the dishes before I have to leave."

But what Suze really believed was wrong with Sheryl was terror. She should never have allowed the argument—call it a discussion—about homelessness to go on so long. She would bet a lot that Sheryl was picturing what her life would be like now, if she were disabled, as she was, but had no family.

While Suze ate pizza, Norm Bennis was in Skokie, a large suburb immediately northwest of Chicago. He had a contact there, and had notified the man to meet him in one of the village parks.

"My gypsy friend," Bennis said when Harold Pigeon strolled past the swing set and over to the bleachers near the small baseball diamond and sat near Norm.

"Haven't I told you, you shouldn't say gypsy? It's considered pejorative."

"Yeah, you told me. I'm not a politician, Harold. I don't have to be p.c. I'm a cop. Everybody knows how insensitive we are."

"You know, what this world needs is a 'Proud To Be a Gypsy' T-shirt."

"Maybe you could make 'em and sell 'em. White on dark green is very nice. I also like blue on cream." Harold had been Bennis's source in a few busts of scams on the elderly. The relationship developed when Bennis had traced three women in their thirties who buddied up to men in their seventies and in one case eighty, took them traveling on the men's money, partied with them, and got them to sign over their bank accounts. Harold had been involved, having introduced the women to their victims. In fact he had been the connection that tied the cases together for Bennis. But he was harder to convict than the women, since he had not been directly involved in touching the money, and there was no paper trail involving him. Nothing had been signed over to him. He got kickbacks in cash from the women. Anyway, he was ultimately more useful to Bennis as an informant.

"Harold, I need somebody to tell me about picking pockets."

"What makes you think I'd know anybody like that?"

"Don't play with me. Elaine would probably love to get her sentence reduced, now that she's had time to think it over. Betty

I'm not so sure of, but Elaine is not a stand-up female. She'd rat."

"Well, there is one guy."

Suze and Norm got out of Norm's car in the CPD parking lot, under the peach-colored lighting. "This is the most horrible color anybody could have picked," Figueroa said. "Green would be better." In the light, Bennis's brown skin looked orange, which was not so bad, but she knew she looked sickly yellow. "Whoever invented this should be sentenced to four years in a detox ward."

"Don't be crabby."

They walked together from the parking lot to the El tracks. The El ran along Holden Court, behind the CPD building at the second-floor level, like railroad tracks in the air. Its great iron legs splayed out and down, elbows at train level, the feet set in concrete pillars on the street level. A giant anchored.

State Street, that great street, paralleled the El tracks, one block west, running in front of the CPD central offices building. Because it was also the headquarters of the First District and many courts, the area was busy by day—and never had anywhere near enough parking. The CPD lot was permitted to officers and CPD employees only, and the many other lots that had been randomly placed here and there along State Street north and south of the CPD had gradually been lost to gentrification. New apartment buildings were required to provide plans for under-building parking for tenants before they received construction permits but that didn't help visitors to the area. And most of the street remained patchily run-down.

It was not quite dark even now. Darkness came late to Chicago in June. It would be full night by ten, but at nine the sun had just set. Still the shadows of the buildings and the tracks gave the place an urban gloom.

"Bennis, did you know that during Prohibition you could

smell the illegal alky brewing on Maxwell Street all the way over here?"

"Never heard that."

"If you brewed for Johnny Torrio, you could make ten times what you earned digging ditches. He'd advance you some corn, some sugar and yeast, and one of the old people in the house who'd be home anyway would sit there and watch the corn likker brew. One house could make a couple of hundred gallons a week. Torrio's trucks would come around and collect the booze in tanks. Thousands and thousands and thousands of gallons. The whole district reeked of fermenting mash."

"And your point is you can't keep people away from booze?"

"No, my point is maybe that's a better use for old people than letting them wander around homeless."

"That's not a bad point."

Figueroa gazed up and down the El track and the darkening street. "You know what, Bennis? It seems smaller here at night. The El looks like a fence, an overhead fence. It clamps down on you, doesn't it?"

She glanced at him as if thinking he'd mock her, but he said, "Yeah. Like a tunnel."

"And State Street with those orange lights on all that asphalt is kind of toxic. It looks like the Deadly Dessert that kept people from getting out of Oz."

"What's the matter with you? People didn't want to get out of Oz."

"They did if their Auntie Em lived in Kansas. Anyway, suppose there was a deadly Oz you did want to get out of?"

"Now you're weirding out. Let's not get nuts. Let's look at it up close and personal."

Figueroa put her hands on her hips. "Okay. You're absolutely right. And let's be systematic while we're at it. The first known murder by our killer was Manualo. Ten days ago now.

Close to the El but not right under it. Let's go look."

Jimmy Manualo had been killed about a block north of the CPD building, past what was known as the Annex. The Annex was an undistinguished blocky structure contiguous to the CPD. It had been cobbled onto the bigger building about thirty years ago when the department found it needed more room. Unfortunately, the Annex had never been intended to be part of the CPD, and its floors were not on the same level. This meant that inside, when you walked from the CPD part on any given floor into the Annex, you walked down a sloping ramp of ugly vinyl tile.

The entrance to the First District Police Station was in the main CPD building, next to the Annex. The east side of the Annex and the east side of the CPD building faced the El. There were upper-floor windows on the Annex's east side, but they looked directly out at the El tracks, just like its sister building did, and there were no lower-floor windows.

Bennis and Figueroa stood in the deep purple gloom between two legs of the El and looked at the Annex with dismay.

Bennis said, "It's no better, is it?"

"Why didn't they just put some damn big windows on the first or second floor?"

"Because there's no view. Nobody wants to look at the El and hear all the noise, Suze."

They walked to the exact spot where Manualo had been found. It was a good block north of the Annex, and not near anything, really. A parking lot between the El and State Street was being torn up, probably for a high-rise. A crane was parked on the cracked asphalt. Nobody would have been sitting in the crane all night, watching for murderers.

And next to the track, even though they knew they were in the right spot from the plat drawing they'd brought along, there was no sign of anything unusual. It was as if Jimmy Manualo had never existed and his dead body had never lain in that alley.

Trash was everywhere. Apparently no one had ordered a complete collection of potential evidence on the ground after Manualo's death, so some of this must have been here when he died ten days before. Bennis and Figueroa kicked through it. There were gum wrappers, candy wrappers, McDonald's, Wendy's, and Burger King bags. There were long red wrappers from microwave burritos, a few dried french fries, and a dozen or so cold drink cups. There were several foam hot drink cups, a muddy squashed mitten, a few condoms, part of a car muffler, a few pennies, and an entire car door, painted light blue. There was a child-size T-shirt, and one smashed Reebok. And there were bottles and cans, mostly beer, and some bottles that had contained cheap wine. Most of the glass bottles were broken. Suze and Norm looked for discarded Handi Wipes or Wet Ones, but didn't see any. There was a lot of Kleenex and other tissues, ranging from fairly new to so deteriorated they were slurry, but you could tell they were paper, not pre-moistened towelettes, when you scuffed them.

Bennis said, "Civilization, huh?"

"Pretty smart to kill under an El track," Figueroa said. "Nobody can see you. And if you pick your moment right, when there's an El going over, people could be standing three feet away and not hear a thing. Even a scream or a struggle."

"Yeah, clever."

"Why do homeless people want to sleep here, of all places? It's noisy."

"They sleep all over town. They get moved out of the bus station and the El stops. And out of O'Hare. Plus none of those places have benches you can sleep on anymore. They've put in armrests every couple of feet so nobody can lie down on them."

"Maybe the homeless feel safer here, near the CPD," Figueroa said sadly.

They walked south.

The site of O'Dowd's death, or to be more accurate, Bennis

pointed out, the place where O'Dowd was found, was a side alley, but just off the El tracks and one block south of the CPD. There was as much trash here as directly under the El, and the area was just as secluded. It looked as if the techs had collected very little trash for examination, just like the Manualo murder.

By now the sky was dark. Only the sickly peach lights made it possible to see. The eye couldn't pick up any details. "I'm glad we came here, Bennis," Figueroa said.

"Yes. It's different at night."

"Seeing it the way they saw it, you begin to realize how long the killer could toy with them. They could have had a two-hour picnic sitting right here with a bottle of scotch or bourbon and watched the trains go by overhead."

"But you can see people driving by on State. Which means they might see you."

"Right. And cars going down the alley to park in the CPD lot. And some pedestrians on State Street."

"Would anybody notice? A couple of homeless people sitting around?"

"You never know." She thought a moment. "I doubt it. But if I were the killer, I'd still be cautious."

"Which tells me that the murders happened after the eleven-to-sevens reported for duty at eleven and the three-to-eleven guys had left."

"Which would be late enough so there wouldn't be any pedestrians at all."

Bennis said, "And which would be consistent with the ME's time of death estimate."

"One murder May twenty-first, then ten days of no attacks, then two in two days, May thirty-first and June first. Depending on how you count—whether they happened before or after midnight. I wonder what that sequence means."

"I hope it doesn't mean he's found out he really enjoys it," Bennis said.

Having got the feel of the area in its own dim light, they took out their multi-cell Kelites and did another search. Holding the flashlights low to the ground, they scanned the broken asphalt and gravel for anything new. The raking light gave them a better view of the contours of the ground and highlighted some small litter that they would not otherwise have seen. But there was nothing that looked like evidence.

They clicked the lights off and walked to the spot a block farther south where Abigail Ward's body had lain. This was still blocked off by yellow CRIME SCENE DO NOT CROSS barrier tape and the AUTHORIZED PERSONNEL ONLY signs.

Figueroa said, "I guess nobody took this down."

"Why should they? Nobody needs this place. You can get into the CPD lot by coming down the alley from the north, and you can get in from State Street."

"Yeah." Peach light discolored the parking lot and the side of the CPD building. It turned the red brick of the apartment building a dreary tomato soup color. But it didn't give much illumination, and in contrast to its odd hue, the shadows became greenish. Figueroa said, "Bennis, did you see that?"

"What?"

"Over there. Somebody's watching us."

Both froze, looking for a sign.

They stood unmoving for several minutes, Figueroa's knees beginning to ache.

There was a hint of movement near one of the legs of the El. Bennis sprinted to top speed from a standing start. Figueroa ran too, but at an angle to Bennis, a little farther under the El, hoping to head off whoever it was. She clicked her flashlight back on, and the light bounced ineffectively off the ground and buildings.

They pounded down the alley toward the rear of the CPD. "Stop! Hold it, sir! Police!"

The figure vanished.

"Stop! Stop!"

"Police!"

But they knew they were yelling only in the hope of getting the man to show himself. They had no idea where he had gone, and after three minutes of running had taken them past the torn-up parking lot with no sign of anybody, they gave up.

"Where'd he go?" Figueroa said, gasping.

"No doors back here. He coulda slipped under a fence. It's too dark to see between buildings."

"Did you see what he looked like?"

"Not much. Wearing a cap. Young, maybe from the way he ran."

"Jeez. I'm creeped out."

"Let's go get a beer."

"Yeah. I can make some phone calls from there."

Far in the distance they heard the El train coming.

The Furlough Bar was two blocks south of the CPD building and just the other side of State Street. They fled there, each more grateful for the other's company than they wanted to say.

Mary Lynne Lee was twenty-three. She had been a popular girl at New Trier High School, a beautiful girl, had lots of dates, and had played a very good game of soccer.

From her first years in school, everybody liked her. In grade school, teachers had called her "sweet," or "a very peaceful child," or "obedient."

Mary Lynne's grandfather on her father's side was Korean. A nuclear physicist, he had taught for many years in the Tech Institute at Northwestern University. His wife was French and had been an early founder of Montessori schools in the rich suburbs north of Chicago—Wilmette, Winnetka, and Glencoe. She had published numerous articles on early childhood education. Mary Lynne's maternal grandparents were both professionals also, her grandmother an architect and her grandfather an architectural engineer. Mary Lynne's mother was an obstetrician practicing at Evanston Hospital, and her father was an electrical engineer who had got in on the ground floor of computer hardware manufacturing and made lots of money, selling parts to Motorola in Schaumburg, among others. This was not a particularly unusual family history for the north shore area.

Mary Lynne's brother was in school at MIT. Her younger sister, Pamela, had won every academic prize in mathematics the New Trier school system had to offer.

Mary Lynne was beautiful and sweet, but not very bright. Always a C student at best, she tried and tried and tried and did her homework, and listened to the teachers, and tried and failed. After she failed ninth-grade algebra, she was put in remedial math for two years. The school advised her not even to attempt the sciences.

New Trier divided students according to levels, which was a politically correct way of saying they had a tracking system. Level four was the hardest class in its category. A level four English class was for the brightest English students, and within that level they were graded A, B, C, or F. A level three course was average, but not bad. Level two was for those who weren't doing very well. Same for math. Same for history. And so on.

Mary Lynne was of low-average intelligence. She did not qualify for special help. She was not placed in level one. All of her classes were level twos, but even there, competing only against the poorer students, she got Cs.

Which might have been all right, if she had not been Mary Lynne Lee. Her teachers liked her. She did her work; and after all, not everybody in the world had to be academically inclined. If they weren't Mary Lynne Lee.

Mary Lynne spent her life in a family entirely made up of high achievers, and she knew she didn't measure up. Every day, every night at dinner, the family talk was about her brother's scholarships or another article her mother was writing on obstetrics. Her grandfather, now in his late seventies, won several major physics awards, for one of which he had to fly to Paris and for another to the Hague. He took Pamela, Mary Lynne's younger sister, with him, since, as her parents told Mary Lynne, "Pamela can appreciate the award." Pamela had been in level five math, which was only for those especially talented.

Meanwhile, Mary Lynne was playing pretty good soccer.

When she graduated from high school, Mary Lynne took a summer job in a Montessori preschool. In the fall, at the advice of her grandmother who knew schools in the area well, she started at a local small private college that gave lots of personal attention. Mary Lynne wanted to study early childhood education, maybe out of a desire to please her grandmother. But the school discouraged that and suggested phys. ed.

But even that was academically too hard for her.

Frustrated by classwork, Mary Lynne started drifting into Chicago for the weekends, hanging out at singles bars, trying to blot out the humiliations of the school week. The weekends began to stretch into noon on Monday and start earlier, right after class Friday, then Thursday night. For a while she told herself that everybody cut Friday classes in college, but it wasn't true.

She drank more, went to the dorm less, and spent nights downtown with a variety of men she met in bars.

She thought she'd take a little room downtown in a cheap SRO hotel, hoping her family might not realize she wasn't in the dorm most nights. But she needed a source of income other than her parents' allowance to make it work.

Mary Lynne became a weekend prostitute.

For months she continued to turn up at classes on Tuesday and Wednesday. But just before Christmas she was called in to the office of her adviser.

Her choice was to get to every class for the rest of the term or withdraw.

Mary Lynne promised to attend class. But the thought was so depressing that she decided she would go party that night and start being really good the next morning.

She never went back to school.

After Mary Lynne Lee started staying in downtown Chicago on a permanent basis, her parents sent a detective to find her. Four times in the first year, she was discovered and brought back to their house in Winnetka. Four times she slipped away again.

Mary Lynne was not particularly expert at covering her tracks. She had never been sly or dishonest, only sad. But the fourth time her parents brought her home, she overheard them talking with the family internist about "protective residential housing." While not certain what that meant, there had been enough hints that her parents thought they couldn't control her, and the school couldn't control her, and therefore they needed a specialist to control her.

They loved her; she knew that. But her whole family, she believed, was not right for her.

The fifth time she disappeared, she didn't go back to her small hotel room. She stayed with a man she hardly knew, because she reasoned that if she hardly knew him, her parents and their detective would have no idea of his existence at all. Nobody could find her and make her feel bad.

That nobody could find her, she was absolutely right. As to whether anybody else could make her feel bad she was dead wrong. The man she stayed with hit her when he was drinking and ignored her when he wasn't. She decided to leave him and sleep on the streets, at least until the weather got cold.

Mary Lynne tried cocaine for a little while, but she didn't like it much. Later on she tried crack at the urging of another prostitute. But she didn't like it, either. Neither one appealed to her as much as alcohol.

When she was tricking for money, Mary Lynne wore a

short, short skirt with cutouts on the side in the shapes of hearts. When she wasn't tricking, she wore sweatshirts and Levi's. But she soon found that if she put her hair up under a baseball cap when she went out in the sweatshirt and Levi's, the world was a nicer place. People thought she was a boy and they didn't hassle her or call her ugly names.

She was minding her own business just wandering Wednesday night near the CPD building on State Street when the two cops almost walked up on her. Automatically, she ran away. What were they doing out there anyway, poking around under the El with nothing criminal going on? She finally lost them simply by burrowing under some trash bags. After they were gone, feeling slimy and gritty from the trash, she got up and wandered north on State Street, back toward the Loop. Maybe later she could come back and sleep here someplace. It seemed kind of safe to be near the police department.

The address on Abigail Ward's long-expired driver's license was in District Thirteen. During the day, one of the officers from Thirteen went to the address, which turned out to be a bed and breakfast. Nobody there had heard of Abigail Ward, but they had records going back years.

"Just ledgers, really," said a motherly woman of about sixty, "but you're welcome to look at them."

The cop did, and found Abigail Ward's check-in information. She claimed to have arrived from Albany, New York. And she had given her address there.

"So I called the Albany, New York, PD," Figueroa said to Bennis as they sat in the Furlough.

"And?"

"They put me on to the local precinct, and maybe it wasn't a busy day, but one of the cops actually went over to the address where the Wards had lived, which wasn't far from the station. That part's the good news."

"The bad news is there's nobody there named Ward anymore."

"Right. However, the next-door neighbor gave the cop the phone number of a Daniel Frank Ward who still lives in the Albany area."

"He say how old?"

"Thirty-eight."

"That's about right. So call."

Suze called.

"Yes, this is Dan Ward."

"Mr. Ward, I'm Susanna Figueroa, from the Chicago Police Department. I need to be sure I'm talking to the right person. Is your mother's name Abigail?"

"What's happened?"

"You're the correct Daniel Ward?"

"If she—yes."

"I'm very sorry to have to tell you, we have an Abigail Ward who is deceased."

"Well, thank you for calling. Good-bye."

"Don't hang up, please. I need to know when you last saw your mother."

"Why?"

"We're trying to trace her movements. Your mother was killed yesterday."

"By a car?"

"We think she was murdered."

"Thank you for calling. Good-bye."

"Please! Do you want to come to Chicago and claim the body?"

"I don't want my mother and I don't want her body. She wasn't there for me. Why should I care? She—we asked her, we all begged her to stop drinking, and she didn't give a rip, Miss Figgero. I haven't seen her in a decade. Don't even try to lay a guilt trip on me. She was an adult when I was an infant. It was not my doing. I don't have a mother now and I never had one when I needed one, either. Don't bother me anymore."

Sinking onto a bar stool, Figueroa blew air up at her eyebrows. "Jeez. Don't ask. Forget Abby Ward's family."

Bennis said, "Okay."

"We've got three murders. They should tell us something. What do we actually *know*?"

"The victim. Did you get background on Manualo?"

"Finally. The investigation those detectives did is only—at best—well, Mossbacher aside, I'd have to call it perfunctory."

"Go ahead. Call it perfunctory."

"You're a saint. Manualo was a jockey, of all things. Raced at Arlington, Maywood, lots of other places. In the seventies and early eighties he won a hell of a lot. He was major. He was actually famous."

"Got it."

"Then—well, this is kind of sad. A lot sad, actually. Then at the age of forty or so, he started to gain weight. He was a little guy, naturally. Five feet one, ninety pounds tops."

"Kind of like you."

"Smaller than me if you can believe such a thing. He started to gain weight. Went to his doctor, apparently. No hormonal problem, no diabetes, no congestive heart failure, no nothing. He was eating the same as ever. His metabolism had changed as he got older."

"I keep telling my mother that. Don't send care packages of food anymore."

"Naturally, as he got heavier, he slipped down the rank of jockeys. Eventually he became unemployable. Lots of people said he should just eat less. He told one jockey friend he'd spent his whole life calling a lettuce leaf and one boiled clam lunch, and he just couldn't go lower than that."

"So he's unemployed."

"And starts to drink. He'd always allowed himself one ounce of red wine to unwind at the end of the day. *One ounce!* That's one third of a normal glass."

"And it got away from him."

"Yup. And he wound up on State Street in May. High blood alcohol level. Smothered with a coat and a sort of pillowlike thing he was carrying. And his face was washed. He had no close relatives in Chicago. Honestly, I don't see following up his possible enemies or heirs. He was in the wrong place at the wrong time."

"So," Bennis said, "what do we got? Well, victims: we got a white guy, a Hispanic guy, and a white woman. So race and gender is no object to our perp."

"Fine, but what do they have in common?" She picked up her beer. "Just one of these. I'm driving."

"I can drive you home."

"Aw, Bennis, you already drove me once today. Thanks, but I can do it."

"You've had a hard day. You deserve two beers if you want them."

"Bennis, you *sweetheart*!" She threw an arm around his shoulder and kissed his cheek.

"Figueroa! Are you insane?" He jumped back and looked around the bar, which was fortunately deserted. "They'll think we're having a cliché squad car romance."

"Okay, okay. Calm down. So—what we know is this. First, all three murders probably took place after midnight."

"All three were homeless people."

"*Visibly* homeless. Unkempt. Unhealthy-looking."

"All three were alcoholic. And all three didn't do dope."

"True. But in the over-forty age group that isn't so unusual. Maybe the asshole is intentionally killing older people. The dusters and crankers and your random dopers tend to be the younger gang."

"And of course all three had their faces washed."

"Exactly."

"Okay. And all three were within two—mmm, call it three blocks of the Chicago Police Department."

Bennis put down his beer and frowned. "There's something about that fact I don't particularly like."

CHAPTER SIXTEEN

FIGUEROA DROVE HOME after just one beer, as she was determined to do. It was past midnight when she got to her part of town. The nearest parking place was four blocks away.

Oh, gee. Extremely bad luck. No, come on! That's absurd. In fact, she thought, it was stupid. The reason there were fewer parking places was the late hour. She usually got home around four-thirty or five, and most nine-to-five workers got home later. No wonder she often had the pick of parking places.

She let herself in the back door with her key, quietly, so as not to wake anybody.

The first thing she always did after locking her gun was to look in on Sheryl. After her sister's distress earlier tonight, Suze was worried about her. Tomorrow she ought to call the doctor and engage in some serious in-depth questioning about how Sheryl was really doing. If she could report that the doctor saw progress, it would be a good idea to make that extremely clear to Sheryl.

And if the doc *didn't* see progress? What then?

Cross that bridge later.

Early in Sheryl's rehabilitation, Suze visited the surgeon who had reset the fragments of her fractured skull. "I seem to be more frustrated every day that she can't talk," Suze said. "And if *I'm* frustrated, think how frustrated she is."

"Be glad she's come this far," the doctor said.

"But she's so—it's like she's locked up in there."

"No she isn't. There actually is a condition called 'locked-in syndrome.' "

"I already don't like the sound of that."

"In that condition, the patient is actually fully awake and thinking, but the body is completely paralyzed. Some of them can communicate by blinking. Some can't. Some can't do anything whatsoever to communicate with the world outside their bodies. As a doctor, you see these patients and you feel absolutely useless."

"That's like—like 'The Premature Burial,' isn't it?"

"Just about. So when you see Sheryl struggling to get words out, and she will have to struggle for months, you know, you need to be aware of how much worse it could be. Even when she gets most of the way well, there'll be setbacks. It's not just Sheryl who will be frustrated. You and her husband and children are all going to be resentful and angry over and over again."

"It makes me so angry for her."

Dr. Sager nodded, not unhappy to hear this. He was a great advocate of involving the family, and a family member empathizing with the patient was no bad thing in his view.

"You're probably more aware of it than she is right now. She's disoriented, and dealing with muscle injuries, and fractured ribs and arm bones that hurt. Her aphasia is only one small thing to her in a sea of things right now."

"Well, even so—"

"Even so, she soon will be aware of it. Let me show you what the problem is."

Sager pulled over a model of the human brain that he kept on his desk. It opened on a hinge, showing the inside.

"Your sister has had several areas of her brain damaged. The paralysis on her left side was caused by an injury to the right side of the brain. Aphasia—the inability to speak—is caused by injury to the cortex of the left hemisphere in the posterior frontal and anterior temporal lobes. Right about here." He pointed to an area that would be roughly in front of Sheryl's ear.

"What she has is called nonfluent aphasia. Sometimes it's called Broca's aphasia because the site of injury is called Broca's area. It's in the frontal lobe close to the area of the motor cortex, and controls the movement of the lips, jaw, tongue, soft palate, and vocal cords. This is very much like the way other motor areas control arms and legs. Damage to Broca's area causes a difficulty in expressing thoughts verbally and in writing. The ability to understand remains intact."

"In other words, she can think of what she wants to say, but she can't produce the sounds."

"Exactly. Broca's contains the memory for motor patterns of speech. There are other kinds of aphasia, fluent aphasia for instance, where the patient can talk up a storm but none of it makes any sense."

"I was hoping she might be able to use her computer instead. You know she worked as a computer engineer before the accident happened."

"Yes, I knew that."

"I thought she could use a word processor to tell us what she was thinking."

"I don't think that's going to happen. I'm sorry. But patients with Broca's can't write, and mostly they can't type, either."

"What *is* going to happen?"

"She'll improve. It'll be slow but it'll come."

"By 'improve' do you mean just a little bit, or will she be entirely well again?"

"I can't tell you that. All I can say is that the biggest improvement will happen in the first three to six months."

Sheryl was asleep. The faint green light of the night-light showed the peaceful rise and fall of her chest.

Breathing a sigh herself in sheer relief, Suze hurried to the back stairs. She had to be up by six, and the sooner she got to bed the sooner she'd get to sleep. And she was just utterly, totally exhausted.

Stepping onto the first stair, she halted. The oddest feeling crept over her.

Now and then, with another cop, she would do an Officer Friendly talk at a grade school or high school. Their goal, besides trying to make children more comfortable with the police, was to steer children away from potentially dangerous situations. One of the difficulties was that bad people often looked perfectly nice, and you had to explain to the child that he or she should listen to his instincts, even if nothing really looked wrong.

Suze felt as if there was something wrong.

Well, take your own prescription, she thought. She removed her foot from the step and walked back down the hall. Sheryl was still asleep and *definitely* breathing. Suze listened carefully through six full breaths to be sure that she was not only breathing but breathing normally. Feeling like a fool, she also crouched down and looked under Sheryl's hospital bed, but there were no monsters there.

Having decided to do a patrol, Suze checked the first-floor bathroom without turning on the light, so as not to wake Sheryl. Her sister found it hard enough to sleep; waking her for no reason would be cruel. Suze could see quite well in the dim night-light by now. There wasn't any monster behind the shower curtain.

She paced into the living room, across to the sun parlor, then turned back and walked slowly through the dining room, finding nobody lurking anyplace, and finally back into the kitchen. Except that the kids had left a few dishes out of the dishwasher, there was nothing wrong.

She leaned to look down the cellar stairs and flicked on the light, knowing it was far away enough not to disturb Sheryl. She walked down to the landing, and from there she could see most of the basement.

She hesitated a few seconds, then decided she was being stupid. She walked down the cellar stairs. The lightbulb Robert had installed was so dim the light looked brown. Suze walked over to the clothes washer and pulled the cord of the bulb overhead.

Bright blue-white light flooded the cement room. Suze stepped slowly past the washer and dryer. Beyond them was a cement room scarred by old dark streaks. She thought it once had been a coal storage space. It was damp and low-ceilinged.

Retreating, she backed up to the stairs. No monsters in the basement either, except for feelings of threat.

By now she was starting to feel distinctly foolish. The house was full of people. Of course there weren't any monsters. This was all happening just because she was overtired. Too long a day and too much stress. She turned and went up the back stairs, pausing for a full minute on the second-floor landing to listen. Robert slept with his door open so as to hear Sheryl's bell or the fire alarm, although both were loud enough to hear through closed doors. Kath and Maria slept with their doors shut. Everything was just as usual.

As she turned to go on upstairs, Suze noticed a patch of lighter color in the corner where the second-floor hall met the main stairs. Trying not to make noise, she crept over and looked down. It was a pink cloth. When she picked it up, she realized it was a pair of Maria's underpants. Maria was going through a stage of wanting "older" underwear, not little-girl cotton anymore. Suze had insisted that whatever she bought had to be either machine washable or Maria had to hand-wash them herself. This was the result—silky pink undies made of nylon that could be machine washed and even machine dried.

It was strange that Maria dropped them here on the landing

of the main stairs. If she'd been carrying laundry up from the basement, she'd drop something near the back stairs, wouldn't she? But really, that was being too analytical. Maybe she'd stopped here to talk with Kath or somebody and not noticed she dropped them.

Suze hung the underwear on Maria's doorknob, where she'd probably be horrified to find them in the morning, and went on upstairs.

On the third floor, she stepped into J J's room. He was making little-boy snuffling sleeping noises. Just as usual.

Good.

She studied the stairs to the attic. Really, she should go on up if she were going to do a thorough job. But there was nothing of value in the attic and no reason anybody would go there. It would just be hot and empty. And besides she was just so tired.

And feeling even more foolish.

In her own room, Suze stripped off clothes that she had worn now for twenty hours. She thought she could take a shower without waking J J. J J was not like Sheryl. He could sleep through everything except the smell of bacon.

But under the shower, water sluicing down her naked body, she still didn't feel comfortable. She was in her own bathroom, in her own home. Why did she feel so exposed? The water was warm. Why did she feel chilly?

THURSDAY

CHAPTER SEVENTEEN

Thursday, 7:00 A.M.

From Your Morning, *the drive-to-work chat show on AM 98:*

This is Steve Mumford sending you a happy good morning. The weather over the Chicagoland area is mild and lovely, with a projected high in the mid-seventies. Traffic with Brand Goddart in four minutes.

At ten past the hour I will be interviewing Sandra Cascolinelli, the new appointee to the post of press rep for the Chicago Police Department. We'll talk about the CAPS program and the recent shooting inside a Seventh District lockup.

The City Council has decided to table any discussion of safe shelters for the homeless until early fall. The underlying thinking seems to be that it's warm out. Well, that's true. It's warm right now. I find it's often warm at the beginning of the summer, don't you?

But do you parents out there remember the story of the monkey's house that we all read our children? The monkey troop was caught in a terrible hurricane. It blew away the bananas they'd collected and drenched the monkeys and kept them wet and miserable for three days. "This is horrible. We've got to put up a shelter," the lead monkey said. "We need a roof and walls. We need a house. We'll build one tomorrow."

Tomorrow came. The storm blew itself out. The sun rose and the land dried off. All was wonderful. One little monkey said, "Shall we build our house now?"

But the boss monkey said, "We don't need one. Look. The sun is shining and the land is warm and dry." So they played and foraged for food and had a wonderful time.

But after a while another hurricane came. And it blew away their food and left them cold and wet and miserable. "We have to build a house," they all said. "We'll start tomorrow."

And then the storm went away and the sun came out. And what do you suppose the boss monkey said?

You guessed it.

In Chicago we know that winter comes every year. We're smart enough to have picked up on that. I've certainly noticed it, haven't you?

We need reliable, clean, permanent shelters for the homeless. Not scraped-together, temporary, unsafe, overnight cots in vermin-filled rooms. And we need to build them while the sun shines.

It was morning in the Figueroa-Birch household and everybody was running late. Suze hadn't had enough sleep and was fighting the mental fuzzies. She'd dropped the frying pan, trying to make scrambled eggs. The frustration of having to clean up slippery raw eggs from the floor and then serve bowls of cold cereal, which she didn't particularly like, almost made her cry. When she looked at the paper towels, printed with a repeating pattern that said, "Home is where the heart is," she was extremely annoyed. Then, when J J and Kath, who loved scrambled eggs and also didn't especially like cereal, were kind and helpful and said, "Never mind, it's okay," she actually did shed a tear. She skillfully concealed it by pouring herself another cup of coffee.

Maria, of course, didn't eat eggs. Or sausage or bacon or sweet rolls. A glass of orange juice and half a bowl of instant oatmeal was all she wanted. She was dieting.

Just as Suze started out the door with J J, Kath, and Maria, she realized she'd left her handcuffs upstairs. "Hold it!" she said. "I'll be right back."

She ran fast up the rear stairs. Most of the time Figueroa used the rear stairs, and she was sorry to admit to herself, one of the reasons was so that she could avoid Robert.

Robert is a good person, really, she constantly told herself. *He goes out every day and works hard to make money for his family. He brings home his earnings and he supplies food, clothing, and shelter.*

Robert's string of five or so dry-cleaning stores made steady money, but it was no way to get rich. There were staff problems, building problems, zoning problems, pilferage problems, and so on. The opening of the sixth store in Ravenswood was taking a lot of his time. And his patience.

Robert's problem was that he was crabby, nit-picking, complaining, impatient, and sarcastic. So Suze avoided him when she could. Especially first thing in the morning.

She ran up the back stairs, trying not to clump too hard in her heavyish work shoes.

She stepped lightest at the second floor, so as not to get

Robert fussed. As she passed the second-floor landing, she smelled male sweat. You couldn't miss it.

How odd. Robert never used the back stairs. And where would he have been going, anyway? He hadn't come down to the kitchen. In fact, ordinarily it would be half an hour before he even got up. Would he have gone up to the third floor? Only J J and Suze lived up there, and he certainly hadn't sought them out this morning to ask them anything.

When she got there, he wasn't on the third floor. Suze found her handcuffs on her nightstand, and there was for sure no Robert around.

Well, what difference did it make if he was roaming around? It was his house. And anyhow, these old houses were weird. There were creaks and groans you could swear were human, but it was just the house breathing. On the third floor, once in a great while, you could actually hear the furnace turn on in the basement. Most of the time you wouldn't. The sound of the water heater turning on might carry up through the pipes. Or not. Sometimes you could smell what was cooking in the kitchen. Other times you could fry enough onions for the whole First District and not get a whiff of it up here.

Must be a combination of wind direction outdoors, and who had which doors and windows open, she thought. And whether the heating system was on or off.

Anyway, as she came back down the stairs there was no sweat smell remaining in the air.

Sergeant Touhy said, "Bennis and Figueroa. Get to Mossbacher at the area ASAP. No, not ASAP, forthwith!"

"Yes, boss," Bennis said.

Mossbacher was angry.

"You can't just run up hours of tech time."

"Look, Sarge, if there's gonna be evidence anyplace it'll be in transfer evidence on the ground."

"There's a limit, kids. I'll allow somebody to fingerprint the crap directly under the body, and even within one foot of it. Also bottles and cans nearby. But let's not get crazy here. And I'm not talking just about the ton of shit from the ground around the body that you wanted examined. I'm also talking about Dr. Percolin ordering some complicated testing of the stomach contents and some weird analysis of face swabbings."

"How'd you know about this so fast?" Bennis asked.

"Are you kidding?" He gestured at his keyboard and monitor. "You think I can let you two inexperienced hotshots blunder around without any supervision? We got a crisis, but thank God for Bill Gates, I can cyber-supervise."

"Boss, we need this info. We may have a serial killer on our hands."

"Serial killer! Don't say that." Mossbacher looked annoyed and a little worried. "On the basis of three dead bums? You're out of your gourd, Bennis. Drop it."

"There's all these similarities—"

"They washed their faces? Spare me. You're suffering from beginner's enthusiasm. The wonders of techno-sleuthing. You've been reading too much crime fiction."

"But, seriously, sir, if we knew what booze they'd been drinking, we might be able to figure out where these people had been just before—"

"The idea that tracing a brand of booze or a face wash, even if there is one, is just too remote. People can pick up good bourbon or bad bourbon anyplace. Listen, Bennis. Let's say you wanted to do a tox screen. Routine. Let's say the standard tox panel costs a thousand dollars."

"That much?"

"Probably more. This is a for-instance. But say it doesn't turn up anything. So you've got a hunch. *Got* to be something there, right? You want to do fifty more rare poisons. Mercury, chokecherry, radium, theophylline, peyote, whatever. Maybe that's ten thousand dollars. With me so far?"

"Yeah, sure, boss. But—"

"Still no result, so you think of another fifty poisons even rarer. Maybe a hundred thousand dollars. There are three to four thousand tests for things people have around the house every day. There are respiratory drug panels and cardiac drug panels. Where do you stop? What about the trace evidence? You could pick up every morsel of dust and crud and flecks of human skin and bits of human hair and wings of flies in the alley and study them, do DNA on the hair and skin fragments, but do you have any idea how much lab time the city'd be paying for? WE DO NOT DO THIS IN CHICAGO! Can't. The city budget is not infinite. You want your potholes patched? You want fire engines?"

Bennis said, "We're not stupid, boss. We know there's a limit. We'd draw the line someplace."

"You're not hearing me, Bennis. You've already drawn the line *too far out*!"

Figueroa said, "If the dead guy was the mayor, you'd order every scrap of evidence eyeballed. Minutely."

Mossbacher surged to his feet. His face was red and congested and his eyes were half buried between lowering brows and bunched cheek muscles.

"Figueroa, if the dead guy was the mayor, *you would not be on the case! Now get out!*"

They hurried out of the door, but not fast enough. Suddenly Mossbacher appeared behind them. "And *don't* talk to the goddamned press!"

His door slammed hard.

"Say, I could be wrong, Bennis, but I kind of get the idea we're on our own."

"Yes, Suze, my man. We're on our own, and I'm not even sure they want us to get anyplace."

"These homeless people are throwaways."

"Murder victims, but negligible human beings."

"Makes my blood boil."

"You bet, Tiger. We'll forge on."

"Three musketeers, Bennis?"

"Two anyhow. One for both and both for one."

"My buddy."

"My pal."

CHAPTER EIGHTEEN

"LET ME GET this straight. You want me to tell you if you have a serial killer?"

"Right," Bennis said. He put the three file folders down on Jody Huffington's desk. It was nine-thirty Thursday morning and coffee was brewing in a pot on the file cabinet. Jody was a middle-aged man starting to show flecks of white at his temples.

"These days everybody thinks they've got a serial killer."

"I suppose. But we just might."

"Actually, to be honest, they're not as rare as you might think. Right now we have three serial killers of prostitutes operating just in the Englewood area."

"So why do people keep telling us not to jump to conclusions?"

"Because you shouldn't jump to conclusions. These days everybody thinks they know all about serial killers," Jody said. "They throw around 'profiling' and 'organized serial killer' and 'disorganized serial killer.' It's the result of an overdose of TV. In the real world, it's not as easy as that."

"Well, we've got three cases with a lot of similarities."

Bennis and Figueroa sat in Huffington's office in the basement of the CPD Annex building. Metal shelving sagged under books and slabs of paper. Figueroa had never seen so many books in any cop's office.

"You need to understand what I do here," Huffington said. "And what I don't do. The FBI runs training courses for officers from police departments around the country training in profiling. This is a help. We can pick up on cases early. There are three of us in the CPD who took the course. But if it really looks to me like there's a serial killer here, I send all the specs to Quantico to get the series analyzed."

"Fine. Whatever you say."

"When the Behavioral Science Unit of the FBI developed the notion of profiling," Huffington went on, "it was considered pretty abstruse stuff. Almost like magic. And there was a lot of doubt about whether it would work."

Bennis said, "I know. I remember hearing cops talk about it. Black magic nonsense."

"Frankly," Huffington said, "they thought it was stupid. But then the predictions started coming out pretty good."

"I saw one of the first questionnaires they ever developed."

"They developed them and then refined them over several years. With questions like the place where the bodies were found—in a house, in a public building, in a store, in a school, outdoors in woods, outdoors on a street, all that kind of thing. You filled it out and sent it along with the crime scene photos and any tech results in to the FBI and they'd score it and send you back what to look for."

"So help us out here. What do we look for?"

"We're not at that stage yet. Leave me the files. Go get coffee or something and come back in half an hour. I'll skim them and see what I can tell you. Then if you want me to do a more thorough analysis, I'll copy them and keep them a day or two."

"I have to say I'm not sure. You've got three different murder methods—"

"But they all stop the breath. Strangulation, smothering, that fire extinguisher stuff."

"And the victims differ about as much as they possibly could. Except for the alcoholic homeless aspect."

"We're aware of that. But the locations are close together and the time of the murder is about the same in every case."

"You don't know the time of death in the first one. He was half-hidden and the ME wouldn't pin it down because several hours had passed."

"Well, it had to have been night at least. Killing somebody there in daylight is too risky."

"Look. I'll give it the benefit of the doubt. Say it is the same killer for all of them. I'm gonna show you something. Two kinds of serial killers, from the 1985 FBI Law Enforcement Bulletin."

"Organized and disorganized?"

"Right. Look." He shoved two sheets of paper at Bennis and Figueroa. The letters were slightly fuzzy, as if they were photocopies made from photocopies of photocopies.

Crime Scene Differences

Organized

Planned offense
Victim a targeted stranger
Personalizes victim
Controlled conversation
Crime scene reflects overall control
Demands submissive victim
Restraints used
Aggressive acts prior to death
Body hidden
Weapon and evidence absent
Transports victim or body

Disorganized

Spontaneous offense
Victim known
Depersonalizes victim
Minimal conversation
Crime scene sloppy
Sudden violence to victim
Minimal use of restraints
Sexual acts after death
Body left in view
Evidence or weapon often present
Body left at death scene

"So see how well you think each fits your crime scenes. Now, let's say for purposes of discussion that the same person actually did commit all three of your killings. The bodies were left in view at the probable death scene. That's disorganized. But the main features—planning, targeting a certain kind of victim, plus weapon and evidence missing. That's organized. Anyway, here are the two profile possibilities."

Profile Characteristics

Organized

Average to above-average intelligence
Socially competent
Skilled work preferred
Sexually competent
High birth order status
Father's work stable
Inconsistent childhood discipline
Controlled mood during crime
Use of alcohol with crime

Precipitating situational stress
Living with partner
Mobility, car in good condition
Follows crime in news media
May change jobs or leave town

Disorganized

Below average intelligence
Socially inadequate
Unskilled work
Sexually incompetent
Low birth order status
Father's work unstable
Harsh discipline as child
Anxious mood during crime
Minimal use of alcohol
Minimal situational stress
Living alone
Lives or works near the crime scene
Minimal interest in news media
Significant behavior changes

"As between the two, to my eye he's organized."

"But, excuse me, Lieutenant Huffington," Figueroa said. "This doesn't point us anyplace. We can't very well go around looking for smart guys with clean cars who read the papers and watch the news. Not in Chicago. Hundreds of thousands of people fit that description. This doesn't give us anyplace to *start*."

"Usually it doesn't at first. What it gives you is a way of narrowing things down when you get suspects."

"We don't have even one so far."

Bennis said, "Huffington, paint me a word picture of these guys."

"All right. A disorganized offender is a loser, living with his mother, maybe, or by himself in a place that's basically a dump. A real mess inside. Most likely it isn't far from the crime scene. The guy is dumb and socially inept. He's probably between eighteen and thirty-five. He doesn't own a car, or if he does, it's crappy and dirty. He's impulsive and kills in a blitz attack. No subtlety. His victims are often people he's seen around his neighborhood. He often mutilates his victims. He's the easier one to catch, of course."

"And an organized offender?"

"All this is hypothetical, you know. But on the average, he's different. Methodical. Smart. Very verbal. Plans carefully. He owns a car or a van and it's in very good repair. He murders fairly far away from home. And probably not near his work. His victims are strangers. But they're a 'type' that he wants to kill. In your case homeless people. He finds some way to control them before killing them. In your case, he's controlling them by getting them drunk, which given their addiction, works remarkably well. He doesn't leave evidence most of the time, and he loves to make fools of the police."

"Man, oh, man, our guy has certainly done that."

"Another thing you need to remember, besides that there's no pure case of organized or disorganized, is that they can change. The disorganized offender doesn't become organized. He doesn't have the self-control. Or the smarts, either. But the organized offender can morph into a disorganized killer as he spins out of control. Or like Ted Bundy, who was very organized, deteriorated into a spree killer near the end. A spree killer kills again and again in fast succession without a cooling-off period."

"If we have one of those, we're in real trouble."

"What I'll do, I'll send this stuff to the FBI and see what

VI-CAP says. See if they think this is a legit serial killer. I'm also gonna advise you to go to a friend of mine. Dr. Ho. He can paint you a better picture of this guy." He paused.

"Assuming there is a guy."

CHAPTER NINETEEN

"You the characters that wanna learn about magic?"

"What?" Bennis said.

"Are you the law enforcement *individuals* who would like *instruction* in the *art* of *prestidigitation*?" The man giggled at his own wit and bopped from foot to foot, dancing up and down the cement esplanade near the lake.

"No, what we're looking for—" Bennis began, but Figueroa kicked him sharply in the shin.

"Yup. That's us," she said.

Eddie Charles was jumpy. He looked like a puppet on strings, thin to the point of scrawniness, long-limbed, with big knees, big elbows, big joints in his fingers. Thin as a one-sided board, Figueroa thought. For a few seconds she wondered if he was nervous about meeting with them, but she soon decided he was just naturally hyper.

It was just past ten-thirty A.M., and both they and Eddie had been on time at the meeting Bennis had set up the night before.

They had met on the lakefront, just north of Navy Pier. And Eddie was walking back and forth while talking. Out in the lake, the Victor Schleger fireboat was doing some sort of practicing, squirting water high up into the air in an arc that caught the sunlight. Rainbows flickered in its mist.

"I ain't a pickpocket, y'know. I'm a magician. I do magic shows."

"Where you played lately?" Bennis asked. Figueroa elbowed him in the ribs, seizing a moment when Eddie looked out at the water.

"And plus I teach magic. I'm only doing this because Harold asked me to help you, y'know."

"We appreciate it," Figueroa said.

Eddie bounced up and down on the balls of his feet. *Coked up?* Figueroa mused, but she didn't think so. He didn't have the signs. *That's just our Eddie*, she thought.

She said, "So tell us, how can a person pick a pocket without being noticed?"

"It comes down to three things. Distraction, distraction, and distraction." He laughed, pretended to punch a punching bag. "Ba-ba-boom!"

"Well, can you be a little more specific, Mr. Charles? I was standing in a crowd behind a woman who had a wallet in a tight back pocket. Suppose I want to take that wallet out. She's looking at a perfume demonstration. Shall I just ease it out slowly?"

"Absolutely wrong, wrong, wrong! Worst thing you can do. Totally wrong technique. Plus that perfume thing prob'ly isn't enough distraction. You bump her, pat her, collapse, whatever you need to do, and at the very same instant as you grab her arm, like this, you whip the wallet out of the pocket."

"Okay—"

"Like this," he said, giggling, and holding out Figueroa's wallet.

"I see we came to the right place," she said grimly, taking her wallet back. Some joggers on the lakefront glanced at the three of them, wondering if there was a crime going on. But Bennis smiled blandly at them and they jogged on.

"The basic thing you need to know is that the human mind can only focus on one thing at once."

"But you just said that it wasn't enough for the woman to be looking at the perfume demonstration."

"It ain't *enough*. Now if she sees a car careening at her kid, *that's* distraction enough. But see, it's the *type* of distraction, too. You want somebody not to feel a physical touch, you gotta give them some bigger physical distraction. Now, when I got a mark—that is, in my magic shows, a member of the audience—and I'm gonna pick his pocket, I say, like 'Now, I need you to stand over here,' and I take his arm real firmly. Squeeze it. I put more pressure on the arm than I'm gonna make removing the wallet. Ya get me?"

"Yes, I think I do."

"Like this. Watch. Now you can keep your hands on your wallets, or whatever," he said, grabbing Figueroa's left wrist and Bennis's right wrist and dragging them toward the very edge of the cement walkway, which was eight feet above the water. Figueroa and Bennis, in fact, both placed their hands on their wallets and paid close attention to their sidearms, which they were really determined not to lose, no matter what.

"So I got your attention by pulling you over here. Right?" He pulled them almost, not quite, to the point where all three of them might fall into the water.

"You bet."

"So where's your watches?"

"What?" Bennis whipped his wrist forward. No watch. Figueroa turned her arm to look at her own wrist. "All right, Eddie, you made your point," she said, not knowing whether to marvel at him or be annoyed.

"Sure. I sure did. Here." He produced both watches. Bennis's was on a clasp band, Figueroa's on an expandable band. Hers was cheap, but she knew Bennis's had cost a fair amount.

"Now tell me something," Eddie said. "Before I told you they were missing, didn't you really *feel* your watches as if they were still in place?"

"Yeah, kind of," Figueroa said, thinking back. Bennis nodded curtly.

"That's because I squeezed your wrist. Your body retains the memory of it, y'know?"

"Okay, but how'd you get them off?"

"Put 'em back on and I'll show you." He put his hand over Figueroa's wrist, slipping his fingers under the expandable band on four sides and moving it forward over her hand. For Bennis's watch, he flicked the tongue of the latch with one finger as he squeezed the wrist. Having released the latch, he let the watchband open up, then just lifted it away.

Bennis growled.

"Course," Eddie said, "I distracted you by walking you a little too close to the edge of the water, too."

"I see," Figueroa said.

"Now that squeeze. Or the grab to the arm before you take the wallet—among us magicians, we call this the distracting force."

"No doubt."

"Distraction, distraction, distraction." Eddie bopped over to the edge of the water, then back. He snapped his fingers half a dozen times, both hands. Figueroa admired this; she could only snap her fingers right-handed.

"Other good things to know," he said, snapping his fingers once more. "Don't look at what your hand is doing. Look away. I looked at you and then the water. Keep a straight face. You're interested in something else, see, not the person you're working on. Lotta times, now this is onstage, y'know, lotta times you can use a false arm. People see both your hands, they ain't gonna think you're picking their pocket, right?"

"Right. But—"

"Course, say that's no good for your perfume demonstration. But then again it might be possible, y'know. Mmm. Might be."

"Like how?"

"Say you put a coat over your arm. Say you put a rod in

the coat or in one of the sleeves so it stays rigid, like your arm is under it? Your other hand just goes and does its work. See?"

"I do see. Except this is warm weather for a coat."

"Shopping bags? Garment bags?"

"Could be."

"Well, hey. Is that all you need?"

"I guess," Figueroa said. "We certainly do appreciate you coming and helping us out this way."

"No prob."

"And before you go, let me and my partner here just make sure we have our wallets and watches and so on."

Eddie laughed raucously. "I like you. You make a good joke."

"I wanted to arrest that little bastard," Bennis said.

"Yeah. You weren't exactly friendly."

"I wasn't feeling friendly."

They got to the lockup by eleven. "So, Herzog, my man," Bennis said to the prisoner. "What we need here is for you to show your good faith."

"My lawyer takin' care of that."

"No, see, we have your lawyer's permission. We wouldn't be talking with you otherwise. You're making yourself one very fine deal, my man."

"Yeah, you're a smart guy, Herzog," Figueroa said, glancing up for lightning bolts.

Herzog did a little side dance with his head.

"So tell us here," Bennis said, "how'd you meet up with Valentine?"

"That his name? Thought it was Sisdel."

"It's his real name. Harold Valentine. Trust me on this."

Herzog thought for a few seconds, but didn't seem to get

much out of the exercise. "Whatever. I was in this bar, see? And this guy comes up to me."

"Okay. Back up just a touch. Was he there first, or did he maybe follow you?"

"No, no. He was there first. I would be onto that, otherwise."

Onto what? Figueroa wondered, but as long as the idiot was talking, what the heck.

"So he'd been drinking a while? Talking with people?"

"Dunno. Drinking, maybe. But he wasn't with anybody. And he didn't talk much. He, like, sat and listened."

"For a long time?"

"Yeah. Like an hour or so. I'm talking with a coupla buddies. You know. And finally he comes over, says he's got a proposition. Picked me out of a crowd, he said."

"Slick talker, huh?"

"Uh. No. Not exactly. Kind of talked in short bursts, you know?"

"Curt? Abrupt?"

"Yeah. Abrupt. But he needed a guy for this job where he knew we could get a lot of cash, see? He'd set it all up, but he needed a guy with brains and guts he said."

"And you were it."

"Well, don't make fun. He was right, you know. There was a lot of cash in that place."

"You willing to identify him?"

"You got him, I'll identify him."

"Well, so far we don't got him."

Noon. The man in the attic, Harold Valentine, knew that the nurse would just be starting her lunch in the sun parlor. For a while he toyed with the idea of paying the spaz a visit. Still, it would be much nicer at night when there would be more time.

Instead, he went over to the place where the roof made a

point, creating a wedge-shaped space in the attic. It was so low that he had to walk in on his knees. At some time in the past, there had been a water leak here—at the place where the wedge met the upswing of the central roof. On the outside, this would be what roofers called a "valley." And that made sense, because that would be right where water might leak in. Inside, several floorboards had warped from water damage. Two of them had bowed upward like rocking-horse runners. That left a hollow space above the ceiling of the third floor. This was where he hid the remaining cash. It wasn't much money. Far less than it should have been, he thought with a surge of anger.

And wasn't it silly of him to check it every few hours? Ridiculous! After all, nobody came up here, ever. Therefore nobody could have taken it. But he couldn't help checking every so often, just in case.

He'd been anxious, ever since the first money flew away. He couldn't have escaped from the cop if he hadn't thrown the money into the air, but he'd been so sure the cash from this robbery would give him a new start. He wanted to have all of it.

When he got away from the cop after the car chase, he had hailed a cab, and there went more money. He'd had the cab follow the two cops and that idiot Herzog back to the cop-shop and drop him there. He'd wait as long as he had to, and get even.

He sat on a fence near the CPD parking lot.

He saw them come out of the cop-shop at three-thirty, and when he got a good look at the Suze bitch, he realized he hated her more than the man. And then, to add insult to injury, they spent an hour in a goddamn bar across the street.

But the Suze bitch came out of the bar first. That was a break. And headed to her car. And while she did, he got another cab.

And after all that bad luck, here he was in a house with a sweet little girl. Who ever said things don't balance out?

CHAPTER TWENTY

Suze Figueroa and Norm Bennis were just talking about lunch when his beeper went off. He called the district.

Sergeant Touhy said, "We have two new pickpocket reports. What are you two doing out there? Painting your toenails?"

"Which stores, Sarge?"

"I want this resolved, Bennis."

"Sarge, we got three murders going on."

"That's Area Four. Not my department. I've got ritzy stores exceedingly upset."

"Okay. Tell me which ones. We're on our way."

While Bennis drove toward the Miracle Mile, Figueroa cellphoned the two stores that had just suffered another pickpocketing. As before, the wallets had been lifted while the women watched product demonstrations. Then she called the other four stores to confirm from the lists they had faxed of the times today the stores were having demonstrations.

There was time to visit the targeted stores first, then the other four.

As Bennis eased the car around a Chicago flexible bus, the kind in two segments with a rubber middle, Figueroa screamed, "Bennis!"

"What?" Bennis hit the brakes.

"No! Don't stop. I've got it!"

"Figueroa, you nearly made me hit the bus. Do you have

to be so mercurial? Why can't you be measured and calm and rational, like me?"

"Babies, Bennis! Babies!"

He cast his eyes at the sky, then immediately back at the road.

"Distraction, just like Eddie said. What's more distracting than a baby? What's more natural in those crowds of women than a couple of babies? What makes it easier to lean forward, lose your balance, and grab somebody's arm than a screaming kid?"

Bennis waved his hand. "Say! What makes it more reasonable to have stuff hung over your arm? Diaper bags, extra clothes. Suze, my man. I think you've got it!"

Cassius Mullen was the head of security at the first Michigan Avenue store they visited. The uniforms had already taken particulars of the pickpocketing.

"Two wallets in the same crowd," Mullen said with disgust. "And I can't imagine how you'll ever find out who did it."

"Were there women with children in the crowd?" Figueroa asked.

"Sure. Almost always are."

"Do you have any other demonstrations lined up? My chart says you plan a lipstick demo at twelve-thirty."

"That's right. Do you think we should call it off?"

"No. Let us observe."

"Mr. Mullen, your demos and the other stores' demos are concentrated around the noon hour, from eleven or so to one-thirty. I would think that's a crowded enough time already. Why do you do that?"

"It's not like the old days. We used to have demos in midmorning or midafternoon. But women work these days. A lot of them only get lunch hour off."

"What about the idle rich?"

"Even the idle rich don't want to be idle any longer."

"Mr. Mullen, I'm going to hang out in the crowd. I have a radio. You and Officer Bennis wait out of sight. And here's how we're gonna do this—"

Nothing out of the ordinary happened at the lipstick demo, except that Figueroa learned she ought to call it "lip gloss."

Fortunately, the stores were clustered in the space of four blocks. There were demos scheduled at two other stores, at one and one-thirty, and because they were so close together Figueroa and Bennis could get to them easily.

At Batchelder Shops at one-thirty, they watched as a sultry woman gave a mascara lesson. And finally, Figueroa hit pay dirt. Two women in the crowd had infants in strollers. Figueroa edged her way into the crowd and stood about equidistant between the two. She didn't notice any suspicious moves, but after a few minutes, one of the children began to cry impatiently, then a few seconds of silence, then cry angrily again. The mother reached forward, giving the baby a bottle, dropped the bottle, fell a stagger-step toward the woman near her, caught her balance, and said, "I'm sorry."

"No problem," the other woman said.

Figueroa's radio was inside her jacket. She mumbled a description into her neckline.

Czielski, the security boss at Batchelder's, had been adamant that he and his staff and only they would stop any suspect and talk with her. Not the cops. So Figueroa just kept watching. The demo came to an end fairly soon. The supposed pickpocket had waited until it was breaking up so as to escape under cover of a lot of people walking off in different directions. Figueroa saw the suspect and baby stroller head off toward a spot where she knew the security man could easily intercept her. Figueroa herself kept an eye on the other woman with a baby in a stroller, so that nobody would confuse her with the suspect. At the same time, she approached the probable victim and showed her police ID.

"Ma'am, Officer Figueroa, Chicago Police Department. I wish you would check your purse. We think there are pickpockets operating in this area."

The woman looked at her purse. It hung open. She gasped.

When the crowd had finally dispersed, and the second stroller had passed out of the doors, Figueroa took the victim with her and caught up with Bennis and security. Czielski stood near a woman with a baby in a stroller. He was saying, "I'm terribly sorry, ma'am, but I certainly appreciate your letting us look."

"I don't mind. It's a good thing that you're trying to protect people." The baby screamed. The woman handed the child a graham cracker.

The woman and the baby and the stroller moved off. Figueroa left Czielski to explain to the victim why they didn't pounce the moment they had a suspicion—not an easy thing to do. Very awkward. "We couldn't tell whether someone touched your purse or not, ma'am—"

Figueroa drew Bennis aside and whispered, "What happened?"

"No stolen wallet. She let us search her own purse, plus the stroller, and the diaper bag, and the baby, and even feel the baby's diaper. And the mother wasn't wearing the kind of clothes that conceal anything."

"Dammit, Bennis!"

"Yeah, yeah, I know."

"We pretty much have to find stolen stuff on the suspect, or we can't arrest 'em."

"Well, we musta got the wrong woman. Did she look like your suspect?"

"I'm not sure. I only saw her from behind in a crowd. They both had fairly long dark hair. But mine had a dark blue shirt,

I think. This one was wearing a black shirt. Shoes—well, I couldn't see mine's feet because of the crowd."

"We got the wrong woman! Hell!"

"It really looked like the same stroller, though. One of those light, foldable ones. Hell. I guess there are a lot of them around."

"And the same baby?"

"Yeah. But then one stroller looks a lot like another. And for that matter, one baby looks a helluva lot like another, too."

"Even more so."

CHAPTER TWENTY-ONE

Mary Lynne Lee woke up a little past noon. Unrested and unhappy, she had tried to fall asleep again. She had been awake until four in the morning, turning tricks in cars that picked her up on Rush Street. The last guy had been a real sweetie and had taken her to a hotel, a cheap hotel, but one with sheets and hot water. When he left at six A.M., he told her he had paid for the room for the whole night and that checkout time was one P.M. He said he wished her well.

They weren't all like that. In fact, they usually weren't like that at all.

She knew the hotel manager would be around on the stroke of one to roust out anybody left. Her one chance to get a real shower was right now.

But she just felt so sad. She wished she had her own place. She wished she had a nice apartment, because then she could have a dog. A medium-size dog, not one of those tiny ones you were always afraid of stepping on. A tan cocker spaniel, maybe. Or an Afghan. She wanted a dog with long, beautiful hair that she could brush and comb.

Mary Lynne started to cry. Somehow time got away from her once she started crying, and it seemed like only five minutes later that she heard knocking at the door.

"All right! All right!" she called. "I'm leaving."

Now she didn't have time for a shower. But at least she had money. She dragged on her horrible-looking clothes, thinking for just a moment that she could buy a new shirt. But before long she was thinking instead about what she would buy when she got to the liquor store. She could afford vodka today. But then, for the same amount of money she could get two big bottles of cheap wine. Better get the wine. It would last longer. And anyway, weren't there some vitamins in wine?

When the hotel housekeeper let herself into the room, Mary Lynne was dressed and ready to walk out.

Figueroa said, "Bennis, today we are going to eat lunch or else."

"I promise."

"Let's go get enchiladas."

"Soon. Right after we see Dr. Ho."

"What your profiler Jody thinks of as disorganized serial killers and organized serial killers I think of a little differently," Dr. Ho said. His office at Northwestern University Medical School was distinctive. Figueroa wondered whether she liked it or hated it. Dr. Ho collected seashells. One entire wall contained nothing but display cases, floor to ceiling. The shells were grouped in categories, hundreds of shells, all labeled with beautifully handwritten calligraphic labels—black conch, cone shell, pectin, lace murex, measeled cowrie, olive shell, juonia, sunrise tellin. The other three walls were filled with bookshelves, and one small window peeked through the books, giving a view out toward Lake Michigan.

"I think of them as psychotics and psychopaths. Disorganized killers are primarily psychotic and organized serial killers are almost always psychopaths. But you need to realize the psychopath who kills is a rarity among the large group of psychopaths out there, just like far and away most psychotics don't kill. Most of what we call crazy people are much more dangerous to themselves than to anybody else."

"Wait," Figueroa said, "aren't psychotics and psychopaths the same thing?"

"No. Small wonder you make that mistake. It's just too bad the words 'psychotic' and 'psychopath' are so similar. Almost everybody confuses the two. For a while I hoped we might use the word 'sociopath' for psychopathic people, but it didn't stick." Ho gave a small but attractive smile. "And I wrote so many extremely convincing articles on the subject, too."

"So what is a psychopath?"

"They're people without a normal sense of empathy. They don't understand why they're supposed to care about other people. They're often described as being without conscience."

"But they don't all kill?"

"Of course not. Why should they? Most of them aren't angry, for one thing. Let me describe a pure psychopath for you. He or she is irresponsible. He doesn't see why he has to fulfill commitments he makes. He loses jobs. He's the kid who says he'll be home for dinner and just doesn't show. He comes in when he darn well pleases. Most of them aren't even very self-protective about it, even though they're smart. A psychopath doesn't really learn from punishment. He steals from his mother's purse and even if you spank him he'll just do it again. A psychopath is very charming. People who don't have to depend on him think he's wonderful. Remember how charming everybody said Ted Bundy was? Well, of *course* psychopaths are charming. They don't have to believe the things they say, like the rest of us do, so they say whatever will please you."

Bennis said, "I just bet a lot of them become politicians."

"Sure. Some mild psychopaths are politicians. Some are doctors. Some are lawyers. They seem 'nice.' They're neatniks, usually, unlike psychotics, who if they're really disorganized, may live in absolute squalor. Psychopaths behave very attractively, like Ted Bundy. If you'd seen his defense table, you'd have thought he was one of the lawyers. So they come in under your radar. And that's the problem. When they're bad, they're very, very bad. The killers among them are the people we really have to warn our kids about—they are people who look nice and act nice, but are deadly dangerous."

"So unless you see them in action for a while, you can't tell who's a psychopath?"

"Pretty much. But not entirely. Psychopaths make mistakes in their charm. They study normal people, and imitate them, but they just don't get the *reasons* why normal people say certain things. So sometimes they'll say something they think is charming and the people they say it to don't think so at all. My mother-in-law is mildly psychopathic, I think."

Bennis laughed, but Ho said, "No, I'm serious. She doesn't kill anybody. But she has very shallow emotions. And considerable charm. People who don't have to depend on her think she's an absolute darling. But she gets her charm just a little bit wrong at times. For example, my wife's brother is very much overweight, and he's sensitive about it. *Every single time* he comes to a family gathering, the minute he walks in the door, Myra says, 'Why, Todd, you've lost weight.' Which, of course, immediately calls attention to the fact that he's fat. I took her aside at one point and said, 'Maybe he doesn't like having you call attention to his weight like that.' And she said, 'But I was complimenting him. I said he'd lost weight.' I said, 'Myra, suppose you're Mikhail Gorbachev and you have a great big birthmark on your face and you're sensitive about it. Would you like it if every time you walked into a room somebody said, 'Gee, Gorby, your birthmark is smaller'?"

"What did she say?"

"She just stared at me. She could *not* understand what I was talking about. She has other psychopathic behaviors too. Starts jobs and quits. Says she'll be home at six and comes in at eight. Nothing major. Indulges in little lies that she calls fibs. Like she'll say she's late getting home because she stopped to pick up a stray dog. But she carries in half a dozen shopping bags from Marshall Field's. Hardly bothering to cover up, see? She just doesn't *get* it."

"She must have been a real treat for your wife to grow up with."

"Psychopaths befuddle and infuriate their families. My wife spent the first thirty years of her life trying to figure out whether her mother just didn't understand her or hated her. In fact, my wife kept thinking she was a deficient daughter in some way. Not a good enough little girl. After we married, I showed her some literature on psychopaths. She kind of jumped up and yelled, 'That's Mom!' "

"But your mother-in-law doesn't kill people."

"She's not angry. And like I said, she's a *mild* psychopath."

"Our guy—"

"I believe you do have a serial killer. And your guy is nasty. He's belittling those homeless people when he washes their faces. We had one man a couple of years ago who was killing prostitutes, and for some reason, after he killed them, he painted their noses green. When we caught him, of course we asked why. The psychoanalytical types were trying to think of reasons—like the term 'blue nose' means prude and 'brown nose' means a suck-up. But green nose doesn't mean anything especially that we could figure out. We were avid to find out what it was. He told us he thought the green color contrasted well with their pink skin tones. And he meant it. He couldn't understand why we looked at him like he was a monster."

"Bad upbringing?"

"No, not necessarily. The current thinking on psychopaths is that there's either a developmental problem or a birth injury. Something in their brains just doesn't develop. Which given the complexity of the human brain isn't that surprising. Remember, thirty years ago psychiatry thought autism was caused by bad mothering. The 'refrigerator mother.' There were families devastated by that, and mothers who killed themselves in remorse. But it now seems clearly to be organic. Some brain-injured people recover from the injuries but come out with totally different personalities."

At this, Figueroa felt a chill. Suppose when Sheryl began to speak, what she showed was a different personality? But she wouldn't, would she? She seemed to be the same person. Figueroa realized that Bennis, aware of her fear, was carefully not looking at her. Dr. Ho sensed something amiss.

"Did I say the wrong thing?"

"No, Doctor," Bennis said. "We were just thinking about a mutual friend. Go ahead, please."

"Well, whatever the cause, some researchers think maybe two to five percent of the population may be psychopathic."

"That's very scary."

"Most of them never kill people. They're con men. Ne'er-do-wells. They're irresponsible mothers or fathers. Petty thieves. They may be quite good surgeons. Or lawyers. Or salesmen. They're the charming young men who prey on older women. And they're the charming young women who prey on older men. Every hospital has a doctor or two who are known to do procedures unnecessarily painfully. The psychopaths you have to be scared of, though, are the ones who happened to be born into a cruel childhood. Without a conscience, they become human monsters."

"But they're not crazy?"

"Not in the usual sense. Perfectly normal children can be made into psychotic killers, usually into what Jody calls 'disorganized serial killers' by a cruel childhood. They kill out of rage. Their killings are often committed impulsively, in a sudden fury. Psychopaths can be made into organized serial killers. They kill because it's fun."

"Jeez!"

"My belief is there are four categories of crooks. The first is the cultural criminal. A child grows up in a family of thieves and turns into a thief."

"Seen a lot of that," Bennis said.

"Anyhow, a cultural criminal is usually not a killer. They just steal stuff."

"Okay."

"Then there's what I call the ruined soul. Someone so abused as a child that he or she just can't develop normally. Some of them have so much anger that they kill. And when they kill over a period of time, they're called disorganized serial killers. But some of them are the sexual predators. They have been damaged at some sexual level, and they play out their lives compulsively on that level."

"Okay."

"Then there are the true psychotics. People with a real mental illness. Sometimes it has a genetic component. Schizophrenia runs in families. So does depression. Sometimes the psychosis is caused by chemical exposure or disease. The man who shot all those people at a McDonald's in California several years ago had been exposed to heavy metals. Cadmium, I think."

Bennis said, "And then there's the psychopath."

"Right. My own belief is that a psychopath is a psychopath from birth. But the psychopathic *killer* probably has also been abused as a child. I often say about killers—some we make, and some we make worse."

CHAPTER TWENTY-TWO

Dr. Ho had brewed a fragrant batch of coffee that Bennis, always attuned to food, found superb. He said so. Dr. Ho said, "Thank you. And to go with it—tah-dah!"

"Oreos?" Bennis said, taking two. "Thanks." Ho passed them to Figueroa, who took one and then Ho took two himself.

"Sure," Ho said, watching Bennis rotate the top and bottom of the cookie apart, exposing the white inside. "I find that how a person eats an Oreo says a great deal about his character."

Figueroa froze, a bite taken out of hers still in her mouth. She had not unscrewed the cookie. She watched as Ho dunked his in his coffee.

Bennis sat still too, his open Oreo held in front of his mouth.

"And you believed that?" Ho said, laughing uproariously. "Eat it any way you want. I can't tell a bloody thing about you from it." He smiled more calmly. "People are just so uneasy with psychiatrists. They think every move gives them away somehow."

"Yeah," Bennis said. "But I'm taking the safe way out." He dunked his Oreo in his coffee. "Say, that's not bad."

Figueroa said, "Describe a psychopath, Dr. Ho. Charm, a history of changing jobs, what else?"

"Petty thievery sometimes. A history of petty crimes. Sometimes silly, unnecessary, obvious crimes. People say, 'He's too smart to have done this.' "

"But even so," Figueroa said, "how do we find somebody like that?"

"It's not easy. Despite what the FBI leads the media to believe, you very rarely *find* an organized serial killer in a large metropolitan area on the basis of the profile. In small towns with a limited suspect group, you might. Organized serial killers usually hide in plain sight. Or to put it another way, unlike the disorganized killers, who usually go to ground, they don't really hide at all. Usually they're caught because they do something foolish and an alert cop spots it. But there are two possibilities that might help you. First the zone of comfort."

"Explain, please."

"You already must know that people go to customary places, where they feel comfortable. For instance, if you have a park you sometimes go to, you'll probably always sit on the same bench. Same in restaurants. If you're allowed to choose your own table, it's probably always the same table."

"But isn't that because I like that table? Maybe it's against a far wall and I can see the door?"

"A cop table? To watch the door? Sure, maybe it is. And maybe your bench in the park is far from the street so you don't smell the car exhaust. But what difference does that make? It's your choice and you'll go back to it. Plus, if there are two benches equally far from the car exhaust or five tables against the back wall, you'll still go to the same one if you can."

"All right. That's a normal human behavior."

"But don't you see? Killers have mostly normal human behaviors. And a screw loose."

"That's a technical description, Dr. Ho?"

He smiled. "Ought to be. On the whole, organized serial killers try to pick a place to kill or to dispose of their victims that won't be directly connected to them. That's your challenge, I guess. But usually in fact it's a place they know. And a whole lot of them choose places close to them. We had a bunch of bodies that were discovered in Wisconsin when a cow barn, a milking barn, actually, was bulldozed to make a foundation for a new house. The bodies had been buried there over a period of years, from about 1969 to three weeks before we arrived. Naturally, we tore the life histories of everybody who had worked there into little tiny threads. Nothing. All the owners, absolutely every little scrap of their entire lives. Nothing. After literally months, we worked our way back to a man who had been a custodian, cleaning up the barn in the 1958–1961 period. People who remembered him said he abused the cows. Hit them when they wouldn't stand still for milking. He was let go. Apparently you can't do that. A happy cow gives more milk."

"He killed the victims?"

"No, he was dead. Been dead fifteen years, which was why he hadn't appeared on our lists. But his wife and son had lived there at the time, and his son accompanied his dad to work. We think he was abusive to both of them. So to make a long story short, that was the place the son remembered and felt comfortable in. Comfort zones. Sometimes they're far in the past, but sometimes they're close. Remember Ed Gein, the Wisconsin grave robber and cannibal who, if memory serves me, hung the home-tanned skins of his victims in his own barn? Or John Wayne Gacy, whom I am sure you remember—"

"Who could forget?"

"Right. Buried his victims in the crawl space under his *own house*! Imagine the risk! But that's not at all unknown in these cases. Or Jeffrey Dahmer. He kept his victims in his *apartment*, for God's sake. Some of their heads on a shelf."

"So we look for somebody who lives in the area?"

"Lives or works in the area. And I'm sorry to add this—or who *used to* live or work there."

"Well, okay, I can buy that," Bennis said. "We could get records on everybody who has lived in that brick apartment building over the years."

Figueroa said, "Plus DOT workers, El employees, garbage pickup men, electric workers, maybe?"

"Maybe," Bennis said. "But otherwise—if that doesn't work, there can't be much sentimental connection to the El track."

Dr. Ho said, "You never know."

"I mean, what killer could really be comfortable virtually in the shadow of the police department?"

"I thought you'd never ask."

Figueroa and Bennis were silent. Ho poured more coffee. It was obvious what he meant, and they didn't like it. Finally, Figueroa said, "All right. Maybe he works in the CPD building. Maybe he worked there twenty years ago." She didn't want to say, maybe he's a cop.

"Inadequate personalities gravitate to jobs that give them authority and status. Jobs like security guard, rent-a-cop, cop, paramedic, firefighter. And when a stressor happens in their lives, like loss of a job, or divorce, or whatever, they snap."

"C'mon. Now that you've freaked us out, give us some good news."

"I can do that to a certain extent, as a matter of fact. The second of the two possibilities I mentioned. Psychopaths do have one Achilles' heel. They take risks, sometimes risks that seem insane, given the fact that they're smart and they clean up clues around their killing zone. I don't know whether it's because they think they're so much smarter than the police that they take the risks just to prove it, or whether they love the adrenaline rush of it, or whether they actually want to get caught. If I had to guess, I'd say they don't think they can be caught, or in some weird way they don't think it matters. Ted Bundy carried the heads of his victims around with him. Now, is that self-protective behavior?"

"I wouldn't think so."

"They tend to escalate, kill more often, take more risks, and finally get caught. There was a serial killer in New York named Joel Rifkin. He had committed at least eighteen murders, and he goes out driving in a truck with no rear license plate, without headlights, and the rotting body of a victim in the back of the truck. He gets stopped by some New York State Troopers for a totally unnecessary traffic violation. Gave *them* a surprise."

"What do you think of profiling, Mort?" Bennis asked, back at the Furlough.

"I hate art."

"No, I mean like criminal profiling. Like when the FBI does a profile of a serial killer based on the evidence at the crime scene."

"Ah, that shit ain't worth a bootful of piss."

"Go ahead," Figueroa said. "Don't hold back. Tell us what you really think."

"That psych stuff is crap."

Bennis and Figueroa had picked up a bag of White Castle hamburgers and taken them to the Furlough at three-thirty, hoping to see the gang. This detective job, Figueroa had found, tended to isolate you from your old friends.

Mort started to uncap a beer for the Flying None. She said, "Wait!"

"Wait, what, dammit?"

"I'd like something different for a change. How about a pink lady?"

Mort's mouth dropped open. "Arrr—" he said.

"I'll do it," Corky said. He pulled a bar recipe book from the shelf. "Oops. Can't. Egg white, grenadine, cream, and gin. We only got the gin."

Mileski said, "Drat."

"How about a peach blossom?" Sandi said.

Corky checked. "Needs a peach."

"Sloe gin flip?" she asked.

"No sloe gin."

Mort said, "I'll flip you."

"My dad used to drink Pall Mall cocktails," Kim Duk said.

Mileski said, "A cigarette cocktail?"

"Don't be silly," Bennis said. "It's named after a famous street in London. So are the cigarettes."

Mileski started to say, "How come you know so much?" when Corky cut in.

"But I can make you an orange blossom," he said. "*That* we got."

"Well, get it over with," said Mort, walking out from behind the bar and letting the flap in the counter slam down.

Corky said to Figueroa, "Don't let Mort bother you. There's a lot to that profiling stuff."

"Thanks, Corky."

"Did I ever tell you I spent two years in the Green Berets?"

"No. That's amazing."

"Well, I was young and foolish. But anyhow, we used a lot of the results of early profiling. You know, if you're going into a situation, like, say, you want to rescue a downed airman and he's being held by a rebel group."

"Yes?"

"You need some psych background on the group. What is it they value? Physical strength? Strategy? The ability to negotiate? Might be that more than anything they don't want to lose face. Or are they impulsive, like your disorganized offender? If so, you better get in and out fast and strong. You don't use subtlety with those guys."

"I never heard you had that kind of background."

"Oh, you know me. I like variety. It was fun for a while. Beirut. Eastern Europe. Parts of North Africa."

"I would think it was more dangerous than fun."

"Yeah. That too."

Stanley Mileski said, "I was in the army, but jeez, I wouldn't volunteer for anything like that."

"Aw, c'mon Lead Balls," Bennis said, "you'd give 'em hell."

"You been out all day?" Mileski asked Bennis.

"Us?" Figueroa said. "Yeah. We went to roll call. Been out since then."

"Then you haven't heard. Another one of the detectives died."

"Oh, shit. Of E. coli?"

"Yup. And they say there are eight on dialysis."

Bennis said, "What a goddamn shame."

Figueroa was paged and saw the phone number was Dr. Percolin's. She called back and talked with him. Finished, she went back to Bennis.

"Percolin found one case. It was a homeless man, a black guy, sixty-one, alcoholic. Killed closer to Congress Street, but that's not more than six blocks. The man's face was washed, although that wasn't in the autopsy protocol."

"How come he didn't tell us about it before this?"

"He didn't know about it. It wasn't his case. One of the other pathologists did the post. And Percolin almost missed it in his search. He was just using homeless and alcoholic and this general part of town as parameters."

"So how does he know the guy's face was washed?"

"He was going to pass this one, but he noticed the man was smothered. He had a blanket pushed over his face. So he asked the other doc."

"And he remembered?"

"When he was prompted. Percolin says you couldn't take it to court."

"When was this?"

"A year and a half ago. Percolin's still doing searches."

"Jody Huffington said killers sometimes step up the pace as they deteriorate."

"I know. I know."

By four o'clock Bennis and Figueroa were out of the Furlough and walking to the CPD headquarters. Since the murders had occurred late in the evening, and all of them pretty certainly after eleven P.M., they wanted to question everybody they could find who was on the three-to-eleven shift. They might have seen something out of the windows of the building. Or they might have seen something when they went to the parking lot to get their cars. Or—possibly one of them was the killer, and hung out after work to do his murdering.

They'd have to repeat with the eleven P.M. to seven A.M. people. Fortunately, since this was primarily an office building, there were fewer of them.

Figueroa and Bennis decided to start from the top floor and work down. It was a default decision, one they made without much discussion, since they were both distressed and unhappy with the idea of asking CPD people where they were at the time of the killings. Suze and Norm hoped the cops, secretaries, janitors, and so on would have no idea they were under suspicion. Still, they were edgy. Bennis said, "I couldn't feel any more uncomfortable if there were sea urchins in my underwear." Suze and Norm were genuinely interested in finding out whether any of these people had seen anything, and asking that would help cover the other reason, but underneath they knew one of these people could be the killer.

All shifts had received their memos by now, asking anybody who had noticed anything suspicious on the late night to early morning of May 21, May 31, or June 1 to beep Bennis or Figueroa. So far, nobody had.

The thirteenth floor was the "penthouse," housing the women's lockup. The senior guard, an administrator named Forbes who would have been called "matron" in an earlier era, was a tiny woman who looked like she could be Katie Couric's grandmother.

"Of course you can come in," she said when they explained why they were here.

As in any lockup, they had to deposit their sidearms in a box outside the jail facility itself. That way there was no possibility of prisoners getting their hands on guns.

"I don't know exactly what you can see from here," Forbes said. "But you're welcome to check. Our prisoners couldn't have seen anything at all. They're all housed in inside cells."

Thinking about the Manualo murder, Figueroa said, "Can I get a view to the north from this floor?"

"Sure."

The Annex, which was attached to the main building, was only seven floors. When Figueroa and Bennis looked out of the north windows here, they saw the roof of the Annex and nothing of the ground level just north of it. Nobody could have seen the Manualo murder from this floor.

"Thanks," Figueroa said. Forbes led them back to the lockup. The cells, in two double rows down the center of a huge room, with the cell backs against each other, were tiny and very public. The bars in the front were the full width of the cell and included a door made of bars. The woman yelled, "Man coming through!" as they walked. Some of the women prisoners in underwear made no move to cover up. The ones who were screaming mostly went on screaming. Each cell had a toilet, a sink, a slablike bed, and one—just one—blanket. Therefore the whole facility was kept very warm.

Figueroa noticed the shoes on the floors outside the cells. Tradition said the shoes should always be placed outside so that the prisoners wouldn't hang themselves with their shoelaces, but most of the shoes had no laces and they were outside anyway. Sometime she thought she would ask why. Hanging was also the reason why they weren't given sheets.

"Over here," said Forbes.

The wall that faced the El, the east wall, was almost entirely windowless. Apparently even in a jail nobody wanted to look at El trains. There was a single east window on the corner adjacent to the south wall. The CPD parking lot was to the south.

Against the south wall was a bank of four microwaves above a counter on which stood two coffeemakers. Next to the counter was a refrigerator. There were several chairs and a low table, scuffed around its edges. Figueroa assumed that the scuff marks were from guards sitting on the chairs and resting their feet on the table edge, although none of them were doing that now, with the administrator looking at them. Two stood at the microwaves, warming sandwiches on paper plates.

"Bologna sandwiches," Forbes said. "You know this is a temporary holding facility, not a residence facility, so we don't do real meals."

"You serve—"

"Bologna sandwiches for breakfast, lunch, and dinner. But we do offer them either cold or warm, depending on which way our guests like it best."

"Oh. Gourmet dining."

"So what do you want to see?"

"This." Figueroa and Bennis stared out the single east window. There was a good view of the El, but they couldn't see the alley underneath it. The south windows that overlooked the parking lot gave a diagonal view of the place where Abigail Ward had been killed, but it was a long way away.

"If you could call all the guards together, I'd like to tell them some dates and ask them what they saw."

While the woman was gathering everybody, Figueroa remarked softly to Bennis, "All we can do, I guess, is watch body language and try to get each one of them to talk so we can get an idea of what they're like."

"Looking for Dr. Ho's characteristics?"

"What else can we do? We have to start someplace."

"I don't believe the killer is a woman."

"I doubt it myself. Think positive. Maybe one of the guards actually saw something down there."

One had.

Five female guards shook their heads and shrugged. But one said, "Yeah. May thirty-first."

"What did you see?"

"It wasn't from here. I got out of here late because my relief didn't show. Idiot woman. She's been fired. Good riddance. Anyhow, they got in a replacement twenty after twelve. So I'm in the parking lot and see, I'm short."

"Yes. About my height."

"Right. And I'm standing near my car, trying to figure out why my keys aren't in my key pocket where I always put them. Turned out to be in my hand. And I see this guy crossing the lot. He doesn't see me because the car is taller than I am."

"What did he look like?"

"Well, you gotta realize I'm seeing him through two car windows and they aren't that clean. I just basically noticed him because he passed in front of the light at the far end. Which meant, see, that the light was behind him."

"But what *did* you see?"

"Medium tall. Wore a hat. Baseball cap, I think. Short jacket. Walked like a youngish guy."

"You sure it was a man?"

"Pretty damn sure. Walked like it."

"Heading which way?"

"Well, see, that's why I noticed. He came from the street onto the parking lot, so you figure he's going to a car, right? But he walked right on through and out the other side."

"Toward?"

"Under the El."

"How come you remember the date?"

"My kid's birthday. I hadda work that night, so we were celebrating the next day. Kid was freaked. Who knew that ten-year-olds could be so formal about ceremonies?"

Bennis and Figueroa repeated the process with the men's lockup on twelve. Here they didn't even bother to check from the north windows. The view would only be worse than from thirteen.

None of the guards remembered anything at all out of the ordinary on the nights of the murders. "Nothing unusual outside," one of them said. "In here every day there's weird shit happens."

Eleven, ten, and nine produced next to nothing. On eleven, the suits had several years earlier declared a cafeteria. Almost nobody ever ate there, largely because the food was putrid. A hot table with real, live, and hideously bored cooks ran along the east wall, the wall that backed onto the El. There were no windows whatsoever in it and if there had been they'd have been as steamed up as the plastic covers over the hot table. The only hot foods left in the stainless-steel bins at this hour were creamed chipped beef and some grayish sort of meat, with an orange barbecue sauce half stirred into it, giving a marbleized effect. The cooks stared morosely at thick white plates of wilted iceberg lettuce.

There was a long row of coin-op machines along the south wall. They had been set down in a row regardless of the fact that there were windows behind them. As a result, nobody could possibly have seen down into the parking lot or over toward the El, without standing on top of a coffee machine, which nobody was likely to do casually. If the killer had been looking out to see whether there was a homeless person walking by, he didn't do it from here.

The cooks had seen nothing, knew nothing, and didn't give a good demonstration of caring much, either.

On eight, the Personnel offices still hummed, but showed signs of closing up for the day. A secretary with big hair the color of overripe mangoes showed Bennis and Figueroa her south-facing window, which looked like it hadn't been washed since it was installed. There was another window next to it that was actually rather clean, about as transparent as lightly used dishwater. But the several potted plants growing there would have made it hard for a person to look out without being conspicuous about it.

Except if nobody else was in the office.

"When do you leave for the day?" Figueroa asked.

"Five. Normal time."

"Ever stay late?"

"Hardly ever. Not in the last three-four weeks."

"Can we talk to the commander?"

And they did. Commander Cole, a tall, slender black man with a reputation of being highly professional, was outraged that somebody would do murder near the CPD. However, he couldn't help much. He often worked late, but in the last weeks had been out of there by eight, going to community meetings. He also admitted, after a little chat, that he had not asked to be Commander of Personnel. "Borr-rrring!" he said. He wanted to be back in Detectives or Patrol.

Seven and six were administrative offices. Nobody knew anything and everybody said they left by five, which Bennis and Figueroa thought actually meant four-thirty at the latest.

Five and four were Dispatch.

The Dispatch Center was something else again. Absolutely state of the art when it was built in 1961, it had been visited by police departments from all over the world and copied a thousand or more times. Six months from now, it would all be gone.

Arranged around an open center were stations consisting of desk space, microphones, zone maps, and special maps. A dispatcher staffed each work station, which covered a specific zone of the city. The special maps were of parks, lakes, and such, where giving street addresses didn't work and where fleeing felons could easily get themselves lost. The cops could get lost, too, if no one had a clear map of the area.

911 calls come into Dispatch, but are first categorized by a real live human being. If the concerned citizen has a cat up in a tree, 911 may try to get Fire or Animal Rescue to deal with it. Chicago has been famous—or famously foolish—for decades for trying to run on every 911 call, but no more. In a time of overload, there's prioritization.

However, once vetted, a call goes to the dispatcher appropriate to the district involved. He or she puts it out on the air. The dispatcher is in charge of choosing the most appropriate car, usually the closest, but if he or she knows a car is about to go to lunch, and if the call seems like it will lead to a long interaction, a missing child for example, another car just up from lunch will be chosen. Lunch is the meal in the middle of the tour, regardless of the time of day.

All of this will be completely computerized in the new building, and will include "live" radios in the squad cars, which will read out on the screen exactly where the car is. All will be computerized, that is, except for the dispatcher, who will still be in charge of making the big decisions.

Dispatch is always busy.

When Figueroa and Bennis strode in, lights were flickering on and off along the fronts of consoles, phones were ringing with muted buzzes, like a field full of crickets at night. The air was filled with quiet, flat-voiced talk, dispatchers speaking into mikes, ordinary stuff mostly, issuing assignments, returning wants and warrants. But as they walked past, Figueroa heard one say, "Stay off the air, Thirty-three has an emergency. I have a ten-one at Sixty-third and State—"

She imagined the Third District squad cars all suddenly spinning around wherever they were, running to help a buddy in trouble. It would be only one or two minutes at most before the dispatcher was telling them, "Everybody stay where you are. I have enough units on the scene."

"Well, lookee there," Bennis said, pointing at the wall.

"We knew this, didn't we?"

The windows of Dispatch were covered with sheetrock to keep light off the consoles.

"I guess so," Bennis said. "Damn. Well, maybe it narrows things down."

"It doesn't really. It just makes it hard to talk to people here. Can't exactly say we want to find out if they saw anything."

"Sure we can. They get off at eleven. We can ask what they saw in the lot."

But it came to nothing. They got no information on the third, second, or first floors either, and had to spend ten useless minutes with a press secretary who was a glad-handing idiot. He'd had a dozen different jobs, exuded charm, and had emotions about an inch deep. "Sorry to hear about a murder in our area here. Very sorry."

As they turned away from him, Bennis said, "I'll bet he drives a new car in good condition, too."

"So he's a psychopath. I think he's a happy psychopath."

They did the north side of the Annex and found out nothing of any use. They walked slowly to the parking lot. Bennis said, "Talk with Dr. Ho a few minutes and you start to see psychopaths everywhere."

"Maybe they *are* everywhere. Oh, jeez! I have to get home. It's nearly five, and I want to catch the neurologist!"

"We ought to talk to the first watch in the building."

"Meet you in the Furlough at eleven tonight when they come on?"

"Done."

Of all the doctors and nurses and therapists that had treated Sheryl since the accident—and Suze thought they would number more than a hundred by now—the one she liked best was the neurologist, Dr. Hannah Pettibaker.

The one she liked least was a condescending and sappily cheerful physical therapist who had come just for a couple of weeks after Sheryl got home. He was named Jonathan Roon. His job, he said, was to return Sheryl to a "realistic" level of competence. Whatever that meant. He taught her what he called "activities of daily living," which he shortened to ADLs. He had the habit of bounding into Sheryl's room and asking brightly, "And how are our ADLs today?"

Dr. Pettibaker was straightforward, no nonsense, and not saccharine.

The first time Suze and Robert met with her, about a week after the accident, she said, "I'm going to give you the general background picture, and then we'll apply it specifically to Mrs. Birch. And by the way, I don't approve of doctors calling themselves Dr. Pettibaker and calling the patient by the first name, like Sheryl. But we could be Hannah and Sheryl and Robert and Susannah, okay?"

"Okay, as long as I'm Suze."

"Done. Now that we know Sheryl is not going to die, we move into the next phase. We assess the extent of the injury. You'll hear us use a lot of terms, not necessarily the way laymen use them. We're not trying to impress you with them, and they're not secret. So let me explain them."

When they talked about impairment, she said, they meant damage at the organ level. It was the actual damage done to the tissues of Sheryl's body. "When we use the term 'disability' we're talking at the person level. It's what the person can't do. And when we talk about 'handicap' it's at the societal level. The ways in which the disability interacts with other people."

Robert said, "Is she going to be handicapped?"

"We're not sure yet. Right now we're going to deal with short-term goals, given her acute disability."

"Does that mean she's disabled?"

"She is now. But acute disability is a specific term that refers to early, reversible damage. When we talk about chronic disability, that's permanent. Our short-term goals are to get her sitting, and then maybe walking again."

Suze said, "Maybe?"

"Well, yes. Then we get into the difference between optimal goals and realistic goals. It's realistic to think she'll be able to stand, and probably to walk after a fashion. Optimally, we'd like to get her walking normally."

Suze sighed, pressing her hands together. She was utterly terrified.

"Your sister," Dr. Pettibaker said, having noticed Suze's reaction, "is now into stage two. Stage one, immediately after the accident, was the time when she was in a coma. In stage two the patient shows a lot of spasticity. This is normal. It lasts up to four or five weeks. You'll see her making exaggerated responses to normal stimuli, jumping at ordinary noises, twitching when they draw blood. Her head might jerk back and forth. It will seem strange but it's entirely expected and you shouldn't let it frighten you. There's been a tremendous insult to her brain. After stage two, she will go into stage three. What she will be doing then is called synergy. When she tries to bend her elbow, for example, she will also move her whole shoulder and hand."

"And then?"

"If all goes well she will go into stage four. At that point the patient is nearly normal, or as normal as she is likely to get.

Normal motion comes back proximally first, which just means that she'll regain normal use of the parts near the center of the body, arms and legs, before the more distal parts, like feet and hands."

Robert said, "How long will all this take?"

"Most of what function she's ever going to recover she'll recover in the next six months."

"Dr. Pettibaker, it's great to see you! I mean Hannah," Suze said, coming into the living room. It was always good to see Pettibaker. The world felt better after she'd been there. Suze thought that very few doctors would make house calls. Pettibaker was very much aware of how nervous Sheryl got when she was driven to an appointment outside the house.

"Hi, Suze. Your girl here is doing well."

Sheryl actually smiled. Pettibaker always told Sheryl exactly what she thought.

"Be specific for us," Suze asked.

"Sure. I've just started explaining to Sheryl, but once more is good. You're doing a lot less listing to one side, Sheryl. The leg is stronger. I don't think you realize it, but because I see you once a week, the improvement is more noticeable to me than it is to you."

Sheryl said, "Bastard."

"She often says that when she means 'better,' " Figueroa said.

Pettibaker grinned. "I'm your neurologist, not your physical therapist, but I think you're pushing the exercise kind of hard. Your right side is like iron. Your left side is good and getting better, but my guess is you're overcompensating. Be good to your left side. Help it out."

Sheryl said, "Gah."

"I know it's frustrating and you're frustrated about your

speech. It will get better. It really will. Aphasia can be quite stubborn, but your last MRI was encouraging."

"Ahhhh."

"I think that was an intentional 'ah.' "

Sheryl smiled again, lopsidedly, but genuinely.

You didn't "walk Pettibaker to her car." You wouldn't get any more information anyhow, and she wouldn't get herself into situations where the patient could even think the doctor was telling the family stuff the patient didn't know. Suze admired that.

After Dr. Pettibaker left, and Robert had come home, Suze said, "We're going to celebrate. I'm gonna call for Thai food."

After dinner, Suze, J J, and Maria did the dishes.

"Aunt Suze," Maria said, "Emily's having a sleepover tomorrow night. Can I go?"

"Well, I don't see why not. Your dad has to go out, but I'll be here."

"I'll be here, too," J J said.

Suze said, smiling, "That's right. With me and J J and Kath, your mom should be fully protected. Speaking of which, I have to go back out tonight."

J J said, "Aw, Mom, do you really?"

"Yes. I'm sorry but they pay me for this. I should be back by one A.M."

Valentine was sitting in his favorite spot for the family dinner, halfway down from the second floor. When he heard Suze say, "I should be back by one A.M.," he was quite pleased.

He whispered to himself, "That will work out nicely."

CHAPTER TWENTY-THREE

SUZE GOT TO the Furlough at ten forty-five and found Norm already there. "Miranda stand you up?" she asked.

"Amanda, and no."

"Been working?"

"If you absolutely *must* be nosy, I spent the time since I left you at the laundromat doing my laundry."

"Ohhh. Testy, testy."

"What do you think, Figueroa. Is the Furlough our zone of comfort?"

"Must be."

Corky came down to their end of the bar and said, "It's warm out there tonight. Get you a beer, Figueroa?"

"Not while I'm working. Thanks, though. Afterward, maybe." She looked pointedly at Bennis's beer.

"One beer is like food," Bennis said.

"Can't do it after," Corky said. "We close at twelve."

Bennis chuckled. "Just long enough to mellow up the third shift?"

Mort said, "Jeez, Bennis. Even us bartender types gotta sleep sometime."

"Although some would say," Corky said, laughing happily, "that we spend our days asleep at the switch."

The first-watch guys started to straggle in. Figueroa knew they were not supposed to drink before going on duty, but what was she, their mother? She poked Bennis. "Let's hang out in the lot."

Third watch was leaving, and first watch was arriving. Bennis and Figueroa hung halfway between the parking lot and the CPD building. It was a chance to ask the ones arriving and parking if they'd seen anything on the target dates. And also a chance to catch the ones leaving, of course. Since they arrived over a period of maybe half an hour, you could spend a little one-on-one time. Both shifts had heard the memo read at roll call, but there was always a lot going on at roll call, plus a group doesn't respond like an individual. Besides, Bennis and Figueroa thought that catching these guys outdoors and gesturing at the El and the alley might jog somebody's memory.

For ten minutes Bennis and Figueroa split up, trying to talk with cops one at a time. They spent more time with departing third watch, since they could also run down the arriving first-watch cops again in a few minutes at roll call.

However, when Suze and Norm walked toward each other in front of the CPD, each knew in a glance that the other had found out nothing much.

"Zip," Figueroa said.

"Zero."

"Goose egg."

"Nada, damn it!"

"Well, up and at 'em," Figueroa said. "Into the building."

The women's lockup was much the same as it had been at four o'clock. Mrs. Forbes was gone but her assistant, a burly woman named Ms. Lotogath, was energetically in charge. When the guards were rounded up and asked by Bennis and Figueroa whether they'd seen anything suspicious, Lotogath practically ordered them to come up with something. Figueroa, fearing that one of the cowed women employees might invent a suspect just to please the boss, had to intervene.

"We don't want to put any pressure on you. Don't force it. If you don't remember, you don't remember, that's all."

"We know our guy is trying *not* to be seen," Bennis added.

After they left he said, "Sheesh! I'd hate to run into Lotogath in a dark alley!"

"You don't suppose—"

"No, I don't."

By twelve-thirty they'd cruised the whole building. There was nobody in Personnel or the head honchos' offices. The cafeteria was even more depressing than earlier, if possible. One of the veggie choices for dinner must have been brussels sprouts, and the room still smelled sulphurously of them.

The Dispatch floors were exactly the same as they had been hours earlier. Only the faces had changed. Virtually nothing was going on in the north side of the Annex.

"Another great day for law enforcement," Bennis said.

They walked north on the sidewalk in front of the CPD building. Just north of the Annex, they cut to the right, through the construction area, past the backhoe and bulldozer, and over to the alley under the El.

The night was warm and very still. An El train had passed as they stepped out of the CPD doors, and a few flakes of rust were still sifting down. The trains ran less frequently after midnight. Very few cars were passing on State Street.

"Spooky here," Bennis said.

"Now don't creep me out, Bennis."

"Which means you feel it too."

"Yeah."

They stood without moving for several minutes. Figueroa tried not even to breathe loudly, and after a few seconds she realized Bennis was doing the same. Then, as if they had consulted with each other, both began to stalk quietly south.

They passed silently behind the CPD building, careful not to brush against discarded paper and other trash. Slowly they worked their way south to the fence that backed up against the CPD parking lot. They stopped there and still didn't speak.

They heard a rustling.

Bennis grabbed Figueroa's arm to quiet any idea she might have had of chasing the sound. It was too far away and they'd been fooled before.

It was somewhere in the open area under the tracks, not in the parking lot. But from the faintness of the whispery noise, it had to be more than half a block away, farther south.

Bennis put his head down, right against Figueroa's ear.

"Either you or I gotta walk back around to the front of the building. Come in from that side."

She took his head with her hands and turned it, leaning her mouth to his ear.

"I'll stay here. You go walk around front, and unless I yell, get into your car. Go out of the lot by the front, and if I still don't yell, go around the block and park and come in the alley from the south end."

"Good. Except you go. I'll stay here."

"Bennis, do *not* patronize me. We've been together too long."

He sighed very, very softly, then faded down the alley northward, without a sound.

Figueroa stood unmoving in the shadow of a telephone pole. Very little of the peach light from the streetlamps reached back here, but why take a chance? Really, the only two things that would attract attention were sound and motion. If she had not already been spotted, standing still should take care of it. And if whoever was out there believed someone had been here, the motion of Bennis walking away down the alley might satisfy him.

A minute and a half went by. Figueroa felt a shiver of fear

run up her back. She would never admit it to a soul. Well, she'd admit it to Bennis, but nobody else. A partner was unique.

Finally—finally!—she saw Bennis walking south on the sidewalk in front of the CPD. He turned into the parking lot and without a glance in her direction headed toward his car. He got in and started the engine with a sound that seemed louder than it had ever been before. He flicked on his lights, backed out of his space, and drove slowly down the row of cars toward the exit to State Street. As he turned, his headlights had passed across the east side of the lot and shined into the alley under the El.

Figueroa had expected this. They hadn't talked about it, but they'd worked together a long time and she knew he'd swing his lights into the alley for her. It was also part of the reason she had placed herself behind the telephone pole. As the lights swept the darkened alley area, she thought she saw a round shape move.

Somebody's head?

It was hard to be sure, since the motion of the headlights made everything seem to move, but this moved differently, against the direction of the other shadows. She focused on exactly where it was, and spotted objects nearby so as to be able to find the place, then looked slightly to one side of where it was. The tail of the eye picked up motion better than the center of focus, she knew. That old mammalian need to see things sneaking up to eat you.

Bennis would now be parking somewhere around the block. He would come into the alley from the south, while she held her position here, behind the north corner of the CPD building.

She heard a scrape. A rat? A cat? A human being?

Nothing moved.

Figueroa tensed and released the muscles of her legs without making any external movement. She wanted to be ready to jump into action if she had to. And she probably would have to get going fast, once the hidden man realized Bennis was coming down the alley. This was no box canyon. There were openings to Wabash Street between the buildings on the east. The brick apartment building had narrow walkways on both sides of it. The CPD was not fenced, and even though the parking lot was fenced on three sides, there were driveway openings on both west and east.

After two or three minutes, Bennis appeared at the far end of the alley, half a block away. He had changed his jacket, so he didn't show the same silhouette against the streetlights. He came shuffling into the alley with the exaggeratedly careful walk of a drunk, as if he were trying hard to balance his head on his neck.

Figueroa stayed where she was, unmoving.

He came closer, slowly, looking about as unthreatening as anybody could.

Closer still, past the far end of the CPD parking lot, along the fence, closer to where Figueroa had glimpsed a person. He neared the gate into the lot. In another ten feet, she thought, he should be near the spot.

Suddenly, a runner broke out of the shadows, racing down the alley and into the walkway next to the brick building. Figueroa went to a run from a standing start. Bennis changed in a split second from a drunk to a sprinter.

The fleeing person ran like a young boy, but with a floppy gait. His cap flew off. Figueroa put on a burst of speed. She jumped the cap, Bennis right after her. They came out on Wabash, amid garbage Dumpsters and parked cars. The runner was ducking and weaving. Now there were a few street people on the sidewalk, a group standing around an all-night diner entrance.

The runner ducked around the group, between cars, and into an area-way littered with cans. There were several ways out, Figueroa saw. She couldn't see the runner, but picked one of the possible routes, knowing Bennis would pick another.

Hers was a dead end, and no other person was in it.

She ran back to the Wabash entrance.

She heard Bennis running down a sidewalk into an enclosed courtyard and heard him say "Damn!"

She ran past, catching sight of him coming back.

"Where'd he go?"

"Could be anyplace," he said. "Damn it!"

They stood quiet and listened for running feet or toppling cans. Nothing.

"Hell," Figueroa said.

On the way back to the CPD lot, they picked up the cap. Figueroa put it in one of the paper evidence bags she carried in her car.

"Why do that?" Bennis said.

"Who knows? Maybe Trace can find something on it. Hair anyhow."

"No, I mean why bag it? Let's take it up now."

"They don't work at night."

"So? They can get started first thing in the morning."

They went into the building and up to the tech floor. Suze filled out the forms. She took the cap out of her paper bag. The evidence bag to put it in was also paper. Plastic kept out air and some biological material would degrade in it, so you weren't supposed to put evidence, especially blood or anything they might get DNA from, like hair follicles, in plastic. "Look at this," she said to Bennis.

There were several hairs caught in the clasp at the back where you could snap a band to make the cap larger or smaller.

"Long, aren't they?" he said.

The hairs were black and straight and very long.

Figueroa said, "Well, this isn't so bad. We know something

already. It's straight. So our guy is probably not African-American."

"Yup, you're right."

"Also, it's coarse hair, a thick shaft, don't you think?"

"I guess."

"So probably not one of the very northern of the northern Europeans."

"Like you're a hair and fibers expert."

"Help me here, Bennis. We lost him. We've had no luck so far. Send me home happy."

"Well, the lab will tell you. But—don't hit me—I think in general you're right. An analysis of this oughta give a pretty decent description of the perp. Maybe even age. This doesn't say old guy to me."

Figueroa stared at the hairs. "I thought it was a boy when he was running. Do you think it was a girl?"

"With all the guys out there wearing long ponytails? I wouldn't want to guess."

"What do you think this is—fifteen, sixteen inches?"

"My spread hand is eight inches. Yeah," he said, measuring from the end of his little finger to the end of his thumb without touching the hair. "Sixteen it is."

"Of course, this guy could be anybody. Doesn't have to be the killer."

Bennis said, "Why'd he run?"

"Didn't want to be questioned by the cops."

"Well, maybe."

Figueroa said, "Maybe he had drugs on him."

"Look, he didn't run quite the way a homeless person runs. Most of them are pretty deteriorated. This isn't a big area for drug sales. It's too near the CPD. Drug use, maybe. Small amounts don't get you in big trouble. He could be anybody, but I think the odds are decent that he's our killer."

"As I said before, send me home happy."

Lying flat in the shadows underneath a Dumpster just off Wabash, Mary Lynne Lee cowered and shivered, peeking out at a thin slice of pavement. Their feet had disappeared several minutes ago, and she thought she was safe.

They'd almost got her. And if they did, they'd throw her in a squad car and drag her home. She started to cry soundlessly. The whole world just wouldn't leave her alone, and it was so wrong. Why couldn't she just live her own life? She wasn't hurting anybody. When in her entire life had she ever hurt anybody?

Well, actually she had. Her mother and father. They were terribly, terribly disappointed in her. And her grandmothers, both of them, and her grandfathers, both of them. They expected more. Especially her grandfather Lee who had said, "I expected more of you, Mary Lynne," and almost tore her heart out saying it. She loved her grandfather Lee.

They were terribly disappointed, and probably very worried, too. The best thing would be if they never heard of her again. That way, they would never know how bad it was. If they never saw her again, they wouldn't ever know for sure how she'd been living.

When those cops chased her, the running had consumed the little bit of energy she had gotten from a short bottle of red wine. Wine had made her sleepy when she first started drinking; that was one of the things she liked about it. But a half bottle hardly affected her now. Briefly, it had made her invincible once she started to run flat-out. Now it was all gone. All the energy and all the—what?—protection. And all her stash of wine was gone, too.

She didn't dare stay here. Peering out from beneath the Dumpster, she saw a large homeless guy with flowing hair, a familiar figure she thought of as BAD, strolling up the alley.

Over her months in the streets, she had got used to categorizing people as good or bad on the instant.

There was a bad guy lying on the sidewalk where the alley met Wabash, too. She was way past the naive stage where she thought anybody without a shave and who smelled sweaty was a bad guy. But she'd seen this man push a smaller person into the path of a car a couple of days before, and she didn't want to get near him.

What she had to do was slip really sneakily around back to the police department building. She could sleep there.

But before that, she needed a drink.

Figueroa drove Bennis to his car. He gave her a good-night gesture, shooting his index finger at her. Figueroa shot back. She said, "Well, tomorrow is another day."

Bennis said, "Fiddle-de-dee."

CHAPTER TWENTY-FOUR

SUZE SANK GRATEFULLY into bed. Her knees hurt, her eyes hurt; her feet hurt; her head hurt. Finally she took an inventory of what didn't hurt, and since there were more of those—her eyebrows didn't hurt, or her nose, elbows, neck, ears, and a few more—she told herself to quit bellyaching, be grateful, and get some sleep. It was nearly two A.M. and she had to be up at six.

She couldn't stand too many more days like this. If there had been more progress, or if she and Norm had achieved some major success, she knew she would feel less exhausted.

There were only two windows in the attic. Neither one was much use. They were very small, one at the far north under the peak at the top of the roof, and one at the southwest, under the lower peak of a dormer. Both were in the positions where you ought to have attic vents if you had any sense, Valentine thought. In fact, he believed that they had once been the positions of attic louvered vents and the vents had been removed and replaced with windows in the early seventies during the fuel crisis. They were framed in a certain kind of matte aluminum that he knew was seventies-period.

But trying to save on heat in the winter meant that moist air would accumulate up here and eventually the wood would rot.

People were so shortsighted. They just didn't *know* anything.

Neither window opened, so he got all the stale air from the

house. Wouldn't you think almost anybody, however stupid and penny-pinching and inconsiderate, would provide decent air for a guest? A minimum gesture, wasn't it?

Of course, he was an uninvited guest, he reflected, giggling softly.

Outside one of the windows was the top of a huge sycamore tree that obscured his view from the north, toward the street. The other window looked down on the backyard, which wasn't particularly interesting. And both were terribly dirty. Shiftless, these people.

He picked up the screwdriver he had taken from the basement. The aluminum window was held in place by eight screws, two on each side near the corners. He had previously removed them all, then replaced and screwed in only the two in the top bar. The other six he simply pushed back in as far as they'd go, which was not all the way. In an emergency, he might possibly be able to jump out of the window into the tree and escape.

But it was even more useful than that. He pulled the window out and set it down on the floor. Then he urinated out into the tree.

This got around a lot of the danger of being heard flushing toilets. And truth to tell, it also gave him a good laugh.

Now he put the window back in place and pushed the screws in. As far as he could determine from looking out both windows, this and the one at the other side, all the lights were off downstairs. There were no patches of light in the yard or on the tree. His watch, which was still running, told him it was two-thirty A.M.

He crept down to the third floor. Stopping at one of his favorite spots, just inside the third-floor hall, he listened. There was no sound from the door at the end, which he now knew to be the lady cop's room. He stuck his head into the little boy's room, knowing the kid didn't wake easily. Yes, there he was, dead to the world.

Now down to the second floor. There was a light halfway along the hall, but it was dim and green. The night-light in the bathroom.

And on down to the first floor. Valentine entered the kitchen. On the counter was half a loaf of whole wheat bread. He took out two slices, buttered them heavily with the butter he found on the counter. Okay, where do you keep jam? He opened one cupboard, found it in the second place he looked. A good omen for a fun night.

He spread jam thickly on the other slice of bread and then put them together, giving the two slices of bread a little extra push, because he didn't like sandwiches that fell apart, then sat down at the small kitchen table, and ate, with great satisfaction. He popped a can of Coke. He put his feet up on the other chair. Excellent.

Finally he wiped crumbs from his hands, wiped and replaced the knife, and—he was ready.

Sheryl lay on her back in the faint glow of a blue night-light. The call buzzer hung over the bed rail almost touching the knuckles of her right hand. He stepped quickly to the bed and lifted the buzzer over the rail, letting it fall quietly the length of its cord, to a point an inch above the floor. Out of her reach. It would take her a long time to get it into her hand, even left to herself.

Then he tickled her foot.

Sheryl woke slowly, which surprised him because he assumed that lying around all day would make her sleep lightly. Valentine watched consciousness come gradually to her eyes, and watched her focus on him. He leaned right over her, up to within a foot of her face. Awareness came more slowly than consciousness. As her eyes widened, first going to the place on the bed rail where the buzzer should be, he recognized the very instant when she was going to scream or call for help, or whatever she was able to do in her condition. When she drew in a breath, he moved fast, picking up the extra pillow near her head and bringing it down over her face.

Sheryl's body arched and she thrashed from side to side, trying to free herself. Her right hand grabbed at the pillow, and her left hand tried to, but repeatedly scrabbled ineffectively down the length of the cloth, as if the fabric were slippery. Her right hand was strong, stronger than he had expected, but he held it down on top of the pillow.

Valentine giggled a little, careful to make hardly any noise.

When Sheryl's struggles had all but stopped, he pulled the pillow away. With wide eyes, Sheryl stared up at him, sucking in air. She was pale, but not quite blue. She took in three whooping breaths, which he judged too faint for anybody in the house to hear. With great interest, he watched the pink come back into her cheeks. "Whit-ne-" she said, meaning nothing he could decipher, but he knew it meant "why?" or "who are you?"

"A nightmare," he said, and put the pillow back over her face.

CHAPTER TWENTY-FIVE

SUZE JUMPED STRAIGHT out of bed and started to run in place before she realized where she was. What was going on? She was sure that she was in the Academy and the trainer had just blown the whistle that meant run the track.

Buzzer, not a whistle. Oh, God.

Sheryl!

Suze ran for the door, never mind she was wearing just a nightshirt. Hyperventilating, she kept saying, "She rang the bell, she must be okay, rang the bell, must be okay, rang the bell, must be okay—"

Taking the back stairs two or three at a time, she practically crashed into Kath on the last flight. Robert was pounding down the front stairs.

They piled into Sheryl's room together.

"Oh, God, you're okay!" Suze said, seeing Sheryl sitting half up, half tangled in the bell cord that she had apparently pulled toward herself through the bed-rail bars, even though it should be looped over the top rail.

She wasn't okay, though. She was alive. But Suze immediately took in Sheryl's gasping breaths. Her face was blotchy, both red and pale, tear-streaked, her hair pushed upward. She was trying to talk and saying, "Aah, gah, gah, ahh, ack."

Robert said, "What's the matter, Sheryl?"

"What happened, Mom?" Kath asked.

Maria came into the room. "Mom! What's going on?"

"Gah-gah-gah-evil."

"She's had a nightmare," Robert said.

"GUH-det!" Sheryl said. "Hose."

Robert said, "She must have knocked the buzzer off the rail."

Suze almost said, "Don't talk about her as if she isn't here." But she had trained herself not to interfere between Sheryl and Robert. In the long run, she could only make trouble if she did.

But how could she have knocked the buzzer off? The cord was always wound around the rail.

"Sheryl, honey." Suze took her hand. "What happened? Are you sick?"

"Uh-uh-uh." If Sheryl was upset she spoke more poorly than usual.

"Take a breath, honey. There. Again. Did you have a dream?"

Sheryl twisted around, almost as if indignant at the thought. But Suze saw what she considered a touch of doubt in her eyes.

"You're not sure?"

"Gastrop."

Kath took Sheryl's other hand. "Mommy, can I sit here with you a little while?"

Sheryl settled back, not quite as panicky. Suze went for the sedative the doctor had prescribed for times that Sheryl was agitated. They tried to use it very sparingly, but this seemed like the sort of thing it was intended for. "Sheryl?" she said, holding up the bottle of tablets. "How about it?"

But Sheryl thrashed around, nearly as desperate as when they had first arrived.

"I guess not."

Robert said, "What happened? Tell us."

Tears came to Sheryl's eyes.

"Honey," Suze said. "It's three A.M. How about we get the kids back to bed and then either Robert or I sit here and sleep in the chair with you."

Sheryl smiled.

Robert and Suze sent the children back to bed in order to get two minutes in the kitchen to talk softly.

"All right," Suze said, "what do you think happened?"

"Like I said, a dream."

"She hasn't had any this bad."

"She hasn't had any this bad in the last month."

"Okay. True."

"Look, what else could it be? Do you think she's having some sort of seizure?"

"Didn't look like it."

"No," Robert said. "I don't think so either."

"She got quieter as soon as she realized it was us. It was almost like some monster got in and scared her."

"A monster in a dream," Robert said.

"I don't think it was a seizure. You know Dr. Pettibaker was here today and she said she 'likes' how Sheryl's doing."

"Good."

"Do you think Pettibaker's the reason? She put her through a lot of tests today."

"Pettibaker's very professional, and very soft-spoken."

"I know that, Robert. But Sheryl still knows she's being assessed, no matter how subtly it's done. Maybe Pettibaker thinks Sheryl's doing well, but the tests made her think she's not. You know she's never as good as she wants to be."

"Maybe. We'll probably never know."

"We will when she's well. She's going to tell us about all this stuff. Robert, you don't think—I know this may be dumb, but what if we had a real burglar and she saw him?"

"Don't be silly. The rest of us didn't see anybody."

Just then Kath came around the door.

"Honey," Suze said, "you should be in bed."

"Well, I was just wondering—"

"Wondering what, sweetie?"

"I wondered if Mommy saw the ghost."

"The ghost?" Figueroa felt chilly. "What ghost?"

"Last night. A ghost looked into my room."

"What did it look like?"

"It looked just like a regular man, except it was pale."

"Did it do anything?"

"No, it just stared at me real hard."

Annoyed, Robert said, "Kath, that's enough. We have real problems to deal with. We don't have time for foolish stuff."

"But it was real."

"A real ghost?" Robert said scornfully.

"Well—I really saw it."

"You were dreaming. Go back to bed."

Kath caught her lower lip in her teeth. Suze said, "Honey, whatever it was, we're here to protect you. Don't worry."

"Okay." Reluctantly, Kath went upstairs.

Robert said, "Suze, you have to back me up when one of the children is acting stupid."

"Look, I don't know what she saw, but Kath is a very reliable child. I can't just automatically 'back you up' until I know the facts."

"Well, you'd better."

"What? Why?"

"We're putting you and J J up here, you know."

"Putting us up? I pay rent."

"You pay rent for accommodation in this big house, with use of a big kitchen, clothes washer and dryer, two TVs, a whole floor to yourselves, basement, and a big backyard with play equipment. If you rented an apartment for the same money, you'd get a tiny bathroom, a kitchenette, and two tiny bedrooms if you were lucky."

"Robert, I do *all* the grocery shopping, *all* the cooking. What would you do if I weren't here? Send out for pizza seven nights a week? Which would cost more, too, by the way. Plus, I do *all* the laundry except a small amount that Maria does. And probably half of the Sheryl care. It would cost you a fortune to replace me."

"Maria could do the cooking."

"Not only can she *not* do the cooking, in the sense that she doesn't know how to cook more than one or two things, but she shouldn't. Maria needs to concentrate on her schoolwork."

"She's not doing that now. She spends all her time thinking about boys and clothes and makeup."

"Exactly. I have to keep after her just to get her to finish her homework. This is not the time to take up her energies working as 'little mother' to a family."

"Oh, I guess you know everything. If you're so overworked, why do you stay?"

"Sheryl." She said it simply and quietly.

He said, "Sheryl. Right." And there was something in his tone that told Suze a lot. Oh, no. God, no. *No, no, no.* Robert has a girlfriend. Hell, hell, hell, damn!

Holding her annoyance in, Suze said, "Whatever Kath thinks she saw, we'd better check the house."

"You're catering to her."

"There is nothing wrong with reassuring a child, let alone the fact that she won't even know we're doing it. She's gone to bed. Tell you what, Robert. You go in and sleep in the chair, and I'll check that the windows and doors are locked."

"Can't. I have a busy day tomorrow. I need my sleep. You go sit with her, and I'll check the windows and doors."

"Well, listen. I had a hell of a day today—oh, never mind. Go ahead. I'll stay with her."

FRIDAY

CHAPTER TWENTY-SIX

Friday, June 3

From "City Beat" by Charles Horgue

Sandra Jordan gets up each morning and gives her daughter Casey, eleven, a breakfast of peanut butter and jelly on whole wheat bread, Casey's favorite. Then Sandra walks Casey to school. During the morning, Sandra goes to the laundromat and washes her clothes and Casey's, leaving some in the dryers while she waits table at lunch at a local diner.

Casey plays basketball after school. Her mother picks her up there at four-thirty and they walk home together.

Casey would like to invite friends home after school to play, but she doesn't, and she very rarely goes to her friends' houses because she can't reciprocate. In fact, she's not supposed to tell anybody, including the school, where they live. Since Casey's father left, they get their mail at the home of a friend of Sandra's.

Casey and Sandra live in Sandra's car.

SERGEANT TOUHY WAS on a rampage. "I'm getting pretty damn sick of half of you getting pulled off to play detective. Most of you are only half alive anyhow!"

"Where's Bohannon?" Bennis asked, trying to deflect her. "And Moose Weatherspoon?"

Touhy ground her teeth. "You wouldn't believe," she said.

"Aw, c'mon. Tell us."

Touhy had started roll call a little early, which she often did when she was mad. It made everybody have a minute of worry that they were late. She thought starting their day with a little dose of fear was a good thing. Kept the troops in line.

Finally, she said, "They're being interviewed by the commander."

"Sarge, why would that be?" Bennis said.

"Might as well tell you, Norman," she said. "You'll only find out sooner or later."

"Sooner," Figueroa muttered under her breath. She didn't think Touhy heard. Touhy gave Figueroa a nasty look because she deduced approximately what Figueroa had said.

"Officers Bohannon and Weatherspoon were sitting on an apartment while the detectives swept up witnesses after a homicide last week. Unfortunately"—Sergeant Touhy paused for effect—"they decided to while away a weary hour watching porno on the guy's TV."

"Is that so bad?" the Flying None asked.

"It was pay per view. The lawyer for the family closed everything down last night—gas, electric, phone, charge cards, like that—to make sure there were no extra expenses. Everything buttoned up, up to the minute. My goodness, he says, the ME told us Mr. Sharpe had been dead for three days when he was found. How could he possibly have been watching TV on Thursday? *And run up all these charges?*"

Bennis said, "Oh, dear."

Touhy said, "Indeed. Then those two shit-for-brains said they just turned it on to check out whether the TV was working. Why they imagined they had to do that we don't know.

And, wonder of wonders, they just happened to hit the porno pay per view in passing."

"That's possible," Bennis said.

"For six and a half hours?"

"Oops."

"I want this to be a lesson to all of you. You don't drink the victim's Coca-Cola, or his Macallan, you don't eat his Frango mints, you don't nuke his leftover pizza, you don't watch his TV. You're really, really parsimonious about breathing his air."

Bennis started to say, "Parsimonious—" But he thought Touhy was in no mood for jokes about using big words. While he considered asking whether parsimonious were those vegetables you used in soup, Touhy's cell phone rang. She answered.

Then Figueroa could say, no, that's parsnips and he could say aren't parsnips like ministers, and she could say that's parsons and he could say aren't parsons like missing parsons—but then again maybe this was better kept for the Furlough—

"BENNIS!"

"Oh, yes, boss."

"I've been talking to you."

"Sorry, ma'am."

"You and Figueroa, up and out."

"Where to, sir, ma'am?"

"Don't wind me up, Bennis. Get out back. Under the El."

Bennis looked at Figueroa. Figueroa looked at Bennis. They both mouthed, "Oh, shit!"

It was all happening again. Mossbacher was standing near a squad car. There was a different evidence tech. Today's evidence tech was a middle-aged black woman who was circling the body, photographing absolutely everything, as far as Figueroa could tell. The body was half hidden between two Dumpsters, but appeared to be a young man dressed in the dirty clothing of the homeless. It was located a little bit farther south than Abigail Ward's body had been, leading Figueroa to wonder if the killer was moving farther from the CPD to be safer.

Figueroa didn't get close enough to be sure. Mossbacher grabbed them as they came down the alley. "Do what you need to, wrap this up, and come and see me."

"I'd like to give Dr. Percolin a heads-up," Bennis said. "Have him ready to do the autopsy."

"I have no problem with that. If he can do it right away, fine. But come see me right after. And *don't talk to the press.*"

"Yes, boss."

Mossbacher strode away. A first-watch uniform started to string barrier tape. An elderly man from the ME's office arrived to pronounce death. Figueroa pulled out her cell phone. "Bennis, want me to call Percolin?"

"Yeah. Sure."

While she spoke into the phone, Bennis located the first uniform on the scene.

Figueroa said, "Percolin will be there waiting. He's just finishing one up. By the way, he says Abigail Ward's blood alcohol was 'paralytic.' "

"That's consistent. I guess she wouldn't have fought being sprayed with the fire extinguisher. Figueroa, this is Officer Meeks. Meeks is gonna tell us who found the dead guy."

"Great."

"Secretary coming in to work saw the body."

Obviously, Meeks was not a chatty type. "Coming to work at the CPD?" Figueroa asked.

"Yup."

"What is her name?"

"His. Bill Marcantonio."

"Meeks, help us out here," Figueroa said. "Try to be a little more narrative about this. Start with who he's a secretary for."

"Chief of Patrol Archibald Davis."

Figueroa thought, *Oh-oh.* Meeks went on. "He sees the shoe, parks, goes back to look, sees the body, comes inna the building, and tells us."

"What made him see the body? It's pretty well hidden."

"Dunno. He said he thought it was funny a shoe bein' there and sticking up. Toe-up, like. I guess he figured a shoe oughta fall down."

"He's right, too. Then what?"

"Well, I was goin' off. I was practically out the door. I mean, I had one foot in the locker room, but Sarge says go see. Came out. Saw the body. Stabilized the crime scene. Didn't let nobody touch nothin'. Called the honchos. If I'd'a been just a little faster gettin' to the locker room, I'd'a been home by now."

"I feel your pain."

The tech, whose name was Barbara Carter, came over to Bennis and Figueroa. "What specific extra stuff do you want me to do?"

Hot damn! Figueroa thought. Somebody is finally treating us as if we know what we're doing.

Bennis said, "We need the trash around the body collected."

"Then the pavement underneath Dustbusted," Figueroa said.

"Sure thing. Anything else?"

Figueroa said, "Keep an eye open for Handi Wipes kinds of things." Bennis glanced at her face. She knew he could tell she didn't want to see the body, or any dead person in this place. She felt like a failure. What should they have done? Stayed here all night? If they had, would they have prevented a murder?

Bennis said, "Let's go take a look."

The evidence tech had not disturbed the body, and the doc had seen at once that there was no chance of resuscitation, so he had not moved it very much, either. Figueroa and Bennis approached the shoe. It was indeed vertical, and attached to a leg wearing very ratty blue denim.

The other leg was bent up and leaned against one of the Dumpsters. "It's a kid," Bennis said. "A teenage boy."

The doc said, "No, it's a girl."

"We got all the pictures we need?"

Figueroa thought Bennis, too, hesitated to take that last step. She said, "I think so."

"Well, let's do it."

The tech was already wearing gloves. She laid a body bag on the ground while Figueroa and Bennis pulled on gloves. Then they and the doc pushed their way between the Dumpsters.

Rigor mortis had begun in the jaw, neck, and most of the upper body, but the legs had some flexibility. They carried her like a log out onto the body bag. The young woman wore a flannel plaid shirt over a white T-shirt, but both were soiled and torn. A plastic carryall bag lay on the ground where her body had been.

Figueroa glanced at the bag, which was flattened. A glittery gold material stuck out of it a little way. Well, they'd see to that in a minute. But experience told her the bag contained the young woman's trick clothes.

Gently, they lowered the woman onto the open body bag, where her hair made a dark spill around her face. Figueroa at last looked directly at her.

"Oh, God," she said.

Bennis said, "What?"

"How long would you say her hair is?"

"Oh, man, oh, man. About sixteen inches."

CHAPTER TWENTY-SEVEN

"IF WE'D CAUGHT her last night, Bennis, we might have saved her life."

"I know. Don't beat it into the ground."

"I'm not forgiving myself."

"Listen, Figueroa, she ran away from us. It isn't as if we made her go hang out in the alley."

Not consoled, not even really listening to him, Suze said, "And there we were, running after her, probably scaring her, and all the time we were so convinced that we were chasing the killer!"

"If we'd scared her away from there, she would have been all right."

The body had arrived at the morgue separately from Bennis and Figueroa. The two cops caught Dr. Percolin as he entered the autopsy suite. Percolin saw them and lifted his arms out to the side, as if he felt helpless. Then with a sideways lean of his head, gestured them in to the autopsy suite.

"Did you know," he said, "that they're not authorizing an analysis of the face swabbings?"

"What!" Bennis said.

"They who?" Figueroa barked.

"The Chief ME." Percolin held up his hand as Figueroa drew breath. "Don't yell at me. This is a governmental agency with a budget—just like yours, and the President, and Streets and Sanitation. They review what gets requested, and they decide whether the chances of results are worth the costs. They say in this case the potential results don't justify the cost. And frankly, it *would* be expensive. What I wanted was an analysis of all the stuff on the faces of O'Dowd, Ward, and this one, so we could tell what kind of wipes the killer used."

Figueroa said, "Suppose we get a suspect and he has wipes in his pocket or car. What are we supposed to do?"

"Bag 'em I suppose. Meanwhile I'll keep the swabbings."

"I'm sorry, Dr. Percolin."

"Not your fault. Dammit! This is stupid! This is short-sighted!"

"Yes."

"It is also"—here his voice rose higher—"not what they hire us for! Damn! We're supposed to be highly trained and highly qualified investigators? Give me a break! Let us investigate! Hey! Is that too much to ask?"

Figueroa was stunned. It was a shock to see Santa Claus well and truly pissed. Bennis, however, agreed and was furious himself.

"Shit, shit, shit!" Bennis said.

Figueroa said, "He doesn't usually swear much."

Percolin said, "God! I feel exactly like he does. All I know at this point is that the faces have propylene glycol on them." Technical stuff seemed to quiet him. "And that's not too much help, because three-fourths of all the individually packaged Wet Wipes kinds of towelettes have propylene glycol in the liquid formula."

They turned toward the tables. There were several other autopsies going on, but Figueroa and Bennis saw their corpse at once.

She lay on the cold steel, covered to the chin with a sheet. The sheet was tented over her knee, where the leg remained bent as it had been on the pavement under the El. Her black hair spread out around her head and a wave of it fell over the table edge. She had been a beautiful young woman, even though she was much too thin, and her color was unhealthy.

"A poorly nourished female, possibly of part Asian ancestry," Percolin said into the mike. He gestured at her.

"Her face is clean," he said. "Like the others. Although, for that matter, her hands are pretty clean." He leaned over and smelled her face. "You too," he said to Bennis.

Bennis smelled the face. "Lemons." He smelled her hands. "Soap."

Percolin drew fluid from the eyeball for a check of ethanol and other drugs. Figueroa knew it was necessary. That didn't make her hate any less seeing the thick needle go into the eye.

The diener and Percolin turned the body over. Rigor was well established now, and the young woman turned like a log of wood, even the bent leg holding its position.

"Scratches," Percolin said, pointing to lateral red marks on the rib cage.

"He scratched her?" Bennis said. "That's different."

"Doubt it. She's been working as a hooker, I think. Probably got scratched a day or so ago. Look. They're dry," he said, rubbing one of the marks. It made a rough sound.

The diener and Bennis rolled the body onto its back again, while Percolin dictated into the recorder.

Now the woman lay facing up at the light, unblinking. A few strands of the long black hair had pasted themselves to her forehead and another swatch lay across her neck like a cut. Figueroa stared.

She said, "Why is there so much mucus in her nose and mouth?"

Dr. Percolin hesitated. "It's not mucus," he said finally.

"What is it, then?"

He picked up a hemostat and touched the material in her nose. It resisted, firm but rubbery. "Translucent, slightly whitish, rubbery," he said to the recorder. "I think it's silicone caulk."

Figueroa ran from the room.

After ten minutes she came back, sheepish. Bennis said nothing. Percolin only said, "Figueroa, look at this."

He had eased the plug of caulk out of the young woman's throat. Two smaller plugs, the ones from the nostrils, lay in a shallow stainless-steel tray.

"I do believe we've got something."

"What?" She came closer, fighting back her nausea.

"I think our man has made his first mistake."

Dr. Percolin pointed at what appeared to be a short brownish thread embedded in the silicone caulk. "It's a hair," he said. He already had a magnifying loupe focused at it.

"How do we know it's not from the victim?"

"It's a little lighter color than her hair, and it curves just a bit. See?"

Bennis had grabbed up a magnifier from the instrument counter along the wall. "I see."

"Fate has smiled on us at last. It's not a cut piece of hair, like might be left in your collar after a haircut. See the taper at the end? I'll bet our man shot the caulk into her nose first. And I'll bet the tip of the caulk tube was sticky after that, and it brushed his arm and pulled out one of his hairs. And that means—"

"I know what it means," Bennis said. "The root is still on the hair."

"And that means that when you catch the guy, we can match his DNA and pin it on him. You can get DNA from cut pieces of hair without the root, but this is *very* much better."

Figueroa said, "And *that* means all we have to do is catch him."

"Okay, Figueroa," Bennis said in the car. "Let's go feed you. You missed lunch the last two days. We'll have midmorning breakfast. Brunch. Whatever. It'll be good."

"I can't. I feel sick."

"You've been up late too many nights. You're worn out. I always say, if you can't sleep, at least eat."

"You're ashamed of me."

"I am *not*! You're one of the strongest people I know."

"But I couldn't stand it. I ran out on the autopsy."

"You came back. Anyway, Suze, if I'm gonna think less of you because you had a runaway attack of sympathy for the dead, what kind of person am I?"

CHAPTER TWENTY-EIGHT

Sheryl Birch lay in bed, exhausted from her morning set of exercises. She found her mind wandering as Alma Sturdley talked about the problem her sister was having with varicose veins.

"And her husband said, if you can believe it, that her legs looked just like a road map! Can you *believe* the insensitivity of the man? I said, you should have told him you would have been just as pleased if *he'd* been the one to carry four children to term."

Sheryl did not really hear her. She was tormenting herself about the ghost, or the nightmare, or the devil she had fought with the night before. Was it really possible that she had imagined that evil face? She did sometimes experience things that weren't real. She accepted that. Dr. Pettibaker had told her to expect it for some time to come.

There couldn't be a real intruder in the house. The house was full of people.

"The brain is coping with a lot of changes. You have to expect that the wires get crossed occasionally."

Wires crossed indeed. It was more like the world turned inside out.

No! She needed to tell somebody. Last night *couldn't* have been a dream or hallucination. She could still feel the pillow over her face. She had been sure she was going to die. If she could only speak a whole, clear sentence, she would have asked Suze to check the pillow. Surely she had bitten it or slobbered on it or maybe she had torn it when she struggled with the man.

Or—that would be true even if she had had a dream or hallucination, wouldn't it? Oh, God.

And anyway, she couldn't speak a whole clear sentence or even a whole clear three words.

Bennis was eager to put some space between the autopsy and Suze. The autopsy itself had confirmed what they knew already. The woman, Mary Lynne Lee, was twenty-three. She had grown up in Winnetka, which was unusual for homeless, but not entirely unknown for high-priced call girls. Which she wasn't. Clearly something bad had happened to Mary Lynne at home or as a young person. But what it was would take some finding out.

She showed signs of having used IV drugs, but not recently. Like the other three dead homeless, she liked alcohol. She lived on the street most of the time, to judge by her clothes. Even her trick bag clothing was cheap and worn. She had some health problems related to homelessness, like skin parasites, and some VD related to prostitution, but Bennis did not think any of these were going to lead to her killer.

Dr. Percolin didn't think so either.

Her stomach had been full of scotch.

"Enough to put her so far under that somebody could squirt silicone caulk in her mouth and nose?" Bennis had asked him.

"Absolutely. Enough to make her absolutely paralytic. Yes," Percolin told him. "But she wasn't forced to drink it. There's no sign at all of a physical attack, in the sense of anybody pouring stuff down her throat. Maybe—poor thing—she was just thrilled to get the very best stuff for a change. This guy has access to good scotch and good bourbon."

Bennis said, "Suze, I have today's schedule of store demos."

"Okay. As a matter of fact, I've got this extremely excellent idea about that," Figueroa said.

"Oh, that'll be a first."

"Bennis, you know all my ideas are good."

"Look, I don't want to be the Grinch. Let me say that you have occasionally had an idea that worked out very well. What's this one, anyhow?"

"Let me try it out and we'll see."

"That's hardly the scientific approach. You should tell me first, for purposes of external verification."

Figueroa and Bennis began at eleven-thirty to make the rounds of the large stores. Four were presenting demos, the first at eleven-thirty. Having informed the security chiefs on the way there about what they would be looking for, the setups, including radio communication, were very much better than they had been on Thursday. Figueroa had brought along a change of clothes and a pair of glasses on the theory that the pickpocket yesterday might have seen her. On the way over, she tugged her hair back into a fairly neat chignon and applied more makeup than she usually used. She began to have misgivings, though, the closer they got, and thought she needed an even better disguise.

She asked the security chief at their first stop, "Mr. Lermontov, can you give me a scarf or a cheap wig?"

"We don't sell cheap wigs," he said somewhat huffily. Then he relented and entered into the spirit of the thing. "Let's see what we can do."

He took Figueroa to the "better jewelry" counter, and consulted with the head buyer. "Something just a touch too flashy," he said.

After a moment's thought, the buyer gave Figueroa a pair of amethyst earrings. She studied herself in the mirror as she put them on. They weren't anything she'd ever wear, but she thought they looked very nice. Not too flashy at all. But then, what did she know?

Lermontov next escorted her to scarves. He himself pointed to the one he wanted—a head scarf, lavender to match the earrings, the fabric shot with fine fibers of silver. Suze fumbled around with it until the saleswoman tied it for her.

Bennis said, "I guess we shouldn't've missed that scarf-tying demonstration."

Today's demo was mascara. The representative of a cosmetics company, a thin, birdlike woman, stood on a little dais that raised her twelve inches above the sales floor. With her were two absolutely gorgeous women, wrapped in powder-blue smocks, seated on high silver stools. One woman was a pale blonde, with fair skin, ash-blond hair, and light eyes, which Figueroa had to agree would look brighter with a little makeup. The other was an equally beautiful black woman, with sleek cocoa skin, hair that was black but with reddish highlights, and dark eyes that were highlighted by long dark lashes. Figueroa couldn't imagine how mascara would improve woman number two.

"Now, we're going to take a Polaroid photo of my two lovely assistants before we begin, so that you can compare later," the thin woman said. "This is Margo, and this is Elaine. I'm going to start with Elaine."

Elaine was the blonde.

Figueroa watched the demo with what she hoped was fascinated attention to eye shadow and liner. The blonde grew brighter eyed—or as the thin woman put it, the eyes began to "pop." Figueroa considered this an unfortunate choice of words. She scanned the crowd from her position to the rear of the group. There was only one baby present. This one was sound asleep in a white and blue padded stroller that did not look like the foldable ones from the day before. Of course, you couldn't go by that. The pickpockets could have any number of strollers and costumes.

These demos were always short. Unfortunately, by the time Margo's eyes were done—and Figueroa admitted that they, too, looked more defined, even though the difference was less noticeable than in Elaine's case—nobody had shouted out that their wallet was missing. And Figueroa herself had noticed no suspicious moves by the woman with the baby or anybody else. The Polaroids had been passed around, amid exclamations of delight, and the crowd dispersed. Many of the women bought products, which was the point, of course.

Sighing, she met Lermontov at the elevators. "We'd better get over to Cadbury and Mason. They're doing perfume at noon."

Lermontov said, "Would you like to keep the earrings and scarf for the day?"

"You trust me with them?"

"Hey, you're the police."

When they got to Cadbury and Mason, Brandon Ely told them, "I don't really believe the pickpocket will come back. After all, she's been here twice that we know of. It's taking too much risk. She'd have to be terribly overconfident."

"And your point is?" Figueroa muttered.

Bennis said, "Yeah, she's right, Mr. Ely. That's why they get caught. They keep doing it."

Ely, who had shown signs of liking Figueroa before, chuckled understandingly.

Figueroa said, "She's gotten away with it every single time. You have to assume this whole sequence of events is making her overconfident."

Neither Figueroa nor Bennis thought the pickpocket had seen them yesterday. "But the woman and baby might have seen you, Bennis, when they were stopped and searched."

"I know that. I'm staying well in the background. I'm back in Swiss chocolates."

Cadbury and Mason's perfume counter was a thing of beauty. Backed with forty feet of mirrored panels six feet high laid out in a gentle curve, and fronted with thirty feet of beveled glass display counters, it sparkled in much the same way as a high-priced bar. In front of the mirrors were ranged hundreds of beautiful bottles on glass and gold shelves. Cut-glass bottles, blue glass bottles the intense shade of Noxema containers, ruby-red bottles, clear bottles shot with gold or silver filaments, tiny silver flasks, big balloon-shaped spray bottles for cologne, and all the brand names known in the world of fashion—Chanel, Armani, Estée Lauder, Clinique.

The demo woman was glossy too, wearing a gold lamé wraparound sarong.

"Today," the woman said, "we are going to consider only the herbal fragrances. These have become tremendously popular of late. As I'm sure you know, florals were terribly popular in the 1920s and 1930s. One can almost picture Theda Bara floating along on the scent of camellias. We all wore simple scents during the World War II years when women worked in defense plants. Then the fruitier scents came in. But of late the more natural herbals have made a big advance, especially among young people, who don't care for artifice—"

There were perhaps thirty people in the audience, Figueroa thought. Several of the women looked vaguely like some of yesterday's crowd. Three of them had children in strollers, one cuddled a tiny baby in a papoose carrier.

Without appearing to study the audience, she pushed in a little way and was able to keep in view the three women with strollers. This position made it impossible for her to see the fringes or back of the crowd without turning her head, and she just had to hope that her guess about babies was right.

She had a view of the left shoulder of one woman and the

back of her stroller, the back of another but not much of her stroller, and the right arm and most of the baby in the case of the third.

By using the edge of her vision, she could be aware of movement of these parts of these three women without moving her head or even cutting her eyes back and forth very much.

The baby on her left started to cry. The mother leaned forward and plucked a bottle out of a diaper bag. She handed it to the baby, slightly jostling the arm of a woman next to her. The woman to Figueroa's right jumped when her child threw his pacifier into the air. In so doing, she grabbed the sleeve of a woman ahead of her and said, "Oh, I'm sorry."

"No problem," the other woman said.

The woman directly in front of Figueroa plucked her baby out of its stroller. This meant Figueroa got her first look at the child, a little boy eight months old or so in a plaid baby suit, just at the moment that the baby kicked the woman in front of her. Figueroa had never before realized how much physical activity occurred in a group watching a demo.

Also at that moment, one of the older women in the front of the bunch decided that she didn't want to stay for the rest of the demonstration. She turned and pushed her way out, right past Figueroa. The older woman was wearing pointy-toed high-heeled shoes—the kind Figueroa believed had been developed by orthopedic surgeons to create more business—and as she neared Figueroa she turned her ankle, falling heavily against two people, the woman with the baby on Figueroa's left and a young girl standing nearby.

The older woman said, "Oh!"

The teenager said, "Are you all right?"

"Yes, I think so, dear," the older woman said. Her face had flushed with embarrassment. She patted the teenager and smiled as if she were fine, but as she moved away she limped heavily.

Figueroa had now seen so many "contacts" she didn't know who to watch. Two of the four babies present started crying. The demo came to an end. The group broke up like an expanding bubble, people moving off in all directions. Figueroa was utterly at a loss about whom to suspect. When a chubby little woman started to yell, "Where's my wallet?" Figueroa had nothing useful to say into her microphone.

She walked fast, but she hoped unobtrusively over to Bennis and Ely, who stood next to the elevators.

"Who was it?" Bennis asked.

"I have to go take care of that woman," Ely said, looking at Figueroa as if she weren't as much fun as he'd thought.

"Bennis, stay right here. Don't get any nearer; we don't want the pickpocket to see you. But watch me; watch where I go."

Suze strolled to the women's rest room and pushed her way inside. There was a young woman washing her hands at the sink. She had long brown hair, dangling earrings, and wore a red silky shirt. A large black purse was next to her feet. Figueroa could not specifically remember whether she had been at the demo. There was no one else in the place. Figueroa went to a sink, looked into her left eye, pulling the lids apart, blinked a few times, rinsed her face with water, and after drying her hands left the rest room.

She went immediately to a long rack of pastel summer jackets and hid behind them, watching the rest-room door. She was aware that Ely would be looking for her soon, but this was more urgent.

Several minutes went by. An older woman went into the rest room and came out two minutes later. Still the young woman remained inside. Then Figueroa saw the rest-room door open and somebody peer out.

She waited.

A teenage boy emerged, carrying a gym bag with a baseball

mitt hung over the strap. He wore a ponytail, a Cubs T-shirt, and Levi's.

Figueroa pounced on him and said, "Gotcha!"

"The bag turned inside out," Brandon Ely said. "The earrings came off, of course. The hair became a boy's ponytail. The makeup came off in the bathroom sink. And Levi's are unisex, of course. But the 'boy' was really a young woman."

"You carry a baseball mitt," Bennis said, "you look like a boy."

"Who would not have been watching a perfume demo," Figueroa said.

"She handed the stroller and the baby to a confederate. She kept the stolen wallet because the person with the stroller might be searched, and she went to the bathroom, figuring that if anybody got followed it would be the woman with the baby."

"Who was dressed similarly," Bennis said. "What I'm sorry about is that the confederate got away."

"Well, we can follow up on this one's associates. Now that we know where she lives, we can find her relatives. Somebody will talk."

"What I don't get," Ely said, "is how you knew she'd be in the *women's* rest room."

"She had to watch the demos as a female, or she'd really look out of place. So at some point she had to change to a boy. She had to do it right after the demo ended; she couldn't control that. So for all she knew, she'd be going into a rest room that had other people in it. So it couldn't be the men's. They'd freak. Once she changed clothes, she could wait around inside the women's rest room until it was empty. If somebody came in she could duck into a stall. She could peek out and make sure nobody was especially watching. By the time she got outside, a few feet away from the door, nobody would notice that a boy had come out of the ladies' room."

When Figueroa went back to the other store to return the scarf and earrings, she found she had lost one of the earrings in the brief scuffle.

Lermontov said, “Forget about it. It’s a small price to pay. Congratulations.”

CHAPTER TWENTY-NINE

"I AM SO psyched," Figueroa said.

"Well, it was good work," Bennis said. "Just the same, I think it's unseemly to crow about it quite so much."

"When you gotta crow you gotta crow."

Even Sergeant Touhy had been pleased when they walked in with their pickpocket. Touhy showed this by not snarling. However, she said, "I have a couple of new jobs to give you."

Bennis said, "We have to canvass on the murder, Sarge."

"All right. I'm giving you the benefit of the doubt. For now."

As they started to turn away, she added, closing one eye and looking sideways at them, "Oh, gee. I guess I must've just forgotten. Go see Mossbacher."

"Figueroa. Bennis. Sit down."

Mossbacher was more subdued than usual. He can't possibly doubt that we have a serial killer now, Figueroa thought. And then she had a sudden throb of apprehension. If he thought it was an important case, he'd put somebody else on it.

He said, "I want to know what you've got so far."

Figueroa looked to Bennis. He flicked a glance back at her, but courageously started to explain.

"A series, boss. The cause of death in all four cases has been a variation of smothering—choking, smothering with a bunch of fabric, cutting off the woman's oxygen with a gas fire extinguisher, and now stopping the mouth and nose with silicone caulk. There's a pattern there."

"Not much of one."

"And there's a pattern in the selection of the victims. All homeless. All poorly or raggedly dressed. All alcoholics."

"And all different ages and genders and races," Mossbacher said.

"And all with their faces washed," Bennis said.

"All of them?"

"Including the last one. Mary Lynne Lee."

Mossbacher steepled his fingers in a gesture Figueroa thought was rehearsed rather than genuine. Nevertheless he looked genuinely annoyed. "And so?"

"A serial killer isn't going to stop. We need to get proactive. We need to put out decoys. We need to let the community know he's out there. We particularly have to get word out to the homeless to stay away. They should be warned."

"No. The press would get wind of it."

"Use the press. The press can warn them. That's one way the press is actually useful. And warn anybody else in the area. Maybe the press doesn't care so much about the homeless, but we can't be sure that he won't turn to drunken party-goers next."

"No can do, Bennis. Won't make Chicago look like fun city. We're right at the beginning of the tourist season. We got the Air and Water Show coming up, then the Taste of Chicago. The Fourth of July celebration. One thing right after another. They may be homeless, but murder still isn't good advertising. We're gonna handle this quietly."

"But he's hitting fast now—"

"And what's more, you don't know who Mary Lynne Lee is."

"We've got an address. We want to talk with her relatives next."

"I've already sent somebody to do that."

Bennis said, "What?"

Figueroa was shocked. Why wouldn't he let them do the investigating? Meanwhile Bennis, who had only paused half a second, was asking, "Who is she, then?"

"Well, matter of fact, as herself she isn't anybody. But her parents and grandparents are. They're doctors and engineers and corporation CEOs, and the whole lot of them live in Winnetka."

"Oh."

"Oh is right. They're hopping mad already. We do *not* need them to know that she wandered into a serial killer situation. One that we haven't been able to solve."

Figueroa couldn't stand it any longer. "Boss, if we got some support, we *might* solve it now. Dr. Percolin can't do the tests he wants. The stomach contents. The face swabbings. The trace evidence around the bodies wasn't—that is, you didn't let us—I mean, we only got about a tenth of it analyzed."

"It will be now, Figueroa."

"Thank you, sir. That'll help."

"Well, it may help, Figueroa, but it won't help *you*."

"Sir?"

"By tomorrow, barring any E. coli relapses, I should be able to get a couple of detectives on the case. Real detectives, I mean."

Bennis said, "Sir, we should have started earlier. A tox screen is going to take another two weeks."

Figueroa said, "Boss, we've put in a lot of time on the case. We've got leads."

"Then I suggest you follow them up. You've got twenty-four hours. Surprise me."

As they went out the door, he called after them, "And make sure you've written up all your notes so your replacements can get right up to speed."

When they were far enough away not to be heard, Figueroa

said, "Is that his technique? Waits until you're practically out the door and hits you with another punch?"

"Still think you want to be a detective?"

At three-thirty, carrying brown bags filled with pastrami and mustard on onion rolls, Figueroa and Bennis arrived at the Furlough Bar.

"Man!" Figueroa said. "I'm dead on my feet."

"Don't fold yet," Bennis said.

Mort, never chatty, said, "Beer?"

"One. We gotta go back out soon."

Mort pulled the beers and then leaned back against the dishwasher door and stared at the ceiling. Corky gave them a big smile, though. "How's the murder investigation going, guys?"

Bennis said, "Slow."

Kim Duk O'Hara came in, with Mileski and the Flying None right behind him.

"Man!" Kim Duk said, "Am I ever tired of prostitutes!"

Everybody laughed. "Well, I mean, I've interviewed twenty working ladies today, and all they do is make fun of me."

Everybody said, "Aw!"

Mileski said, "Wish they'd make fun with me."

"You can laugh, but you'd think when one of their own gets killed they'd try to help."

Mileski said, "Yeah. I really would have thought so."

"Hadn't seen anything, hadn't heard anything."

"Did you say please?" Sandi the Flying None asked.

Mileski said, "I solved both of my cases."

Sandi said, "Both of *our* cases. One of 'em, we get sent to a call of a woman screaming and find her husband on the floor dead, and she's standing over him with a knife. We say, 'Who stabbed him?' She says, 'I did.' This detective stuff isn't so hard. Corky, can you make a maiden's blush cocktail?"

"Do *not* make any jokes," Figueroa said.

Mileski said to Figueroa, "I hear you're working with ASA Malley."

Figueroa said, "And?"

"He used to be in private practice. Had a guy once come to him to defend him against a sexual harassment thing. Making lewd remarks about a woman in his office. So they go to court. Daley Center, civil case, see? On the way in, they're following this really great looking babe and Malley says, 'Was she like that? Just look at the ass on that woman!' The woman turns the corner, he says, 'And great hooters.' He says, 'Harassment or no harassment, you just gotta burst out with comments sometimes.' "

"And?"

"And the woman turned out to be the judge."

Figueroa said, "You know, that sounds like Malley."

Corky said, "Bennis and Figueroa were just going to tell us how their case is going."

"Oh, man," Bennis said. "We got four homeless people dead. And nobody sees anything. Most recent one last night."

Figueroa said, "We canvassed the area on the first three cases—"

"You need to canvass all over again," Mileski said firmly. "I mean, the fact that hardly anybody saw anything the first three times doesn't mean they didn't see anybody this time."

"I know. Easy for you to say, though."

"And you know what else you have to do? Interview the people who found the bodies. In a lot of cases, the person who reports a murder is the killer."

"They were all different people."

"Right," Bennis said. "And they were all cops. Like, Harry Pressfield, who's a uniform, found Abby Ward's body, for instance."

Figueroa said, "Except the secretary who found Mary Lynne Lee."

"Oh, all right."

Mileski said, "Listen, I take it back. I sure don't think a cop is going around killing people."

Challenging that, Bennis said, "Dr. Ho, our friendly serial killer expert, says killers often kill where they're comfortable. Cops are comfortable near the CPD. Serial killers are control freaks. Cops are often control freaks. Well, don't look at me that way! You never met a cop who was a control freak?"

"Oh, all right! Maybe."

"This kind of killer is a control freak for sure. Immobilizes the victims and kills them. The ultimate control. People become cops to clean up the city. Well, this guy is cleaning out the bums."

And cleaning their faces, Figueroa thought, but she didn't mention it aloud. Best keep something in reserve. Another thing about cops—cops were the world's worst gossips.

"I hate the idea of a killer cop," Mileski said.

"Well, you were right the first time," Bennis said. "The first thing we have to do is find out where the cops who found the bodies were at the times of the murders."

"*And* canvass the neighborhood," Figueroa said, getting off the bar stool. "Again."

"I'm coming." Bennis followed her over to the door. "All right. Let's get efficient here, Suze. Let's split up. I'll take one and you take one. Which do you want?"

"I'd a hell of a lot rather run around to all those apartments and all the CPD offices than ask some cops where they were at the time of the murder."

"Fine. Meet you back at the district at—when?"

"Five? Maria is making dinner tonight, so I don't have to be home until sixish."

CHAPTER THIRTY

Henry Lumpkin smiled almost all the time. A black man of fifty-nine, he had the face for smiling, a round face like a moon, with jolly plump cheeks. He had smiled pretty much all the way from St. Louis, up Interstate 55, through Springfield, the capital of Illinois, through Bloomington-Normal. Up what used to be famous old Route 66. And they were now closing in on Chicago.

The guy in the big rig who had picked him up thought Henry was the greatest hitchhiker he'd ever had. Hitchhikers all helped pass the time, but some were dangerous, which was why Jon Smigla kept a sawed-off baseball bat on the floor to the left of the driver's seat.

Most of the hitchhikers had their problems. And he had figured out what Henry's was when he wanted to stop for beer or wine in Springfield. Smigla didn't care if Lumpkin drank, but he had to do it while they were stopped. There were a zillion Illinois State Police around, plus truck weighing stations, and he wasn't going to have open alcohol in the cab.

So while Smigla fueled up and got himself a burger and fries in Springfield, Lumpkin knocked back a couple of beers. Later, when Smigla stopped for coffee, Lumpkin got another couple of beers.

Lumpkin was running out of money, though. He knew that by the time they got to Chicago, he was going to have to start panhandling, and he hated that.

"Why are you going to Chicago?" Smigla asked.

"My hometown, Chicago. Lost my job downstate. I useta drive a street-sweeper. I loved that job. You're out at night when the streets are practically empty. I useta pull circles up and down the streets. Like waltzing on a highway."

He lost the job drinking, and his wife had died a few years back. He'd lived twenty-five years in St. Louis, because it was Adelaide's hometown, but somehow now he just wanted to go back to Chicago.

Lumpkin was just as pleased with Smigla as a fellow traveler as Smigla was with him. Smigla had that kind of wiry curly hair that looked like he'd stuck his finger in a light socket. And the fact that it was red made it look even more so.

When they came up into the greater Chicago area, and Interstate 55 became the Stevenson Expressway, Smigla said, "I hate to see you go, Henry."

"Me too."

Smigla was well aware that Lumpkin had done nothing but drink all day. "You gonna be all right?"

"Absolutely."

"Well. Where can I drop you?"

"Don't want to put you out."

"I'm going right downtown. Going to Congress Street."

"That's good for me. Can you let me off at Congress and State?"

At five o'clock Figueroa walked into the First District canteen and found Bennis drinking coffee. "Get anything?" she said.

"Most of them can prove where they were most of the time but not the whole time from eleven P.M. to three A.M. all four nights. Small wonder. I mean, even when you're working, there's usually a half hour here or there when nobody sees you."

"I suppose if a guy is alibied for one of the killings, he's clear."

"If so, we got two in the clear and two not. You get anything?"

"One of the women's lockup guards saw somebody ducking around when she got off work at midnight. Couldn't describe him. Otherwise nothing. Except this. Ta-da."

She poured a bag full of small boxes onto the table.

"Walgreen's Antibacterial Moist Wipes?"

"Wet Ones Lunchkins Antibacterial Wipes."

"Baby Wipes."

"Wet Ones Moist Towelettes with Aloe."

"Yum."

Figueroa took out a second bag and piled another four brands of wipes on the table in the middle of the canteen. Then she opened her laptop to make notes.

"Benzalkonium chloride."

"How come you can pronounce that, Bennis?"

"I thought you always said I knew everything."

"Of course. Go on."

"Water, SD alcohol, PEG 75, lanolin, fragrance, propylparaben."

"Sounds delicious. Next?"

"This one is water, SD alcohol, propylene glycol, aloe vera gel, sodium nonoxynol, fragrance, lanolin, citric acid."

"Next."

"Water, propylene glycol, aloe gel, PEG 75 lanolin, polysorbate 20, methylparaben, fragrance, citric acid."

"Next."

"Water, propylene glycol, lanolin, aloe gel—"

"That's the same one. You just did that."

"No. Different order."

"Well, how are the analysts supposed to tell them apart?"

"Some of these have more lanolin, and some have more antibacterial stuff—"

"Sure. But on the skin of a dead person who's been lying outdoors all night, aren't they all going to evaporate?"

"Look, I don't know. What am I? A chemist? Let's do what we planned. Let's smell them."

"The Lunchkins won't work. They're not lemon. They're berry."

"Don't prejudge. You close your eyes. I'll hand you the wipes." Bennis closed his eyes and Figueroa opened the first mini-pack.

"Fruit of some kind," Bennis said. "But not lemon."

"Right. Lunchkins watermelon scent."

Two of the wipes smelled like a hospital, quite antiseptic. One hardly smelled like anything. The CVP Baby Wipes smelled like baby powder. Figueroa held it to her nose for a few seconds, letting it take her back to J J's infancy in the way only scents could do.

Osco Baby Wipes also smelled like baby powder.

"Funny," Bennis said. "I thought more of them would smell like lemon."

"Me too. I wonder why I thought so, now."

"Beats me."

They had gone through seven of the eight packs when Bennis said, "Lemon!"

Figueroa read from the box. "Best-Wipes."

"Where'd you get them?"

"Drugstore on State Street. They're sold in pocket-size carry-packs and large 'economy-size' boxes."

"Okay. They smell like lemon. But are they the *only* ones that smell like lemon?"

"Who knows? They're the only ones of these that do. We do what we can, right?"

"Also, does the lemon scent evaporate?"

"Here, Bennis. You rub one on your arm or face and I'll rub one on me. We'll see in the morning."

"It'll come off when I shower."

"Bennis, I don't want to shock you, but this one day, forget about your shower."

CHAPTER THIRTY-ONE

ROBERT, OF COURSE, was not at home. He was working at the new store, and when it closed at nine would take the manager of the new store to dinner with the more experienced ones from the older stores.

J J met Suze at the back door, very excited because his best friend Doug—who used to be called Dougie until this year—wanted him to sleep over. Suze nevertheless called Doug's mother, made sure it was all right, and then said yes. She felt guilty that Maria was not going to be able to go out too.

Maria had cooked. She made steak, baked potatoes, and green salad, and was very, very proud of herself.

Figueroa said, "This is such a great dinner, I feel guilty about what I have to tell you."

"What is it?"

"I know you had a sleepover planned. But I've absolutely got to go back out. And we need you to stay home and take care of things."

Maria was silent. Figueroa quailed inwardly. She knew the thoughts going through Maria's mind. Guilt that she wanted to go out while her mother was half paralyzed. Resentment that her life was so changed. Unwillingness to hurt her mother's feelings by saying how upset she was.

Kath and even little J J knew how disappointed Maria was. You could tell because they kept dead silent. So did Sheryl, which made Suze sadder still. Sheryl was perfectly aware that if she had been well *she* could take care of Kath, and Maria could go out.

Finally, Maria said, "Do you *have* to go? I mean, they have a whole police department. I mean, thousands of cops, right?"

"Yes, but just Bennis and I have this case. And I told you about the detectives getting sick."

"I know. I know."

"I don't want to claim it's life or death exactly, but we really are trying to prevent another murder."

She heard Sheryl gasp. Sheryl had never been quite at ease with Suze's job.

"Your dad won't be home before eleven at the earliest. And I might have to be out a lot later than that." She didn't say, didn't have to say, that Kath was just too young to leave alone with a paralyzed woman. Too much could go wrong—fire, break-ins, who knew?

"I'll make it up to you, Maria. In fact, my first day off, which now that I think of it is day after tomorrow, I'll take you to the mall and get you—let's see—I promise two sweaters." To Sheryl, she said, "Some people call this bribery. I prefer to go along with the psych students and call it positive reinforcement."

Maria said, "Thanks, Aunt Suze."

"So I'd better get going. J J, get your overnight stuff and I'll drop you at Doug's. Maria and Kath, take charge. And Sheryl, keep on trucking."

Sheryl smiled with the right side of her face.

The man on the stairs smiled with his entire face.

On the way in, Figueroa caught the news on her car radio. Mary Lynne Lee's mother said to a reporter, "The police knew there was a killer loose. They knew it and they didn't do anything about it."

An interviewer said, "Do you feel they neglected these cases because they involved the homeless?" Figueroa cringed. The guy was hoping the mother would say something nastier than he himself would be allowed to.

"My daughter wasn't homeless! She was just going through a difficult, but very human, period of transition."

Cutting off the sound bite of Mary Lynne's mother, the radio voice said, "The Chicago Police Department, reacting to the recent illness of many officers in the Detective Division, appears to have assigned two inexperienced patrol officers to investigate this series of killings of the homeless. Ironically, all these murders occurred a stone's throw from the central office building of the police department itself. Whether experienced detectives could have brought this series of murders to a close earlier will never be known. Whether the murders were not given priority because of the nature of the victims is a question the City Council plans to take up in days to come. This is Dave Hodges reporting from the Chicago Police Department at Eleventh and State. Back to you, Art."

Figueroa ground her teeth and kept driving.

CHAPTER THIRTY-TWO

THE HOUSE WAS like those boxes of chocolates with all the different centers. There was a woman or girl in every room, practically, and all different. He might just sample that one and sample this one. Like nougat, and caramel and raspberry cream. Mmm, his favorites—soft centers.

Valentine giggled. What it came right down to, they were all soft centers, weren't they?

Henry Lumpkin was having a wonderful time. He would have smiled continuously, except that he knew if you walked around panhandling and smiling broadly, sooner or later somebody would think you were a psycho and call the cops. So he held out his hat and only smiled broadly when a person dropped coins into it. Other people, seeing this, would drop in coins too. Henry was not really aware that it was the sweetness of his smile to the earlier donor that made the next several people give him coins.

There were occasionally crabby people, as there were anyplace, but in general he thought Chicago was wonderful.

The main reason he wanted to smile, though, was that he recognized so much of it. It was Chicago, like he remembered it all these years. He stood on the steps to the Art Institute for a while, getting several dollars in coins and just remembering, remembering those music school buildings across the street, whatever they were called, and good times with his family at festivals in Grant Park.

True, there were huge new office buildings and glitzy architecture that was unfamiliar, but that only made him proud. He walked west on Congress as evening came on, figuring the tourists near the Art Institute would taper off.

Since Smigla dropped him on State Street, he had made a full circle north along Michigan Avenue and south on LaSalle and now he was back on State, with night coming on, looking for a liquor store or a bar. He had a whole *lot* of coins now, and he was running through his head what he could buy.

On Wabash in a lower rent area, he sighted a package store and went in. He expected to be treated with some rudeness, because he was poorly dressed, but in fact the clerk, who looked Greek to Henry's experienced eye, was very nice. He let Henry put his pocketful of coins out on the counter, and they discovered Henry could afford to buy two bottles of cheap red wine. "Thank you," the clerk said when Henry paid.

"And thank *you*," Henry said.

"How about a package of cheese crackers? On the house."

"Sure. Thanks." The guy was trying to make him eat, which made Henry feel he might not look so healthy, but nice was nice.

Henry was not naive. He realized that a store like this made their money from people like him. But some such places were courteous and some weren't. Some would make their money from you and all but kick you out the door afterward.

Henry wandered on to State Street to sit somewhere, drink, and watch the El trains go by.

Bennis and Figueroa met in the CPD parking lot and stared at the alley. The sun was setting somewhere over The Land Beyond O'Hare, and the sky was purple.

"You know, I really thought I'd see some patrols out here," Bennis said.

"There's one." A squad car drove slowly down the alley

under the El, carefully avoiding potholes. When it got to the south end, beyond the parking lot, it turned east and headed toward Michigan Avenue.

"Oh, great," Bennis said. "That's *it*? They need plainclothes guys hiding in the alley, dressed like the homeless. Any killer with two neurons between his ears can hide while a squad car goes by."

"I was afraid of this."

"And even if they scare the guy away for a few nights, how does that help?"

Suze said, "Well, let's go see if they have some decoys in the alley."

But even though they walked the alley from Roosevelt Road all the way north to Balbo, they didn't see any cops. There was one old black guy who might have been a disguised cop, trying to look like a homeless man. But the instant he saw them he got up and moved away.

"Hey, don't stay here, sir!" Figueroa yelled. "It's not safe for transient people here."

"He's gonna think you just wanted to move him along because cops always move homeless people along."

"Right now I don't care what he thinks about the reason. I don't want another murder."

"Problem is, he'll probably just come back."

It was only eight-fifteen P.M., too early for the killer to show, so they went back to the Furlough to think.

The Furlough Bar was deserted. Corky watched Figueroa and Bennis come in, looking troubled.

He said, "Hey, Bennis, Figueroa. Did you hear three of the sick detectives, three of the ones that were on dialysis, are planning to retire?"

"Why?"

"Well, it's not because they're scared of cop banquets."

This was not so funny and neither Figueroa nor Bennis laughed. Corky went on. "They've got permanent kidney damage. They go to dialysis three times a week."

"That's awful!" Figueroa said. "Last week they were healthy, active people and now they're permanently handicapped?"

"Well, at least it's a job-related disability. Full pension."

When Corky wiped and swabbed his way down to the end of the bar, Figueroa said, "Okay. Focus, Bennis. Our killer is somebody who lives or works in this area."

"Or used to live or work here."

"Or played around here as a child?"

"Like that case of Dr. Ho's? I doubt if kids have played around here in decades. There hasn't been any real residential housing here in years, except maybe that building behind the CPD. And those kids don't play out on these streets. It's too dangerous. And if it was somebody who played here forty years ago, they'd be in the wrong age group for the profile."

"Right. So—somebody who lives or works here, or used to, probably not too long ago."

Corky said, "I'm gonna go out and have a smoke."

Mort said, "Don't take too long."

"Oh, right. Somebody's gotta handle all the rush orders."

Mort growled.

Figueroa said to Corky, "I never knew you smoked."

"Well, how would you? With the lifestyle police out telling everybody they're gonna die from secondhand smoke. I mean, can I run my life or not, baby, right?"

"Right. It's a problem."

They watched him leave. Bennis thought about it a couple of minutes.

"Hey, Mort. Is there a law about not smoking in bars?"

"Don't think so. One more regulation and I'm going postal."

Figueroa said, "Bennis, you ever heard about Corky smoking?"

"Nope. But who knows? Everybody's got stresses. That's when those bad old habits return."

Corky crossed the street and angled toward the CPD. One didn't want to be too casual, take too many risks, but sometimes the excitement just started to build. He decided to make a turn through the parking lot, holding the lighted cigarette that he didn't really need or want.

The cars all sat there like dead cows, or as he thought about it, like dead hippos. The whole world was like that, mostly dead. Dead to the world, how funny.

It was only eight-thirty, so he was just scoping out the situation. See which members of the lame civilian community were in the area. What members of the even lamer cop community were trying to play detective.

He stood around, pretending to smoke his cigarette, which validated his presence to anybody. For a few seconds, he reflected on how the cigarette police had made all kinds of hanging around on street corners and in alcoves and so on perfectly explainable. Nonsmokers saw your discomfort with glee. You never needed an excuse for standing in some otherwise weird place smoking a cigarette.

You were a cigarette pariah! A nicotine outlaw. A fume felon. A toxic toker. You could go anywhere outdoors and no questions asked.

Cigarette in hand, he strolled through the parking lot and into the alley under the El. He headed north, behind the CPD building itself. Just past the Annex, he took another puff and leaned one shoulder on the wall. About a hundred yards away, down in the construction area, an old black bum was sitting on the ground, his back resting comfortably against the big rubber tire of a dump truck.

Corky watched as the old guy unstoppered a wine bottle, put it to his lips, and turned it bottom up. Corky could almost see the man's throat work as he drank. He frowned at the ugly sight.

CHAPTER THIRTY-THREE

AT EIGHT-THIRTY KATH and Maria decided they would give their mother a new hairstyle. It was necessary, of course, to get her agreement, and they marched into her room together. Alma Sturdley had given Sheryl a shampoo today, along with her bath, so they were being quite honest when Maria said, "Gee Mom, your hair is so nice and shiny."

"And fluffy," Kath said.

"And so out-of-date," said Maria.

"Yeah, I mean, it's so *twentieth century*!"

They watched for her reaction. They could not always tell whether Sheryl was trying to convey yes or no, or whether she was pleased or not pleased by something. Life would be much easier if they could. But now she smiled, just on the right side of her face, but nevertheless it was a wide, definite smile.

"So we thought it was time for a change," Kath said, holding up the scissors. Part of Sheryl's hair had been shaved off at the hospital after the accident and the brain injury. The rest had been cut short. It was now uneven lengths.

Maria had brought a big sheet. They transferred Sheryl to the upright chair, a movement that she could mostly do on her own as long as they watched so she wouldn't fall. Then they spread the sheet to catch hair clippings and Maria went to work, with directions and giggles from Kath.

Wasn't that cute, Valentine thought, from his position on the stairs. It would keep them busy a little while, too, which was good. He went up to the attic floor and assembled his kit, which included duct tape, a change of shirt, a pillowcase, scissors, a screwdriver, and some other odds and ends.

Then he went down to the third floor and let himself into the cop's room. On the whole, he was glad the little boy they called J J was not going to be home tonight. He didn't like little boys—nasty, loud, dirty creatures. He didn't want to have to deal with one.

He took the picture of Mono Lake at sunrise down from the wall and pulled the key off the backing. Then, just to be on the safe side, he replaced the picture on the wall and made sure it was straight.

The handgun was on the closet shelf in its special place. The key fitted, as he had known it would. He unlocked the trigger guard, put the earmuff-shaped pieces in the drawer, made sure the gun was loaded, opened the window, and just for amusement, threw the key out into the yard. Ultimately, maybe somebody would blame the cop bitch for having an unsecured handgun in the house.

CHAPTER THIRTY-FOUR

CORKY PITCHED HIS cigarette stub in the gutter and returned to the Furlough. Mort stood at the bar with his arms folded, studiously ignoring a gaggle of unwashed beer glasses on the drainboard.

"Oh, come on!" Corky said. He opened the dishwasher and loaded them into it. As he slammed the dishwasher closed, the door of the Furlough opened. An elderly black man entered. Figueroa thought he looked like the man she and Bennis had tried to move along.

"Can I buy a bottle of wine here?" he asked. He wasn't drunk exactly, but walking very, very carefully.

Mort said, "No!"

Corky said, "Sorry, but we don't have a package store license."

Henry Lumpkin stood trying not to sway. He said, "Uh—do you know where the nearest—?"

Mort said, "Get outta here."

"Wait, wait." Figueroa got to her feet and approached the man. She drew him toward the door. He was such a sweet-looking man, with such a lovely smile; she could not bear the thought of seeing him on a steel table in the autopsy suite tomorrow morning. Could she arrest him to save his life? There was nothing to arrest him for. "Look, let me take you outside." She walked him out to the curb. "If you head up that way"—she pointed north—"there's a package store up at Congress. But please, sir, don't come back here."

"Why's that, officer?"

"There's a killer around here at night. Really. I'm serious. Please. Don't come back."

He smiled at her.

She saw him mosey north, calling, "Thank you, officer," but she also saw him shrug a little when he thought she was no longer watching. He didn't believe her.

Sitting at the bar, Bennis dropped his head in his hands. He'd drunk just one beer, so Figueroa knew he wasn't overcome by hops and alcohol. In fact, he looked like she felt. It was just as well there weren't any other customers in the place.

"We gotta do something," she said.

"No kidding. What?"

"Well, sitting here is just wasting time. We could go back and look around the alley. We could hide in the alley for that matter."

"I think we should. But it's nine o'clock. We've got over two hours before there's any point."

"That's true. Where'll we hide?"

Bennis said, "What about me pretending to be a homeless guy? I got some truly beat-up clothes in the car."

"And if I fill you up with beer it won't even be an act."

"Pour it over me instead. I need my wits about me."

Corky sauntered over, polishing a glass. "You gonna get up a disguise?"

"Lordy, I don't know," Bennis said, wondering why the guy was so interested. Bored, most likely. "Maybe. Maybe it's the best I can think of."

Mort opened the flap in the bar and went out, letting it fall with a slam as he did. The falling flap made a terrific crash, but nobody jumped. They were used to it.

"What's his problem?" Figueroa asked.

Mort went on his way to the men's rest room.

Corky said, "Nothing, probably. He's always like that."

Figueroa and Bennis sat without speaking for a minute or so and Corky stepped over to the rack of glasses to put some away.

"At this rate," Figueroa said, "I might just as well be home."

"No. Can't do that," Bennis said. "We're going to be replaced tomorrow. We'll slip out there and slide out of sight and wait and we'll catch him."

"Darn right."

"You know, when we were canvassing the CPD, we also should have questioned Mileski and the Flying None and Kim Duk and all the guys."

Figueroa said, "Why?"

" 'Cause they're right here after work every day. They might have seen something."

"No, they leave before five, most of them. Latest by six. Hey, you're not suggesting that one of them is the—our—no, you're not. Right?"

"I'm not. Right."

Mort came back, slamming the flap again. "You guys gonna nurse one beer all night?"

Bennis said, "Yup."

Figueroa said, "Yup."

Corky said, "That's perfectly all right."

"Be right back," Figueroa said. She went to the women's rest room, way down the hall from the men's. It was less convenient, and although she had never been in the men's room, she heard their room was bigger.

She figured a bathroom break right now would be a good idea because she and Norm were going to go back out and spend several hours hiding in the alley. It would also be a good idea to call home. She had told them she'd be back by midnight, which was stupid of her. She should have realized it could take longer.

Yeah, take longer and maybe achieve nothing, she thought.

Still, with Maria in charge and Kath as backup, and Robert getting home by twelve, there shouldn't be a problem.

She'd call anyhow.

She washed her hands, dried them on one of the brown paper towels from the dispenser, and grabbed one of the prepackaged towelettes that had appeared in a dispenser in the washroom a year or so ago.

She gave her face a good, brisk wiping off. Nice lemon fragrance.

Lemon fragrance? Oh, my God!

Figueroa came up behind Bennis at the bar. "Mort, we both could use one more beer, but I'm going to take it to a table. Okay, Norm?"

"You all right?" Bennis said. "You don't look well."

"Yeah, everything all right?" Corky said.

"So-so. That bar stool is getting to my back."

Bennis took both beers and followed Figueroa to a table, one of only four in the place, where she sat stiffly down, her back to the bar. This pretty much forced him to face the bar.

"Sheesh! What's the trouble? You need a doctor?" he said. He knew she never made a fuss unless there was a real problem.

"Look right at me and no place else. Right into my eyes."

"Suze, you're all funny. It's all white around your lips and you're trembling."

"Forget about how I look, Bennis!" she hissed. "Just listen. We're looking for somebody used to being around here. Comfortable with cops. Somebody glib. Somebody who's frequently changed jobs. Somebody superficial. Somebody who is free after midnight."

"Suze, shit. You're giving me chills. All right, I hear you. But Mort doesn't fit the profile. He's a slob and he's charmless."

"Not Mort. Corky!"

"What—"

"Don't look up! *Look at me, not him!*"

Bennis sat thinking, staring down at the table. That was one of the things Figueroa liked best about him; he didn't make light of anything that mattered, and he took her seriously. "And who," he said, agreeing, "has access to all the best booze in the world without having to buy it?"

When Bennis looked about finished with processing the idea, she reached into a pocket and took out a Best-Wipes towelette, which she placed on the table. It smelled of lemons.

Bennis said, "From?"

"The women's rest room."

"Oh, shit."

"So what do we do now?"

"Corky," Bennis said, "I'd like you to accompany us to the First District."

"Why?" Corky stood next to Mort, behind the bar. He looked, Figueroa thought, as innocent as the day was long.

"Step out from behind the bar, please," Bennis said.

"What is this?"

Corky opened the flap and left it open, coming out in front of the bar.

"We'd like to ask you some questions about the homeless people killed here recently."

"Me? I don't know anything."

"Look, just come along with us to the District. If you can explain everything, we'll forget about it."

"I don't *have* to explain anything. What's to explain?"

He looked so good, so innocent, so handsome, really, so charming, that Figueroa lost her cool. "Well, actually, there's some DNA evidence, and we thought you might like to supply a blood sample to clear yourself."

Corky shouted at her, a loud wordless yell, but it was a

diversion. At the same instant, he was grabbing Bennis's gun, swiping the snap tab up, and pulling the gun out of the holster. Bennis turned with a roar, clutching at the weapon, pushing it up to point at the ceiling. Corky dragged it down from Bennis's grip, toward Bennis's chest, just as Figueroa drew her own sidearm.

Bennis was between her and Corky, but she dove at both of them, jamming her gun up under Bennis's armpit, trying to push the muzzle past his flesh, where she could fire at Corky.

She saw Corky bring the gun closer to Bennis's skull. She knew if she fired now, she might crease Bennis's side. She didn't know what damage the blowback and muzzle flash would do to him. It would burn him, for sure. Would it blow a gas hole in his chest?

The three of them rolled against the bar, slamming each other into the wood edge, but their relative positions didn't change. Corky held a death grip on Bennis's gun. One more inch and it would be in Bennis's ear, and she would have to take the chance and shoot. She'd do it, too. Five, four, three, two—

Then there was a crack and Corky's eyes went unfocused. He fell like a sack of rocks, the gun spinning off uselessly onto the floor.

Mort stood over Corky, holding a large bottle of Aquavit by its neck.

He said, "I always knew he wasn't worth a bucket of warm spit."

CHAPTER THIRTY-FIVE

AT NINE O'CLOCK, Valentine decided that the house was just right. Kath was in her room playing some music CDs. Her door was closed. Maria was talking on the telephone. Apparently her parents allowed her to have her own phone, he thought, and he was angry with them for being so indulgent. You could spoil a child so easily. And they're spoiled forever. But then he realized it was probably a portable phone that belonged to the whole family.

He tiptoed down the hall and stood outside Maria's door. She sat on the edge of her bed.

"Well, I *wish*!" Maria said. Pause. "Oh, that's fun! It would go with your coloring. Not mine. I have some peach pink—what do they call it?—oh, here it is. 'Rose Tapestry.' It has little sparkles in it."

Pause.

"Next week. And she's going to buy me something. A sweater, I guess. Oh, I know, I know. She really *tries*! Okay. You go ahead. But I'll call you back in an hour. Okay?"

The instant she hung up, he pounced on her from behind. She made a little "Ooof!" sound, but he had his hand over her mouth instantly and pushed her face into the pillow. He whispered in her ear, "Hold still or I'll kill you," and he had the point of the screwdriver in her back as he said it. Would feel just like a knife. She stopped struggling but trembled from head to foot. A bottle of nail polish rolled onto the floor and spilled enamel into the rug.

He slapped a short piece of duct tape over her mouth. Then he ran tape around the back of her head, pulled the head up by the hair and covered her mouth more securely. She started to fight him again, but now that he didn't have to worry about her screaming, he flipped her over on the bed, knelt on her stomach, and grabbed her hands. He ran the tape around one wrist. She pulled the other away, but he had lassoed the first hand with the tape and he held the second hand next to it, pulling it so that both were together. Then he wrapped the tape around both of her wrists, three or four times.

He did the same with her ankles.

He picked her up like a package and straightened her out. The bound feet he moved near to the rail of the bed's footboard. Wrapping the sticky tape back and forth around her ankles and the rail, he attached her firmly to the bed.

Just to be on the extra safe side, he wrapped one long piece around her elbow and from there to the post of the headboard.

"If you stay right here and keep quiet, you won't get hurt. Understand me?"

After the arrest, and the caution, which Figueroa read to Corky in the presence of two third-watch cops she didn't even know but was using for extra witnesses, there was a raft of paperwork. The arrest slip, the call to the detectives, the felony minute sheet, the call to the state's attorney, the booking and charge, everything had to be done and Figueroa wanted it done to perfection.

Fingerprinting was simple these days. You rolled the fingertips on a glass screen and the machine did the rest. It would automatically go into the AFIS computer. Corky's fingerprints would be on record from his time as a cop. Maybe they'd find that those fingers had committed a crime someplace else in the country. If they were in the system, AFIS would probably pop them out. There were still some fingerprint systems around the country that didn't talk to AFIS, but not many.

By nine-thirty, Mossbacher had arrived. So had the ASA, fortunately not Malley. The felony review unit responded twenty-four hours a day, but they didn't send the senior people late at night. It was a young guy named Fritz Haber, whose blond hair stuck up straight, despite his nervous habit of running his hands over it constantly. His job was to determine whether they had enough for a charge.

Figueroa spent half an hour on the arrest paperwork, the general offense case report, while Bennis shepherded the other procedures. She eavesdropped on what he and Mossbacher were saying.

ASA Haber told Bennis and Mossbacher, "This is quite tenuous. You can only hold him twenty-four hours."

Figueroa said, "What about assaulting an officer?"

"Yeah, I suppose you could use that as a hammer."

"Why not?" Bennis said. "Otherwise, we could be here all night. He's not talking."

Mossbacher added, "Plus he's lawyering up."

"Well, he'd better," Figueroa said. "I bet we'll find a caulking gun in the supplies room at the Furlough. The ME has a hair with the root on it. They'll be looking at a DNA match."

"Found?" Haber asked.

"Inside the mouth of the most recent victim. Stuck there with the weapon."

"Which is?"

"Silicone caulk. The clear kind." Since he was still staring at her as if she was making it all up, she lost her cool and said, "You know. The kind that looks like snot. He has a sense of humor, our Corky."

Outside Kath's door Valentine had to stop and breathe methodically for a minute—in-out, in-out. This was so exciting he could hardly stand it. Much as he might hate Suze, he loved Kath. Kath was the one he really wanted.

He estimated that Suze the Cop Bitch wouldn't be back before midnight. And Robert had said he'd be back by midnight, but Valentine would bet that meant closer to one A.M. People always said midnight when they just meant really late, and the guy was a selfish bastard anyhow.

Plenty of time. Take a deep breath. Pull another short piece of tape from the roll. Eight inches is good. Cut it with the scissors. Turn the knob slowly.

He burst into Kath's room even faster than he had Maria's. She was sitting at a pine desk, making pictures with markers, the music playing loudly in the background. With her back to the door and the music playing, she never heard him at all until he seized her and slapped the tape over her mouth. Her little soft mouth, half open in a soft little "O" before he covered it.

Such big, beautiful brown eyes, with soft eyelashes, looking over the top of the tape.

She tried to kick and fight, but he just picked her up from behind and held her in the air. She couldn't get any leverage that way, and when he held her tightly up against his side, she couldn't even kick him, although she tried to. With both of his arms around her arms, squeezing her, she couldn't raise a hand against him.

She was wearing a little, little light blue fuzzy robe that zipped up the front.

So fast that she didn't expect it, he dropped her onto the bed on her back and whipped a length of duct tape around her wrists. He was very careful to make the tape just tight enough so that she couldn't pull the wrists apart or twist them around, but not so tight as to cut off her circulation.

She kicked her feet while he did this, but it didn't matter. He took one or two blows on his forearm and then grabbed both ankles and taped them. He also wound her knees to immobilize her legs completely.

The little girl lay on a twin bed, and now he had a really good, new idea. He ran tape over her waist, over the mattress, and down the side to the floor. There he unwound more tape and gave the roll a little shove, until it was far enough under that he could reach it from the other side of the bed and pull it out. From there it was up, over her waist again, and down the other side, plastered down to stick to itself.

Two more turns and she was nicely anchored to the bed. Much more elegant than what he had done to Maria.

Learning by doing. How nice!

Then he sat down on the bed.

He stroked the sweet little leg. It was soft and smooth. That was what he loved so much about little girls. They were smooth. There was no ugly hair on them, on their legs, or crotch, or armpits, just creamy softness.

He brushed the ankle, then the knee. Only in little girls was the knee this beautiful. By the time they were women, the knee had grown bony and coarse and ugly.

Smooth. So smooth and soft.

He bent over the thigh. Closer, he put his lips down on the soft flesh. It smelled fresh and clean. Then like a kiss, he took a bite.

Kath thrashed back and forth but she could hardly move because of the tape, and it was no trouble to hold her leg still. No trouble at all.

He bit until the flesh was firmly in his mouth and then he began to suck. The soft, smooth flesh and skin came up into his mouth.

As Mossbacher and the detective brought a smirking Corky Corcoran out of the interrogation room, Suze impulsively said, "Hi, Corky! We got you!"

Corky, who was handcuffed, nevertheless halted and stood as unafraid and calm as if he were the Pope. He stared several seconds at Figueroa.

"You really think that?" he said.

"You're going to jail and I'm going home," she said.

"Nobody catches Corky, you know. Corky is too smart. You didn't find me. I gave up. Corky arranged it this way."

Somebody, it may have been Mossbacher, said, "Mr. Corcoran. You know you've been cautioned. Anything you say—"

But Corky went on, overriding the words. "Corky could have been more elusive. More deceptive. You know that. Corky could have cleaned out a bum here and a bum there. On Lake Shore, on Michigan Avenue, down on Sixty-third Street, up at Belmont. Way west. Corky could have cleaned out a new one every night. And you would never have known. Or cared, would you?"

"I would have cared if I'd known."

"No. People just say that. Who moves the bums out of O'Hare? Huh, Figueroa? Bad guys?"

"No. Cops."

"Damn right, the cops. Nobody wants bums. Bad for tourism. Bad for everybody. They're ugly, dirty, smelly, and cause crime. Corky has been helping, making the city cleaner. The city will realize this. And it won't be long from now. Really, in their hearts everybody feels just the same as Corky does. Everybody. Everybody hates drunken bums. All the clean, nice people like you and me and the sergeant here and all the people who aren't sloppy drunks lying in the street."

CHAPTER THIRTY-SIX

"I REALLY HAVE to get home," Suze said. They had finished the paperwork and Bennis thought they should celebrate.

He said, "I thought Maria was in charge."

"She is, and that's fine as far as it goes. She's very responsible. But still, I feel better being there when Robert is out. Plus, I'm totally tired." She caught the skeptical look on Bennis's face. "Well, okay. So I'm pretty damn energized by the arrest. But I still need sleep."

Bennis said, "We did good."

"We did great!"

"Damn right."

"This has gotta go in our personnel jackets, don't you think?" Suze said. "I mean, we're the heroes of the hour."

"It can't hurt. You really want to put in for detective?"

"Yeah. Don't you? Let's both do it. We're good at this, aren't we?"

Bennis said, "We missed Corky for quite a while, though."

"It's funny how something can be right there in front of you and you don't see it."

"It's like when I go to get a piece of cold pizza in the refrigerator. I know it's there, 'cause I put it there the night before. But I look all through the fridge, move things around in back, push stuff aside, and I can't find it. Why can't I find it? Because it's right in front, that's why. I looked right past it. And that's the thing. It's what's right in front of you that you don't see."

Now that he had Maria and Kath immobilized, he had time to get ready. He went to the master bathroom on the second floor and turned the water on in the shower. While it warmed up, he padded into the master bedroom—or Robert's bedroom actually, since Mrs. Robert was downstairs being a spaz.

The closet in Robert's room held a lot of nice clothes. Valentine picked out a soft cotton shirt in a nice powder-blue. *Matching Kath's little robe.* He thought a pair of navy deck pants would go nicely with it. And of course these good quality cotton briefs. Clean socks. Navy to match the pants.

He carried the clothes into the bathroom, placing them carefully on the top of the hamper, out of the way of any spray. Likewise the gun, screwdriver, scissors, and roll of tape.

Robert's clothes. They all called him Robert. Self-important sounding guy. You just knew he never let them call him Bob, or even Rob. *Maybe I'll call him Robbie-boy when he comes home tonight. I ought to have some real fun with him.*

The shower water was glorious, that was what he whispered to himself, glorious, after all those days in the attic. Those days of purgatory were the cop's fault. Suze. Bitch Suze. But in the shower, he felt as if it all washed off him. There was beautiful, wonderful, hot, hot, *hot* water sluicing down all over him. And on the wall shelf was Ivory soap, minty soap, coconut soap, or oatmeal soap, and three kinds of body wash. Three kinds!

He smelled each bottle of body wash with great care and chose the cinnamon one. Hey! You only live once.

Then he washed all over his whole body, going very quickly, as usual, over the nasty parts. When he was done, he stood under the hot water, and slowly turned the hot tap down until it became warm, then lukewarm. He didn't go to cold, even though he knew that everybody should. He giggled a bit, thinking that he could do exactly what he wanted.

When he stepped out of the shower, he realized he had not brought in a towel. He didn't want to use any on the racks, because they had probably been used to wipe somebody else's body. Robert's, probably. And that idea was very unpleasant. But he opened a door under the sink and found a whole pile of towels. He took two, both dark blue.

He rubbed them briskly over his skin. It felt so good to be clean.

CHAPTER THIRTY-SEVEN

"ALL RIGHT," MOSSBACHER said. "It's up to the suits now."

Figueroa said, "I can go home. Yay."

Mossbacher said, "Figueroa, Bennis, you did a good job. I have to admit it. A really good job."

"Thanks, boss."

"I'm proud of you."

They walked out to the parking lot. Bennis jiggled his keys. Hesitating, he said, "Well, we've earned a rest."

"Right. Good night, Norm."

"Suze—what's wrong?"

"Wrong? Nothing. I'm tired."

"You're not yourself. And you haven't been all week. Something at home?"

"Not that I know of. I mean, all the usual. Sheryl's recovery is *so* slow. And uncertain. We don't know how far she'll get, either. And Robert—well, you know Robert."

"Yeah, but that's always going on. It feels to me like something else. Kids okay?"

"Yes, they're fine. Don't worry about me. There's nothing wrong. I'm heading home and it's high time for a full night's sleep."

She revved up the car and headed north on State Street. It was ten-thirty. Home was twenty minutes away.

Valentine had everything planned. While he believed that Suze and Robert wouldn't get home until midnight at the earliest, he still needed to be warned if they came in unexpectedly early. He got the bags of trash out of the two garbage cans, the one in the kitchen and the one at the head of the basement stairs. He piled one near the back door, just overlapping the frame so that the door would brush it when it opened. Then he opened the second bag at the top, partway, and piled it on top of the first. Rummaging inside, he found two empty cans and an empty glass bottle and balanced them precariously at the very top. When the bottom bag was jiggled, even a little bit, the cans and the bottle would fall over on the floor and make a lot of noise. And the beauty of it was, it wouldn't alert whoever came in that it was a booby trap. It would just look like one of the kids had started to take the trash out and forgot. Or was too lazy. Whichever.

If it was Robert, he'd probably yell angrily for the kids, which would alert Valentine even further. And Valentine could just shoot him or maybe wound him, if everything went really well, and then play with him awhile. Robert was a bully and they always whimpered like babies when you hurt them.

He went to the front door and bolted it from the inside. As far as he could tell almost everybody came in the back door, but it didn't hurt to be extra cautious. If Suze or Robert tried the front door first, it would seem normal. It certainly made sense for the girls to lock the door when they were going to be home alone.

Home alone. Wasn't that a grand joke? The family hadn't been home alone since Monday.

Suze was the one he had to get even with. As far as Maria and the spaz were concerned, he thought he'd just play with them a little bit and then kill them. His interest in them was superficial. Robert he might shoot slowly, piece by piece, just because he was an asshole. But Robert wasn't by any means the dessert in this banquet.

That was Kath.

If he sequenced the events properly, around about two A.M., after everybody else was dead, he would be left alone with Kath. And then he'd have all night. Maybe well into the next morning. Surely that kid J J would play at his friend's house for quite a while on Saturday before wanting to come home.

Kath and he might have many, many wonderful, exciting hours.

Excellent. Couldn't be more perfect.

Valentine walked firmly along the hall to Sheryl's room. Whoever said he didn't have a sense of humor? he thought as he strolled smartly in.

He said, "I'm baaa-aack!"

CHAPTER THIRTY-EIGHT

Suze felt good. After all, she and Norm had made a very, very seriously major arrest. At the same time, she was slightly unsettled. What Bennis had said as she was leaving stuck in her mind.

Was there something wrong with one of the children, something just below the level of consciousness? There was a time, when she was in high school, that she had a strange sense of something wrong in the house. A couple of days later, her mother was rushed to the hospital with appendicitis. Thinking about it later, she realized her mother had winced now and then in the days leading up to the crisis. But she hadn't said anything about pains and nobody, including Suze, had really paid attention.

J J seemed fine. So did Kath and Maria. And Robert—maybe Robert was the problem.

Well, she'd call home. Let them know she was on the way. It was kind of late to call, or would be if it was a school night. But one thing was certain. Maria would be up. Teenagers had a union rule—no going to bed on Fridays or Saturdays until after midnight.

Suze dialed her car phone with one hand and listened while it rang.

It rang eight times, no answer. Ten times.

I must have misdialed. They're there. They really can't go anyplace else.

That's what you got for dialing one-handed. She dialed again, more carefully, and it rang again.

And rang and rang.

Valentine pulled the buzzer button out of Sheryl's hand and dropped it down to the floor. "Even if you used that thing it wouldn't help you."

Sheryl made gulping noises, but Valentine responded as if she'd asked him a question.

"That's because the girls are all tied up."

At that, Sheryl went very still. There was no sound in the room, not even the sound of Sheryl breathing, until Valentine laughed.

"Now, you," he said, "you couldn't identify me. I mean, I could certainly let you live." He looked in her eyes for any sign of relief there, but didn't see it. "But then again, I'm sure you wouldn't want to go on living with your beloved husband and daughter gone. You notice I said daughter. By that I mean older daughter. I haven't quite decided about the little one yet. I might just take her with me."

Sheryl's eyes were huge, but she didn't make any effort to speak.

"I could stay here a day or so I suppose," he said. "I can't believe anybody would seriously look for you all on Sunday. Oh, what am I thinking? J J will be coming home. Why yes, we really do have to get this all done tonight. Then I can take Kath and the car—Robert's car. Suze's car is too old and unpleasant."

He reached out and lifted the bed safety rail nearest him, clicking it sideways and letting it down. This gave him better access to Sheryl.

"I've never been the kind of person to pick on the handicapped," he said. "Plus, this part isn't my favorite. This part I just plan to get over with."

He lifted one of the three pillows lying on the bed and brought it down on her face.

CHAPTER THIRTY-NINE

For about three minutes, Figueroa told herself that Maria and Kath must be playing their music too loudly. They simply didn't hear the phone ringing. It was kept on a recharger stand in the hall. And Sheryl, of course, would hear it but couldn't do anything about it.

Suze was ten blocks from home when she realized she didn't believe this. Not only did she think it was improbable, but she felt an increasing general uneasiness. Bennis was absolutely right. There was something wrong, or something odd, going on at home, and it wasn't as simple as stupid Robert having a stupid affair.

Maria? Could *Maria* be having a sexual relationship with some boy? Could she be pregnant? Could she have gone out with the boy and left Kath alone to take care of Sheryl?

Or could the boy be there in Maria's room and that was why she wasn't answering the phone? Kath didn't have a phone, and she did play loud music.

Or could Maria have gone out to the sleepover? Disobeyed?

But Maria was too responsible for that, surely. And too kind. She was a teenager, and they could be nuts, but Maria was not that nuts.

Suze hoped. A minute or two to home.

As she came down the street to their house she found she was trembling. When she saw that the house was still standing and not on fire, she let out a huge breath of relief.

The only parking place she could find was three blocks away. Bad luck. *Oh, don't be silly. The house looks fine.*

She ran all the way from the car to the house, though.

She came up the alley into the backyard and put her key in the door. Turned it. Pushed open the back door.

There was a crash of breaking glass, a rattle like falling cans. Frightened, she pushed the door open fast.

It was just a bag of trash. Two bags in fact, that the kids had forgotten to take out.

Sheryl felt the pillow come down over her face for the third time. Why had he even bothered to tell her he didn't torture the handicapped? Just to torture her further, she realized. Just like he had done before. It was fun for him.

She fought for air. She felt herself smothering, actually felt herself dying. Then over the roaring in her ears, she heard a crash.

The pillow lifted up.

She saw the man turn and listen. He was on her far side, away from the door, and now he ducked down behind her. From somewhere in the kitchen came Suze's voice saying, "Hi, guys! I'm home early."

The man took a gun out of his waistband. Suze's footsteps were coming down the hall. Sheryl yelled, "Awka! Daddnot!"

The man hissed, "Shut up!" Sheryl knew Suze could not hear him.

Suze walked into Sheryl's room, saying, "Hi, kiddo. How is everything? I called, but—"

Valentine stood up. He fired a shot at Suze, narrowly missing her. Suze drew her sidearm fast. Valentine pushed Sheryl up to a sitting position between them, holding her up with his left arm, firing again, knowing that Suze couldn't return fire without risking hitting Sheryl.

Sheryl grabbed his wrist with her strong right arm, but she couldn't quite get hold of the gun. He fired again, and missed again as Suze jumped sideways. Suze still couldn't shoot because he had Sheryl pulled against him.

Sheryl swiveled her head up into the man's neck and sank her teeth into the strap of muscle there. She bit down and held on. She felt blood leak out, running over her mouth and flowing down her chin, and she was energized! She bit harder. Clamped her teeth in a death grip. She hated him! Hated him!

The man screamed, pulled the trigger, firing into the floor. And Suze came up fast and cracked him on the head with her gun. Sheryl let go. He fell over the bed rail, half on top of Sheryl, then slid bleeding to the floor.

There was blood everywhere. Sheryl trembled.

"Are you okay?" Suze yelled at her. Suze said, "He's down," and pulled the man over to the radiator near the window and handcuffed his wrists around a pipe.

Sheryl twitched and shook. She wanted to talk and couldn't speak. She realized that the girls hadn't appeared, despite all the shouting and shooting. But she couldn't get the words out to tell Suze.

"Oh! Oh, God!" Suze said suddenly. "The girls!"

Sheryl thought, *Oh, God! They're dead. And I'm helpless. My own children and I couldn't save them.*

Suze ran from the room.

Suze was back in three minutes. "It's okay! It's okay!" she yelled.

Sheryl sank back exhausted.

"They're okay. They're taped up but alive. I have to go get some scissors and cut the tape off."

She looked at the man handcuffed to the radiator. Blood was leaking from his neck, forming a pool on the floor. Wondering how long it would take him to bleed to death, Suze said,

"Jugular vein. Shall I call 911? Naw, I'll get the girls first. Let him ooze."

Sheryl said, "Bastard."

They both laughed and then both burst into tears.

CHAPTER FORTY

On Saturday morning, after the police investigation of Valentine had quieted down, long after Valentine was removed to Cook County Hospital and then jail, and all the evidence collected, Robert took Suze to the kitchen to talk. He said, "You brought this on us."

She'd been feeling the same way, herself. "I didn't have any idea, Robert. But I wish it had never happened."

"He followed you here."

"I know."

However, Suze thought Robert had a guilt problem of his own. Last night, three hours went by after Valentine's attack before Robert got home. The girls needed him; Sheryl needed him. But nobody knew where he was. At a restaurant? There were a thousand restaurants. He had said he'd be home by midnight and got home at two A.M., after all the danger was over and the house was full of cops. Suze suspected that he'd spent a couple of hours that night with a woman, probably one of his managers. This was not her business, although it worried and saddened her; ultimately it was up to Robert and Sheryl.

Robert said accusingly, "Well, that's what comes of trying to be a cop."

"Trying?"

"Yes, trying. It's bad for all of us."

Suze didn't lose her temper. She thought seriously for a moment and then said, "Well, Robert, maybe it would be better if J J and I moved out. I know you think we're a drain on you."

Then she watched the wheels go around in his head. She could almost see them turn. He'd have to stop and get groceries on his way home from work. He'd have to pay for an extra nurse or sitter for Sheryl when the kids were in school and Ms. Sturdley wasn't on duty. Somebody would have to be home all day Saturday and Sunday. Somebody would have to cook. And what about the housecleaning and clothes washing?

Suze had an immense feeling of satisfaction when he said, "Don't jump to conclusions, Susanna. You know we value your contributions."

It was a good thing Suze didn't have to go to work Saturday. She spent the whole day watching the girls. Maria had trembled and cried most of the night, and kept her light on, of course, which seemed normal to Suze. Suze slept in Maria's room the whole night and Kath left her door open. When Robert finally got home, Kath slept in his bed.

Maria was no better during the day Saturday. She cringed at sounds and refused to talk about the experience. By lunchtime, Suze told Robert they'd better look for a counselor for her.

"She'll get over it."

"No she won't. I'll call Pettibaker and ask if she can give me a recommendation."

Robert opened his mouth to object, but Sheryl stared at him with such a look that he quit.

Kath, however, bounced back like rubber.

"What a gross, grotty freak!" she said.

Maria said, "Don't talk about it."

"Can if I want. What a crustified idiot. A true jabroni." And she raised her eyebrow and turned her head in a manner that Suze recognized as pre-teen-today.

Suze caught Kath later in the kitchen. "You want me to

find you somebody to talk to? I'm getting somebody for Maria. This was a horrible experience—"

"Truly the worst. Let me tell you about the face he made when he was unrolling that tape. It was *sooooo* scrub."

So, Suze thought, maybe Kath didn't need counseling.

Sheryl was visibly improved. Suze and Kath called her the Vampire. At this, Sheryl actually laughed. Her mood lightened, and to look at her, Suze thought she felt less achy. Her face was less drawn. When she did her afternoon exercises under Suze's supervision, her step was lighter and stronger.

By Saturday night, Suze was calling Sheryl The Vamp. J J was home now, utterly disgusted that he had not been there to "destructo" the intruder. "I'd've smeared him! I'd protect everybody!" he said. Maria burst into tears and ran to her room when he said this, but Kath giggled and Suze said, "Maria's still upset. But I know you'd have done great, kid."

The kids, of course, had no idea what a vamp was, or how sinister and important they were in early movies. But they loved the name and Sheryl, who did know the earlier connotations, appeared to think it was excellent.

Sheryl The Vamp bloomed.

MONDAY

CHAPTER FORTY-ONE

INSIDE CHICAGO

Monday, June 6

In a surprise move, a Chicago City Council subcommittee has moved on the proposal to establish permanent homeless shelters. The proposal was reported out of committee early today, possibly in response to Alderman Paul DeSario's comments to this paper on Sunday, after the arrest of a man who allegedly has murdered five or more homeless in the south Loop area. DeSario, reached for comment this noon, said, "Even if the proposed shelters were built tomorrow, they would house less than a third of the homeless wandering our streets. But it's a start."

[see HOMELESS, p. 21]

MONDAY, IT WAS all back to reasonably normal at the Furlough Bar. Bennis and Figueroa had spent a quiet tour, their first since their four detective days, driving around in a squad car wearing uniforms again, and some of the sick detectives were back on the job. The old gang at the Furlough was trying not to say anything about Mort's part owner who was now in jail. At the first court call on Monday, the judge had refused to grant bail to Corky. But even though everybody else was avoiding the topic, Bennis said, "Hey, Mort, you said you knew Corky was no good. How'd you know that?"

" 'Cause he's an asshole on legs."

"No, seriously. Why?"

"You're a cop bartender and you mix pink squirrelly drinks, you're tryin' to be something you ain't."

Bennis said, "You won't get any sense out of him."

"Maybe he makes more sense than the rest of us," Figueroa said.

The Flying None said, "Say, Mort. My aunt has some money she wants to invest in a business. If you don't have Corky anymore, how about my aunt and me buying in?"

Mort said, "Over my dead body!"

"I could learn to make all the drinks. I just learned a whiskey swizzle. I made some for my mother."

Mort walked out from behind the bar and slammed the flap loudly. They watched his hunched back disappear as he headed to the rest room.

"He needs somebody to help out," the Flying None said.

Bennis and Figueroa left the Furlough at four-thirty as usual. In the parking lot, Figueroa grabbed Bennis's arm. "Look."

"That's the old guy who came into the Furlough."

"Right."

They walked over to where Henry Lumpkin sat, drinking a beer under the El. Bennis said, "Hi, my man."

Lumpkin said, "I remember you. You were movin' me on."

"For good reason. There was a guy killing people out here."

"I read about it."

Figueroa said, "You had a pretty near escape."

"Say, that calls for a celebration. You wanta buy me a drink?"

Bennis and Figueroa laughed. For a minute Figueroa

thought—gee, the man drank way too much already, but then she said, "Sure. Let's go."

Inside the Furlough, Bennis ordered three beers. They both expected Mort to snarl, but Henry smiled at him. Mort didn't go so far as to smile back, but he pulled the beers without complaining.

"You ever need a bartender?" Henry said suddenly.

"Don't need a bartender that drinks up the profits."

"I wouldn't do that."

"How do I know?"

"Try me."

A week later, Bennis and Figueroa came into the Furlough after work, and for the first time were not surprised to see Henry behind the bar. They were actually getting used to it. They ordered their beer.

"Drink fast," Mort said. "We gotta close at five."

"Just for an hour," Henry said smiling. "You can come back."

Figueroa said, "Not once I get home, thanks. Where you guys going?"

"Don't tell 'em," Mort said.

"AA meeting," Henry said.

Figueroa, astonished, realized that in all the time she spent in the Furlough, she had never seen Mort take a drink. After a few seconds, Mileski said, "I heard Corky didn't quit the department like he told us; he got fired. Too often late, too many no-shows."

The first homeless murder had happened a week after Corky had been fired, Figueroa now knew. But she didn't mention it.

Kim Duk said, "I heard his parents were both alcoholics and that's why he hated drinkers."

"And worked in a bar?" the Flying None said.

"Happens that way a lot," Mort said.

Figueroa and Bennis had heard all of that too. They'd heard that Corky's mother had left the family when Corky was a young boy and that Corky had come home one day from high school and found his father dead, choked on his own vomit. Everybody thought that offered some sort of explanation. Figueroa and Bennis had talked about it.

"There's fuel for any point of view," Figueroa said. "Corky seems to have stayed home to take care of his father after his mother left. The social workers say they suspected that he was doing all the cooking and housekeeping, and even washing his clothes. But neither of them would admit it. The father doesn't appear to have been the tidiest person about his personal hygiene."

Bennis said, "On the other hand, both parents are said to have been basically kind. Just what my dad would have called 'weak.' So, who knows?"

"Maybe getting fired was his stressor. Plus the CPD building closing, everything here ending. The cop-shop moving and the Furlough having to move soon."

"Maybe."

Neither one of them could really believe serial murder had a simple explanation.

"Ah, well, let's chalk it up to the deep and abiding mystery of the human animal," Mileski said, and everybody groaned.

Figueroa almost quoted Dr. Ho, "Some we make and some we make worse." But then she decided just to drink her beer in silence.

AUTHOR'S NOTE
PSYCHOPATHS AMONG US

THE QUESTION "WHAT is a psychopath?"—by the name psychopath or another—has fascinated humankind for generations. Who are these people who seem to have no conscience, who have none of the normal human sympathy?

One of the classic and still popular works about psychopathy is *The Mask of Sanity* by Hervey Cleckley.

Among many fictional stories about psychopaths is one by Mary Astor, the actor who among other roles starred in *The Maltese Falcon* with Humphrey Bogart. Astor became a writer in later life and wrote a fascinating novel of a psychopath, *The Incredible Charlie Carewe.*

Oceans of ink have been devoted to the question of whether psychopaths are born or made. An interesting discussion of the human mind comes from Dr. Antonio R. Damasio, University of Iowa College of Medicine. His book *Descartes' Error: Emotion, Reason, and the Human Brain* is filled with fascinating cases.

For a thorough discussion specifically of psychopaths, you might read *Without Conscience: The Disturbing World of the Psychopaths Among Us*, by Robert D. Hare, Ph.D. Hare estimates that there are two to three million psychopaths in North America. He also theorizes that even if every serial killer were a psychopath—which clearly isn't the case—there would be twenty to thirty thousand psychopaths who were not serial killers to every one who is.

PET scans (positron emission tomography) of human brains have shown that psychopaths show a different pattern of cerebral blood flow during the processing of emotional words.

In any case, whether born or made, it is clear that there are such people. Psychopaths move among us and may make up as much as 5 percent of the population—certainly not all homicidal. The rare ones who are killers are likely to look clean; they sound good; they are very pleasant. They are very dangerous.

And after all, every serial killer lives next door to somebody.